Hard-Boiled and Loaded With Sin

HARD-BOILED

and Loaded With Sin (a noir anthology)

Hawkshaw Press | Los Angeles

HARD-BOILED AND LOADED WITH SIN:
A NOIR ANTHOLOGY

Edited by Dianne Pearce
Designed by David Yurkovich

ISBN 978-1-957224-04-6

Find more great titles at
hawkshawpress.com and devilspartypress.com

CONTENTS

Hard-Boiled and Loaded With Sin

Introduction

WELCOME TO HARDBOILED AND LOADED WITH SIN: A NOIR ANTHOLOGY

NOIR IS THE FRENCH WORD for the color black. But what does it mean be an anthology of noir? What are you getting yourself into if you read this book?

Noir is both a genre and an aesthetic.

The genre designation means the stories contain common elements: humans pitted against something that appears to have more power than they do, and the "something" is sometimes bad guys, corrupt systems, or their own better (or worse) natures as the protagonists struggle with their desires or needs versus their morality. We've all faced the struggle of desire against our morality. It can be as simple as driving home, hungry, knowing that dinner is waiting, but the fast-food drive through beckons. Fast food will win, when it does, because it stops the hunger immediately. But will our relationship lose, when we're not then willing to eat the meal waiting at home? Will the grease smell in the car? Will the French fry under the seat, give us away? And you didn't know that you could sometimes be noir!

French fry noir is noir-light, but it easily illustrates the conundrum that is the catalyst for noir. In literature noir exists in the space where desires, wants, and cravings bump up against rational or moral actions and cause trouble. Noir protagonists are generally decent people thrust into mystery, intrigue, and nefarious situations that challenge their morality or their perceptions of the world.

In noir crime fiction the detectives typically have their own codes of honor. Take Dashiell Hammett's Nick Charles, who drinks quite heavily, but is very much in love with his wife and believes in following the law, *to an extent*. Nick doesn't seem to care about the people stuck in the mystery, or the right or wrong of his own methods as much as he cares about finding the truth.

Walter Mosley's Easy Rawlins is at the opposite end of privilege from wealthy Nick Charles, and Easy takes on solving crimes not because he wants to be a hero, but because it's just too simple for the cops to pin it on the person with no power. Easy wants little more than a home and family, but he manages to hold onto to both by a slim thread because that rational side of him that should tell him to keep his nose out of it just can't overcome his desire for a more just world. Easy is the alienated protagonist we can't help but root for.

Noir doesn't have to involve detectives, and can simply be a suspenseful story, perhaps with elements of magical realism present, placing a protagonist in a situation in which the cards are stacked against him or her. Typically the feeling of a noir story is one of alienation from society, and well-written noir transfers that feeling to the reader, making us damn uncomfortable. The characters are up against a lack of understanding of the rules for how the game is played, all while the clock ticks down on the time available for them to save their own necks.

A noir esthetic is a black and white world. The lines of right and wrong are black and white, and often drawn by those with unfair levels of power, and the characters can't find the breathing room they need. The feel is black and white: stark, no warmth, no color. And there is little relief from uncooperative temperature, weather: it's a funeral in a downpour. Folks are often stretched and hungry, and the outlook is not usually one of hope.

And yet, *I love it*. It engages my mind in way that's unique from other genres. I think it's because even without a detective or a mystery, there is always some problem that needs to be solved, a hurtle to overcome, and it distracts me from my own problems, and allows me to focus on a character in a much more high-stakes situation than my own, and to see if I can think of how I'd react in a similar circumstance.

Noir fiction stories wrap in what I think of as a satisfyingly unsatisfying way, meaning that the loose ends are tied up, or the mystery solved, but the ending is not a happy one. Each is a story with tang, umami: it sits on the mind for hours after the reading has concluded, and invades our dreams when we sleep, as we try to work out how it could have ended differently. If you are not a regular reader of noir, you may think that it sounds bleak. Yes, it can be bleak, but there is also the definite unwillingness of the characters to quit, an indefatigable spirit to persevere. They are getting up the next day, and trying again, filled with the belief that it will all work out better the next time. This intrinsic hope rises from endings that typically do conclude the current problem, even if not in the way we, as readers, might prefer. Still, the knot has been untangled.

This book contains noir both with and without detectives. Some of the diverse group of authors in this book follow in Chandler's footsteps (whose quotation is used for the title of this book) and solve a crime, and all the stories create worlds rife with tension, unexpected outcomes, and high stakes for the protagonists. The clock on the device has begun to tick. Will the characters make it?

I recommend you read noir in a wingback chair: covered in rich-looking tufted fabric that hints at comfort, it has a stiff back that won't allow you to get all the way there. If the little voice in your mind suggests you choose a more relaxing seat, while the story won't let you stop reading long enough to move, you've got it just right.

Dianne

Dianne Pearce
Los Angeles

Pride Goeth Before
Suzanne Mattaboni

ALEX AND I BUILT this company from the ground-up. Pun intended, since we're commercial real estate developers. And I do mean up, like thirty-two floors up. Even though we helped this city get a lot of tall, cool shit built over the years, it was still a big day in my life when we moved into this building and set-up shop so many stories in the air.

Even four years after the ribbon-cutting, I still got chills when I stepped into the express elevator and it shot up the center of the building, rumbling like a Harley engine, whizzing past floors like they barely existed. Just like we zoomed past the competition: Carellys & Sheridan, racking up mega contracts from one end of town to the other. Every year, Alex watched me break my ass closing deals and making sure everyone got their shit done, while he sat back on a pile of his dad's seed money and took his cut.

Alex finally got his, though. He should have known better than to try to screw me out of the Tattenham Municipal contract. You wouldn't believe how fast I was able to muscle him out of the company after that.

The poor jerk must have forgotten he gave me his log-in password last time his laptop crapped out. It didn't take much to move some money around and tell the board he was skimming funds. Those rubber stamp-happy bastards totally bought it.

Not only did I take over the Tattenham project, I moved into Alex's fan-freaking-tastic office. I got used to the view quick as hell: It's an all-glass wall looking out onto the river. Now Alex is pounding the pavement for work for the first time in his life. And the name of the firm is changing to Sheridan & Associates.

He's pissed as an acid bath.

Alex's name was printed on every piece of garbage he brought into this place, like he had to remind us that he owned everything. Mother of pearl-inlayed pens. A desk placard, because the brass sign on the door wasn't enough. Coffee mugs with his freaking face on them. Special edition vintage Rolex. Fake cover of GQ. And every. Single. Golf club. Alex Carellys Alex Carellys Alex Carellys.

He'd been keeping personal engravers in business for years. One was on speed dial in his phone.

I threw out as much of his shit as I could once the plate on the door said Joe Sheridan.

When the company really started to blow up, we started bringing groups of business students in to visit, to show them what it looked like when you made it big-time. I'd been playing tour guide every time a group came through. Which gave me an opportunity to show off the view.

I adjusted my imported silk tie and twisted the knob of my office door, swinging it wide to welcome this morning's group. "This is what we call grade-A, prime space, kids."

The city sprawl on the far end of the room revealed itself, sparkling in the sun as the crowd of overeager undergrads milled into the room. You could almost hear a snare drum roll. The ceiling-to-floor wall of glass felt as big as a movie screen. A girl in a long ponytail and a gray dress gasped.

An early morning, peachy glow blasted off the windows of the buildings outside and spangled the river. "Take a look at my playground. From this spot to the edge of the city alone, we're in deals with 11 different commercial properties." I spread out my arms to spotlight the rest of the office. "This is what you get when you're the top dog."

A 20-year-old in an Izod button-down and a sweater vest strolled toward the edge of the glass. His nametag said Jackson. "How do you get to be the top dog?"

"You eat all the other dogs."

I stepped behind my mahogany desk to grab my phone, tapping closed the selfie that Charlene Myer just texted me. She had appeared out of nowhere in my life, impressed as hell with the company. Charlene got a special thrill hearing about how I hosed Alex, almost like she wanted to hear more about him than about me. As long as I was the one she went home with, though, I didn't care how much she wanted to hear about my ex-partner. The girl was so jazzed about our 32nd floor office suite, she insisted I take her up here last night to get busy in front of the glass.

Charlene's goth wardrobe did it for me. She worked at a funeral home downtown. Meanwhile, she didn't realize how close she came to giving 18 college students a view of her black lace outfit this morning, staring out of my phone.

Two of the newbies stepped closer to the glass wall and gaped at the skyline. The girl with the ponytail covered her mouth. Izod Jackson reached a splayed hand to touch the surface of the window.

I jumped out from behind my desk, sending a metal-grate pen holder and some other crap toppling, including a big flathead screwdriver that I didn't realize was behind my laptop. One of the maintenance guys must have left it. They should really pick up after themselves. I ignored the screwdriver as it dropped to the floor.

Jackson practically hopped out of his Vans as I threw myself between him and the glass.

"Please. Fingerprints." I wiped my sleeve to erase the ghost of residue he left.

Jackson shirked his head into his collar like a turtle. "Sorry." A lanky guy behind him gave him a shove.

As I swiped the glass, I noticed some paint chips from the window frame molding were scattered on the floor below. What the hell was the matter with the cleaning crew? I brushed the chips aside with my Oxfords.

"When you work this hard for the glass wall, you want everything to be perfect," I said. Of course, a few months ago it was Alex's wall. Sucks for him.

"The view is gorgeous," said Ponytail Girl, whose nametag said Elle. Her eyes got wide for a second and she turned away. "Don't you get dizzy? I'm afraid of heights."

"Are you kidding?" I said. "I love it." Good thing not all women are afraid of heights, I thought, remembering Charlene against the dark cityscape.

"Imagine if the glass broke." Izod Jackson poked Ponytail Elle in the rib. I couldn't help looking at him like he was some kid my sister might have babysat for just ten years ago, back when I was clawing my way to the top.

"This window wouldn't break if you ran a Hummer into it," I said. "It's military grade."

Jackson tugged his sweater vest. "Like, is that a thing?"

"Indestructible glass? Sure it's a thing." I tapped my knuckles on the surface.

Ponytail Elle rolled her eyes.

"You don't believe me?" Adrenaline started to whizz in my ears. This is the third group I've been able to bait with this line—everybody wanted to know what would happen if the glass broke. It was impossible, that's what would happen. I've done the demo where I run at the glass like a linebacker for every group that's been through here. I did it for Charlene, too. It got her all juiced.

I continue to do it for the head buzz it gives me, watching the landscape speed at me, full-force. The glass doesn't give a shit. The walls vibrate and then you bounce off. The first time I tried it, the staff at the firm was a little shocked. Now they laughed it off.

"Step aside." I carved out some running room, shooing the crowd of young Joe Sheridan wannabes out of the way, and winked at Ponytail Elle. She shook her head.

I took a breath as if I were about to do a swanner off the Olympic high diving board and stared at the river floating in the background. The sun bounced off it like confetti. The highway snaked a border along the river's edge, sewn-in by live Matchbox car traffic. My blood pulsed in my teeth.

The whole scene flew at me as I pummeled my shoulder against the plate glass. I closed my eyes, waiting for the throng and the burst of energy that would shove me back into the room… and…

There was crashing and shrieking, and instead of the bounce I kept going right into the orange-tinged sky, no floorboards underneath me. I was part of the atmosphere, defying all logic in a twisted, surreal dance with a billion-and-two sparkling shards.

I spun around to see the outside of the building suddenly behind me. My office window panel had ripped away from its frame at the bottom and was hanging outside. A mangled corner of the safety glass had pried outward like someone had gone at it with a six-foot bottle opener.

For a split second, I flailed in some physics-defying snow globe full of glass flakes. Then gravity snatched me and shook the globe.

The spider-webbed glass flap flew upward and away as I was

yanked down toward the flatness of the Earth. I screamed and waved and flipped, groping through a space I thought only existed in movies and on the other side of giant picture windows.

My screams rattled as I streaked past floor after floor, the ground racing up faster than the express elevator, wind slapping at me. My eardrums popped, glass still tinkling, the shards above my head like a chandelier hanging in the middle of nothing. The pavement became searingly clear and terror made everything the color of blood.

Then there was cement. And my body became Jell-O up to my waist.

I had no legs anymore. They liquified. And the world sieved into blackness.

In a blink, I was pulled back into the bright sky, my whole being stretching upward like a slick of maple syrup to the accompaniment of a distorted Cure song. I could see my suited half-self below, slumped and impossible against the cement, pants full of melting black cherry jam that painted the sidewalk.

I watched that semi-flattened casing of a man shrink away from me as I floated up the side of the building, past rows of windows with people pressed against them, everyone gawking down at the guy with the puréed legs plastered to the sidewalk. The husk on the ground got smaller and smaller; I kept rising, a helium balloon some kid let go at the park.

I reached the open flap of plate glass of the 32nd floor where the smashed panel bent out into the atmosphere. Without a scratch, I slinked back through the opening.

The sound burst back to life in my office as if someone had unlocked a mute button. Ponytail Elle writhed on the floor, with Izod Jackson and some other Gen Z achiever crouched over her. The rest of the kids were running around the halls past my open office door. Everyone in the firm had shot out of their rolling leather chairs and sprinted toward my office.

I hovered over screaming Ponytail Elle and the boys, bearing down on the scene, which sharpened into high-contrast detail around me. I lamented my bamboo floor full of crushed glass and disturbing paint chips and trickling lines of blood, my prized glass wall desecrated and still crackling as the wind pushed at the broken panel. The pried-out molding and bolts along the bottom of the wall that used to secure the plate glass were tattered and exposed. The floor was littered with a spray of pens, shards, and the flathead screwdriver.

Elle squirmed, knocking the screwdriver. It rolled into a seam between the bamboo floor panels, engraved side up.

A pen I'd never seen before in my life rolled into focus, settling against the screwdriver like it had just met its soulmate. Printed on the pen's side: "Myer Funeral Home—We've Got Dirt on Everyone." As in Charlene Myer, who supposedly had never been in my office until yesterday. And who sure as hell didn't write anything when she was here with me...although I left her alone for ten minutes when she asked me to get her coffee.

What the hell did she do while I was in the office kitchen?

On the bamboo floor, the handle of the mystery screwdriver was engraved in gold letters, staring up at me like a calling card, sidled next to Charlene's inexplicable embossed pen.

Alex Carellys, the screwdriver read. A flake of paint the same off-white as the broken molding was stuck to its beveled head like it had pried at something. Something like my window molding.

As usual, Alex had to remind me that he owned everything that ever appeared in that office. Even Charlene, who it seems didn't materialize in my life out of nowhere after all.

The screaming in the background suddenly started to sound like their laughter.

The Third Refill
Albert Tucher

DIANA WAS HAVING a Tillotson moment.

He spent many hours in the kitchen of her rented Cape Cod, drinking her coffee and listening to her news, but she could never predict when the light would touch him in a certain way, and she would wonder how a hooker had let a cop infiltrate her private life.

She shook the nonsense off and got up to fetch the coffee pot. This relationship worked for both of them.

The caffeine in his bloodstream had to exceed the legal limit before he got down to business, and the third refill usually did it. She topped him up, but she skipped her own cup. She could never match his consumption.

"I'm worried about the new detective," he said. "She's getting obsessed."

Diana took her seat facing him across her grandmother's wooden table.

"The good ones do get obsessed, don't they? Present company not excepted."

"I try to keep my feet on the ground."

"So is this about the Hoberman case?"

The missing wife was getting a lot of space in the Newark Star-Ledger and the TV news.. The northern tip of New Jersey seldom received this much attention.

"It's going to turn out to be a homicide, and it'll be Jackie Spohr's first."

"So the husband did it?"

"That's where the obsession comes in. Odds are it's Hoberman, but Jackie's getting tunnel vision."

"You think maybe he didn't do it?"

"I think she needs evidence, and she doesn't have any."

He drained his cup, and Diana got up again. At this rate she wouldn't have to do her squats in the gym today.

"No evidence at all?"

"We have a missing woman with a husband sixteen years younger," said Tillotson. "Her friends don't like him. That's about it."

"You have a picture?"

He took a photo print from the breast pocket of his poplin suit coat.

"From their wedding."

Grant Hoberman was thirty-ish, dark and hawk-like. Diana could seen him playing sexy bad guys in the movies. She didn't often get to work for men like him, but she didn't trust them anyway.

His blonde bride would have dominated most group photos, even in her mid-forties. She would keep turning heads into her sixties and beyond, assuming she lived.

"Priscilla," said Tillotson.

"Look at her. She makes a name like that work. And everybody in black. Not your average wedding."

"In so many ways."

"So this was, what, five years ago?"

"Here's a more recent pic of her," said Tillotson.

Priscilla was celebrating something with friends in an upscale restaurant.

"To me she looks better than ever," he said, "but I like the road miles."

"A younger guy might get to the point where he didn't anymore. Did Hoberman have a girlfriend on the side?"

"Jackie looked. Hard."

Diana studied the photo, but it had nothing more to tell her.

"You already know Hoberman hasn't come to me."

There was the line she always walked with Tillotson. She was willing to talk about Hoberman only because he wasn't a client. So far, her business ethics had never led to conflict between her and the detective.

"His financials are in good enough shape, if he doesn't acquire any expensive habits," said Tillotson.

"Maybe he wants to."

"Lots of maybes in this case. He signed a prenup, but he still stands to get over a million in life insurance. But now she has to be declared dead. If he killed her, that's either a miscalculation or a very long game he's playing."

"You checked for payments to a hitman?"

"No big checks or withdrawals. No assets liquidated."

"But he could have been saving his allowance."

"I guess. The only hint we have is a .38 revolver he reported stolen a few weeks before she disappeared. That's suspicious, but it doesn't prove anything. And he hasn't replaced it legally."

"Illegally?"

"We leaned on all the usual suspects. They'd have given him up."

Tillotson made a frustrated face.

"It's time for Spohr to step back. The case is going to have to solve itself. Priscilla will turn up. Or somebody knows something but needs a reason to tell us."

Now his expression turned to disgust.

"In the meantime it's getting political."

Diana had an idea what he meant, but she let him spell it out.

"We only have three detectives in Lakeview. It's a big deal when a slot opens up. A lot of guys wanted it, plus Jackie Spohr. I spoke up for her, because she was the best of the bunch. But the dinosaurs in the department were pissed, and now she's giving them some ammunition."

"You want me to talk to her."

It wasn't a question. She had guessed what he was leading up to.

"She won't want to come on your turf, and she probably shouldn't while she's still a probationary detective."

Another thing he didn't need to say—he came to her because his visits got results. If Diana stopped producing information and insights that he couldn't get anywhere else, he would stop speaking up for her with cops in the area.

No pressure on her, or anything.

"I've told her about you. If you can't help her, then I'm hoping she'll take it as a sign to give this thing a rest."

He drained his cup and set it down in a way she recognized. She could turn off the coffee pot.

"Feel like a trip to the mall?"

"Always," she said.

From the same pocket Tillotson took a third photo print. He slid it across the table.

"That's Jackie."

Diana glanced at a typical portrait from a police officer's personnel file. The smiling face didn't look obsessed with anything.

"You're not coming?"

"I'll let you handle it."

Diana blinked. More than anything else she could remember, that comment expressed his confidence in her.

"I told her Starbucks at ten," he said.

On the other hand, he sometimes acted as if he signed her paychecks. As it happened, Diana could do ten o'clock. She didn't need to push back this time.

She drove down the mountain to the mall where it perched over I-80, far enough from Spohr's jurisdiction that the detective wouldn't have to worry about the optics of the meeting. Starbucks had tables in the common area, where the sun streamed down through the glass ceiling. On this crisp fall day Diana enjoyed the effect.

The woman from the photo was already there. Diana gave her points, because a lot of cops would have made her wait.

Diana usually felt pleased with her own dark blonde hair and permanent suntan, but she also admired dark, dramatic coloring like Jackie Spohr's. Diana took the other chair at the table. The detective nodded at the two coffees sitting on the table.

"I didn't put anything in it."

"Black is fine. This is kind of appropriate."

"What is?"

"I sometimes meet new clients at the mall to check them out. If a guy gives me the creeps, I can melt back into the crowd."

"I'm not a client."

"True."

For a while they said nothing more. Spohr had learned how to make the silence work for her, but Diana knew too many cops to find the tactic intimidating.

"I'm here because Tillotson sent me. I earn the same points with him whether we talk or not."

"What a coincidence. I'm only here because I owe him."

"He's sticking with you against the rest of the department."

"Has from the beginning, but I'm not sure how much longer.

Everybody refuses to see what's going on."

"Hoberman."

"She's dead, and he killed her."

"Have you looked at anyone else?"

"Her first husband, but he's in California. He went there when she dumped him, and he's never been back."

"Tillotson said you can't find Hoberman's girlfriend."

"I can't believe he doesn't have one."

"How about Priscilla? Did she have anybody on the side?"

"She's fifty with a gorgeous thirty-four-year-old husband. What else does she need?"

"Maybe an average guy who doesn't give her competition in the gorgeous department."

"Does that make sense?"

"Try hooking for a while. Nothing will surprise you after that. I know guys with wives who would make Priscilla look average, but they come to me."

"How do you know about their wives?"

"They show me pictures. I don't like it, but they insist."

"No, thanks."

"Which? Hooking or marriage?"

"Both."

"You ever been married?"

"Are you a hooker or a shrink?"

"Some guys say I'm both. Including Tillotson."

"I was married for about ten minutes."

Spohr looked as if she wanted to stop there, but the words forced their way out.

"To my father's boss. Sick, or what?"

"I've seen worse. So what was Hoberman like in the interview room?"

"Very cooperative. Answered everything. Never got flustered or pissed off. Never lied that I could catch him at it. I wanted to kill him."

"He sounds either innocent or like a total psychopath."

"Wish I could back up and start over with him."

Spohr fixed Diana with a pretty good cop look.

"Somebody else could. You, for instance."

"If I try, you'll owe me a big one."

Spohr got up.

"I'll get back to you."

She left. Diana finished her coffee and decided that window shopping didn't appeal today. She found her car and drove home.

Tillotson rang Diana's bell five minutes after she got settled in her kitchen. As always, she had scanned her neighborhood for anything out of place, but she had seen no sign of him. One day she would break down and ask him how he knew when to show up.

He got down to business after only one cup.

"How did it go?"

"She wants me to size up Hoberman. I wonder where she got the idea of using me like that."

"Great minds."

He wasn't going to apologize or even look embarrassed. She decided to move on.

"You're right she's obsessed."

"What have I been telling you?"

"But not with the case. With him. She says she wanted to kill him in the interview room. By 'kill him' I think she meant tear his clothes off."

"Great. Now I really need to keep an eye on her."

———

"Tomorrow afternoon," said Spohr on the phone.

Diana refrained from telling the detective that she didn't sign her paychecks either.

According to Spohr, Hoberman liked a bar on Route 15, halfway down the mountain. Diana had passed the place many times, but she had never gone in. She didn't care to encounter clients on her own time, and bars were the place to find many of them.

The time was just after seven, a little late for a suburban happy hour, but early for the party crowd. Diana took a seat three stools to Hoberman's right.

The place had Newcastle Brown Ale on tap, which earned a point in her estimation. When the young man behind the bar asked for six dollars, she made a slight production of getting her wallet out. Hoberman kept looking straight ahead.

Okay.

She accepted her beer glass and pushed a ten across the bar. She made a point of rotating her stool to take the whole place in. There wasn't much to see until she swiveled around to Hoberman. She let her eyes rest on him, but he held up under her scrutiny. Finally he smiled, more to himself than anyone else.

"Where are my manners?" he asked. "You're a guest in my home. Well, not my home, but you know what I mean."

He slid off his seat, picked up his lowball glass, and ambled over. He climbed onto the stool to her left.

"No need. I'm a big girl."

"Next one on me. I insist."

"Okay."

He raised his volume a little.

"Jackie, why don't you come in and join us?"

More than ten years of fielding abrupt comments and requests from clients kept Diana from flinching and spilling her beer, but she wondered how Jackie Spohr was taking the collapse of her plan.

"I've been waiting for someone like you," he said. "Are you a detective?"

"Hardly."

"I didn't kill her. My wife."

"Okay."

"With that out of the way, how do you like the Mets this year?"

"I'm not getting my hopes up. I've been disappointed too many times."

"Me neither."

"And of course I'm lying."

"Me too."

They clicked glasses.

"How did Jackie get you to do this?"

"Jackie. That's interesting."

"She doesn't like it when I call her that."

"Which is why you do it. Me, I have to jump when the cops say jump. You can figure it out."

He gave her a frank inspection.

"What's your hourly rate?"

"Two-fifty. And widowers are part of my business model."

"What if I'm not a widower?"

"No discounts."

"Okay."

In the parking lot Diana started her Taurus and followed him back up the mountain to the bedroom community of Lakeview, which bordered on her hometown of Driscoll and always made her feel defensive about her hardscrabble roots. He pulled into the driveway of one of the McMansions that were driving out the last vestiges of the 1970s.

And in one of those bits of awkwardness that sometimes came up in her business, a regular client lived across the street from Hoberman. It wouldn't cause her any real harm if Phil D'Aquisto saw her, but it would give him more ammunition. Phil was one of those men who found prostitutes fascinating, and he never stopped trying to breach the wall around her private life.

But his house stayed dark and motionless. He might be seeing someone else at one of the local motels. Some women in the business refused to go to a man's home.

In Hoberman's bedroom she went through the familiar undressing routine, but she finished still wearing one item. She would let the experts remove it.

"So that's what a wire looks like," he said. "It's kind of hot knowing she's listening."

Diana didn't comment, but his cruelty impressed her.

He was the kind of man who made the bed every day. As he turned down the spread, he fixed her with a look.

"I know I didn't kill her, but you don't. Does that worry you?"

He needed to stop treating her the way he treated Jackie Spohr, and Diana had just what she needed to slap him down. The story had the advantage of being true.

"A couple of months ago a guy hired me to pick him up from Rahway and drive him straight to a motel. He had a lot of catching up to do. Eleven years for manslaughter."

She met his eyes.

"So no, it doesn't worry me."

He gave her a tolerant smile.

They went through the usual exertions, but this time they felt real to her. That happened once in a while, most often when she had something to prove to a man.

In this case, that she wasn't Jackie Spohr.

She also made a point of giving him exactly an hour. He had bought sixty minutes, not sixty-one. Less than two hours later Diana was back in her kitchen. For once she had a new face for company.

"Did Tillotson teach you to drink coffee?"

"He didn't have to," said Spohr. "Maybe that's what made him think I had detective chops."

Diana studied her. The other woman radiated both calm and energy, as if the evening had purged unnecessary emotions and clarified her purpose.

But what was that?

"You were putting on a good act in there," said Spohr. "Or maybe it wasn't an act."

"Don't worry. He's all yours."

The words came out before Diana knew what she was going to say.

And Spohr didn't dispute them.

—

"You're the one who said I should try it."

"I never thought you'd take me up on it," said Diana.

Jackie Spohr was wearing business casual gray slacks and a plain white blouse. Detectives dressed like that, but so did hookers, and for the same reasons—to look professional and to blend in.

Context made the difference, and this conversation was happening in the parking lot of the Savoy Motel, the premier hot-pillow establishment in the far north of New Jersey.

"I assume you quit the cops."

"Well, yeah. Almost a year ago now."

Diana had heard that defiant tone before, the one that said, "I don't care what anyone thinks."

And she knew what Jackie would say next.

"See if you can guess who's one of my regular clients."

"Not Hoberman."

"Of course Hoberman."

"Even though he killed his wife?"

"Nobody else cares. Why should I?"

Diana looked her up and down.

"You look different. You're not carrying."

"Just what I need—get arrested with a gun. I don't even own one anymore."

"I've never taken a bust. There are ways to avoid it."

"Funny, but Tillotson didn't offer me the same deal as you," said Jackie.

She turned and walked off. Diana watched her knock on a door on the first floor. She knew the man who answered. He was a client she hadn't seen in a while.

Maybe he preferred Jackie.

The next morning Tillotson showed up on Diana's doorstep. It was time for a regular debriefing, but there was something else on his mind. He waited until his third refill to confirm her suspicion.

"I never filled you in on Jackie Spohr, did I?"

"I ran into her yesterday. But you know that."

"Caught me."

She waited, but he didn't tell her how he knew. He must have an informant at the motel that she didn't need to know about.

"So you also know what she's doing these days?"

"Yeah, I know," he said. "I can't believe her. One case goes bad, and she throws her life away. On Hoberman, no less."

"Have you arrested her yet?"

"No, and we won't if she follows the rules. We'll treat her like everybody else."

That comment took Diana back ten years to their first meeting. She heard his voice in her mind: "Tell the cops when you know something, and don't make us look bad."

"There's something else going on with her," she said.

He waited while she put her thoughts together.

"I do this for the money. You know that, right?"

"Right."

"The day I can make more doing something else, I'm out of here. But once in a while a girl goes into this business because it meets a need. With Jackie it might be that she craves the degradation and humiliation. You know about her marriage?"

"To her father's boss."

"Hard to explain any other way."

"If she's that self-destructive, she's not going to last long in your business."

"I wasn't going to point that out."

Tillotson drained his coffee cup.

"Anything more you find out, you know what to do."

16

"I know the rules."

—

Diana's business phone rang.

"Are you free this afternoon?"

The voice sent a charge of something through her. When she had time, she would decide whether it was outrage, attraction, or her fight-or-flight reflex.

Maybe it was all three. Hoberman couldn't really be calling her, could he?

"Jackie gave you my number."

"I did ask nicely. And pay her a referral."

"Why me?" she asked.

"Because you're good at the job."

And probably because he wanted to torment Jackie Spohr some more. A client's money talked, so of course Diana was going to see him. But she decided to make his nasty pleasure cost him.

"My rate is now three-fifty."

"Not for anyone but me, I'm thinking. But okay."

She could hear the "Gotcha" in his tone. She didn't like feeling that she had lost a round, but now she couldn't back down. The best she could do was push back a little.

"Not your house, though."

"Why not?"

"My new policy."

"Okay."

They made a date for four o'clock at a motel in Morristown. When she thought about it, she had two reasons to go there. Phil D'Aquisto still lived across the street from Hoberman.

The drive took a solid forty-five minutes. She parked in the lot and sat behind the wheel, waiting for him to text her the room number.

127

She got ready for verbal sparring and mental gymnastics, but once again he wrong-footed her. He barely spoke, and he performed mechanically.

"Problems at work?"

For three-fifty she owed any client a little effort.

"You could say that."

Or she could just shut her mouth and take his money. He didn't seem to notice when she dressed and left.

Tillotson arrived five minutes after she had finished dinner. He was carrying his battered briefcase, which he set on her kitchen table and opened without asking her permission. Okay, she could skip the coffee.

"Seen Hoberman?"

"Four o'clock in Morristown. Which I suspect you know."

"Got it straight from him.

"Why would you be talking to him?"

"Since you ask."

He took a sheaf of eight by ten photo prints from the briefcase and started dealing them out like evil playing cards. She looked and wished she didn't have to. Tillotson had shown her things like this before, but he usually leaned back and let her deal with them at her own pace. This time he set his forearms on the table and kept the pressure on with his eyes.

Each photo increased the horror. Finally she turned the last one face down.

"She was shot?"

"A lot. And?"

"And what?"

"Who is she?" he asked.

Diana looked again at first picture, a framing shot, and tried to ignore everything but the contours of the face. The gore made it difficult.

"Oh my God. Priscilla."

She looked up at Tillotson. He was still glaring at her like an arresting officer.

"Where is this? Somebody's bathtub, but whose?"

"Sure you don't know?"

"Yes. I'm sure."

"Hoberman's."

"Okay," she said, "who thinks I had something to do with it? You?"

"We're wondering about hooker solidarity."

Diana put it together in an instant.

"Jackie. You think she did it. And you think I'm involved."

"I think you might help her out afterwards."

"If she came to me, I might. But she didn't."

The staring contest continued. Diana refused to break first. Finally Tillotson let his breath out, and the tension left his body.

"She's definitely in the bullseye on this," he said.

"And Hoberman isn't?"

"He has this great alibi. You. Which you realize also makes you look involved."

"He set it up. He even let me think it was my idea to go to Morristown."

She thought about it, and it fit.

"For a year Jackie has been convinced Priscilla was dead. She basically threw her life away because she couldn't bust Hoberman for murder."

She stopped.

"What?" said Tillotson.

"Something just occurred to me. Maybe Jackie quit the police to run her own personal undercover investigation. She was looking forward to showing the department up. And now Priscilla turns up alive? There's no limit on how Jackie might have reacted."

"Killing Priscilla in a rage, definitely. Trying to frame Hoberman also fits. Jackie knows where he lives. She's been to the house a lot. In both of her careers."

"So you're thinking she went there and found Priscilla. How did they get in?"

"Priscilla still had her keys on her, and he never changed the locks. So she's there, and maybe she opens the door for Jackie."

"Who's pretending she's still a detective needing to make sure there was nothing criminal about her disappearance. Who reported it? It's not like somebody found Priscilla lying dead in the street."

"Hoberman did," said Tillotson. "Like he was making was a minor noise complaint. Hate to bother you, but I just found my wife dead in my bathtub. Just like him."

"You might get lucky on finding Jackie. She hasn't been in the business long. I could disappear indefinitely, but she doesn't have the contacts or the know-how that I have."

"One of her contacts is you. You know what to do if she gets in touch."

He still expected her to violate hooker solidarity. She made no reply, and of course he noticed. He packed up his briefcase and left without a word.

But he reappeared at her door the next morning, and his tentative body language told her he had come to make up. She wasn't sure she was ready, but she started brewing coffee anyway.

"Case closed," he said while she was still puttering at the gas range. "In the worst possible way."

"Oh."

"She shot herself in the Savoy."

"Oh," Diana said again. She owed it to Tillotson and to Jackie to do better than that.

"That's some kind of statement," she said.

"Especially since she did it in the bathtub. With a .38."

"Hoberman's?"

"The serial number says it is. But he covered himself by reporting it stolen a year ago."

"I remember. Fingerprints?"

"Just hers."

"Anything more on how Priscilla and Jackie came together in the house?"

"A couple of neighbors did see Priscilla around the house for a day or two. They're new to the area, and it didn't mean anything to them. But nobody saw Jackie. So we still don't know what happened."

"And we probably won't. Which is what drove Jackie crazy."

"Don't let it get to you," he said.

"If it does, I'll warn you first."

———

"There's a thousand in there," said Hoberman. "For your help."

She picked the envelope up.

"What did I help you with?"

"Oh, everything."

"I won't be staying," she said.

"If that's the way you want to play it."

"I have my limits."

"You've already told me you've worked for killers."

"Your wife has only been dead for a week. That's worse."

She studied him.

"By the way, was that a confession?"

"Stick around for some pillow talk. Who knows?"

And once again he had maneuvered her into doing things his way. He watched as she undressed.

"No wire," she said.

"Wouldn't matter."

This time she didn't let herself get carried away during the familiar exertions, and when his breathing returned to normal, she was ready.

"Did Priscilla just show up?"

"Like she'd been out to lunch. I think she might have been a psychopath. No concern for anyone else."

"She might not be the only one."

She put some special effort into here laser-eye look, but it didn't make him wilt.

"Psychopaths don't always become public enemies," he said. "Assuming you're right about me."

"Did she tell you where she had been for a year?"

"You're not going to believe this."

"Try me."

"An ashram in California. To 'get her head straight.' She actually said that."

"Get her head straight about what?"

"Aging. She said she was worried about getting old before me."

"You weren't going to let her get old."

He rolled onto his side to face her with nothing more than polite interest on his face. Diana thought about Jackie Spohr wanting to kill him in the interview room. She sympathized.

"It always bothered me, that million in life insurance. You weren't about to leave that kind of money on the table."

"Now I don't have to," he said.

His tone stayed calm. What did it take to make him blurt something?

"I think you were planning to kill her, and she disappeared just in time to save her own life without knowing it. For a year, anyway."

"Any evidence?"

"You reported the gun stolen. To me that says you were getting ready to use it on her."

"Or maybe it really was stolen."

"Please. Then the gun just happens to turn up in the motel with Jackie? Things have a way of working out for you."

He rolled away from her.

"This was worth a thousand dollars."

"All my clients say that."

But her comeback sounded weak even to her, and he ignored it.

She almost called off her evening date with Phil D'Aquisto. She did feel sick, even if her own anger was the cause. But in this business only clients were allowed to cancel.

At least Phil performed quickly, as usual. She had forty minutes to brood while she pretended to listen to him.

"Want to see something cool?"

"Sure," she said. "Show me something cool."

Diana sometimes wondered how phony her enthusiasm would have to sound before Phil caught on. So far, she hadn't found his limit.

He heaved his bulk out of bed and went to his dresser. She used the moment to get up and part the drapes over his bedroom window, with its perfectly framed view of Hoberman's house. In the last shreds of twilight the hulking structure seemed to grow, as if it were lumbering toward her.

Phil opened the top drawer. She couldn't see what he was doing, until he whirled around with a manic grin on his face and an enormous silver revolver in his hand.

"Careful where you point that."

She backed away from him so fast that she forgot the bed and tumbled onto it.

"It's not loaded."

"You're supposed to treat it like it is."

"Oh. Right."

"Since when are you into guns?"

"I had one for about a year, and I kind of got used to it."

"A year."

She told herself the time frame was coincidental, but a faint breeze of adrenaline stirred.

"You never showed me that one."

"It was just a little thing. Grant gave it to me."

The breeze became a gale.

"Your neighbor. Hoberman."

"Right. But then he took it back, just recently. I mean, it was his in the first place, so I would feel a little weird asking him for it. But I missed having it."

He admired his toy.

"So I got this."

"What kind of gun?"

"A .357 Magnum."

"No, the one Grant gave you."

"A .38 revolver."

"Phil, listen to me. You need to call the police. Ask for Detective Tillotson, and tell him Diana told you to call."

"Since when do you get along with the cops?"

"That's not important. This is."

"Why?"

"Haven't you been following the news?"

"Nah."

She believed him. He was that clueless, and if she knew it, so did his neighbor. Phil had offered Hoberman the perfect hiding place for the gun he had reported stolen.

"Grant killed his wife. He didn't do it himself, but he gave the gun to the killer. And any minute he's going to remember you're a loose end. You can identify the gun and put it in his hands."

Diana might be a loose end too, if Hoberman knew about her and Phil. And she was willing to bet he did.

Phil was still standing and gaping.

"Call Tillotson now. I want to hear you do it."

Once she got him moving, he did well.

"He's coming."

"Then I'm going."

"I thought you got along."

"Trust me. It's less complicated if I'm not here."

She knew how to dress in seconds, but Tillotson's job had taught him speed as well. As she drove her Taurus away from the curb, headlights appeared in her mirror, and somehow she recognized him.

The next morning she was up early for the company she knew would come. The doorbell rang at 7:30.

"Been up all night," said Tillotson.

"I figured."

"I have something, but nobody can know I showed it to you."

"They won't."

He took a laptop computer from his briefcase and set it on the table. He turned the screen toward her.

"Click play."

He had edited a quick and dirty highlights reel for her. Hoberman sat at a table in a room so bare that it could only belong to a police station. He wore his usual expression, somewhere between tolerance and polite boredom. Tillotson started the questioning.

"So what's a guy like you doing paying for sex?"

"It's simpler. Less aggravating."

"Hookers are useful for a lot of things, aren't they? Especially when you know how to handle them."

Did Tillotson handle her? Diana decided to think about that another time.

Tillotson's "just us guys" tone didn't last long. His relentless questioning wore chips off Hoberman's façade until nothing was left but silence and the real man, the one who had contempt for anyone or anything that wasn't him.

Then Tillotson bored in.

"You aimed Jackie like a gun. In fact, you gave her the gun. I can prove you had it. I'll bet you left the .38 on the table next to her envelope with her money. Tell me I'm wrong."

"I'll take my lawyer now," said Hoberman.

Tillotson let the words hang in the kitchen for a long moment, before he closed the computer.

"I think you nailed it," she said. "That's what happened."

"I just thought about the ways Jackie wasn't you."

Diana's throat felt thick, and her voice refused to work.

"I'm not sure what the prosecutor will file," he said. "Conspiracy to commit murder would be my guess."

"Works for me," said Diana.

They exchanged looks, until things threatened to get mushy again.

"I heard there might be coffee around here somewhere," said Tillotson.

"Depends. It's not worth the trouble for less than three refills."

"Let's get started."

Elegy in a City Churchyard
William F. Crandell

FOLLOWING A HUNCH, I drove to the churchyard late Sunday night. I'd packed a .45 Army pistol under my shoulder, a jackknife in my coat pocket. The gravel berm made little noise as I parked my pre-war Nash a distance from the ruined chapel. I slid onto my feet onto the ground, cautioning my client to sit still. The quirky white-haired lady who'd hired me glared at me. The hunch to visit the cemetery had been hers and she insisted on coming. I silently closed my door.

The wind blew hard and high, shredding the silver-edged clouds to show patches of a half-moon sinking in a stormy sea of mist above my head. It had given me just enough illumination to drive the last half-mile in darkness.

An amorphous array of old thin tombstones kept watch, ghostly in themselves. Passing the tumble-down sanctuary, I began hearing voices, muted at first but louder as I advanced. At least two men, cursing in German. How in hell, I grumbled to myself, half a mile from my car, did I let this oddball woman con me into this strange meeting?

—

I hadn't thought of her as bad news that morning when she waltzed into my office, a formidable crone—perhaps seventy. Stately in an expensive navy blue linen suit, white cotton gloves, and a veiled hat perched atop snow-colored hair that curled to her neck, the lady carried a slim black leather satchel and a matching purse.

She offered no hand. "I am Mrs. Gwendolyn Ellendale," she told me in strong but pleasant tones as she sat on the faded couch facing my army surplus desk. "My late husband, Colonel Milton Ellendale, lost his life in the war. I cannot tell you how many times I've strolled past this building and glanced at the gilt lettering on your window, there in your bizarre little mock turret. Today I thought, 'Perhaps a private investigator can clear up this situation.' Is that what you do, Mister—ah—Griffin?"

I stood up. "Yes, ma'am, I'm Jack Griffin."

As she crossed her right knee over her left, her hem hiked up nearly to her knee. A nice knee, I noted, seeing her eyes notice my pupils glancing down toward black high-heeled shoes and stockings. The slightest smile creased her mouth. "Praying, Mr. Griffin?"

Humor. The grin made her wrinkles less sharp-edged. Maybe she was as young as sixty, maybe a year or so less than that. I sat back down. "Let's not discuss theology, Mrs. Ellendale. As to your first question, yes, people hire me to clear thing up. Do you have a puzzle on your plate?"

She brought her grin under control. "Other than why Harry Truman thinks he can be re-elected this year? Or do you avoid politics as well?"

I do when I'm a Democrat with a potential client who looks as Republican as the Queen of Diamonds, I told myself. "Mrs. Ellendale, I don't generally chat with attractive ladies about politics, religion or atom bomb secrets. I do discuss mysteries, though. What's yours?"

She smiled again, giving me the impression of a woman glad to know her game still worked. "You might better call it a problem, Mr. Griffin. Early this morning, I let my dear little Pekingese, Princess Moonflower, out into my fenced back yard without her leash, as I do three times a day. When I returned for her in fifteen minutes, my dog had vanished with no signs of digging under the gate."

"You—"

The lady continued, the Titanic pressing on to shove an iceberg aside. "Within five minutes, my telephone rang. I answered it, thinking that Princess Moonflower's collar held a tag with her name and my number and some kind person had found her. But a man's voice—he sounded dreadfully gravel-throated and obscenely fat—as I say, a man swore at me and threatened to kill my dog cruelly unless I pay him $10,000 by tonight at midnight. He spoke in a European accent. German, I surmise, or possibly Dutch." You could see her brown eyes moisten.

"Mrs. Ellendale," I said, in the kindliest tone I could muster, "you need to go to—"

"The police. Yes, that's what my attorney advised, though the horrid criminal specified that I am not to contact 'the FBI or the politzei.' Nonetheless, I went to the police department immediately. The desk sergeant and his superior grinned as they told me Washington 'has a great many serious crimes to investigate and cannot spare anybody to search for runaway dogs.' Well, of course Washington has more serious crimes to investigate, starting with Congress. But has society sunk so low that we cannot care whether a beloved pedigreed dog is tortured to death?"

"But, you—"

The Ellendale woman sprang to her feet, fists on her hips and her long legs astride. "I'll pay you, of course. Please do not sat no."

"Lady," I said to her as I stood up, "I haven't turned you down. But how am I going to find this guy?"

A mocking grin rearranged her wrinkles. Now she looked more like a gracefully aging film star than a map of the Front in World War I. If she had reached seventy, she'd be twice my age, but I revised my estimate downward a decade or so. Mrs. Ellendale had kept in shape, probably swatting tennis balls, riding thoroughbreds and swimming on the French Riviera. I could see how an older guy might still find her attractive.

The lady laid her gloved hands on my lapels. I'd noticed her scent earlier, something French, I guessed.

"You're a decent man, Mr. Griffin," she murmured. "I don't think this will be either difficult or dangerous. An obese lummox wants to meet me in a deserted graveyard at midnight tonight, trying to intimidate me, I assume. He'll trade Princess Moonflower for a satchel full of cash that I'll pick up at my bank this afternoon. I cannot imagine the lout will try anything. Still, I'd like a strong man as an armed escort. I told him I'd bring somebody to carry the money. You'll do better than I had hoped."

"What cemetery?"

"Anacostia Baptist Cemetery. Down by the Anacostia River off Dunley Street."

Rang a bell distantly. "Across the river?"

Mrs. Ellendale nodded. "Yes. My librarian says a dozen Virginia yay-hoos burned the pathetic little church to cinders maybe sixty years ago, because Negroes were teaching each other reading and mathematics there. The Baptists abandoned it."

—

She offered me two hundred bucks—a bit on the generous side—for the job. Well, I'd met enough Germans in the dark back three or four years to last me a lifetime, when I had a hundred or so guys for backup. But I took it, if only for nostalgia's sake. We both signed a standard contract form. Seating her in the back seat of my Nash, I drove her down the block to her bank and waited while she went in. After fifteen or so minutes she came out, her leather satchel looked less starved. Snapping four crisp fifty-dollar bills out of the black bag, she tucked them into my shirt pocket.

Then she directed me to an apartment building, maybe halfway between my office and the Navy Yard, and I parked along the curb. Birds chirped as I held the door for her, and the sun had begun to fade. Just like Bastogne, but warmer, I thought. The Ellendale lady unlocked her apartment and I carried her satchel inside.

The interior trumpeted money with a muted horn. Artwork a hundred years old in double-matted frames, walls in soft hues, a bronze floor lamp that she turned on, giving off a gentle light. She gestured toward a chair in the Chippendale style and said, "Excuse me for a minute, please. Serve yourself a drink if you like."

Doesn't seem like a good idea, I coached myself. Let's keep my wits sober. I looked over her bookshelves and then sat on a wine red chintz-covered sofa. The window in another room let in a cool nighttime breeze.

Mrs. Ellendale floated out into the living room like a lily on a pond, clad in an ebony silk nightgown and black high-heeled shoes and stockings. I popped to my feet. She poured a small Scotch and sipped it. Setting the heavy glass on a ceramic coaster, the lady asked softly, "Nothing for you, Mr. Griffin? Let me fix that." She began to pour, but I waved her off. "I'll dress shortly, in hunting trousers and boots."

Her left palm lay upon my not-entirely-surprised cheek, while her left hand undid the robe's sash and pulled it askew. Other than her open nightgown and, a garter belt and her stockings and high-heels—all of it midnight black—she wore nothing.

"You've already paid me, lady," I said.

28

"I'm a great tipper," she murmured with a laugh.

"And you've got great tips." And more. What—?

Clasping her red-nailed hands onto my shoulders and pulling herself up so her warm red lips reached my mouth, she kissed me as if she hadn't done such a thing for years, or perhaps for days. I wrapped an arm around her waist and cinched it tight, my other hand covering a breast and thumbing its nipple aflame. My necktie disappeared, my shirt came away, and my shoes dropped under a coffee table. In a marvelous rush, my client snapped my belt out of my pants and pulled them away with my shorts. She cared nothing about my socks, and neither did I.

Then she pushed me onto my back, mounted me, kissed me nearly breathless. All I can tell you is I managed to take my time and so did she. Then, we rode hell for leather. Finally she rolled over onto her back and I stayed on mine till we could breathe slowly

Days earlier, don't ask me why, I'd promised myself to cut down on meaningless sex, as if tapering off of cigarettes. Well, soon, probably. Mrs. Ellendale smiled, rolling onto her side, stroking me in two or three places and kissing my mouth with conviction. "You're better than I had expected, Mr. Griffin."

Outside, the sun hadn't yet reached the horizon, and the dog-napper had specified midnight. The lady snaked one arm around my back and tugged my shoulder with the other. I pitched in and let her pull over on top of her, a very nice place to be.

—

"I've got a hunch, Mr. Griffin," she murmured across a table at Hogate's on the waterfront, where she'd taken me for dinner. I could have eaten a double order of their crab cakes, but the place was noisy and I cupped a hand by my ear to signal her to speak a trifle louder.

She did. "Let's drive to the churchyard as soon as we've eaten. That will give us at least two hours ahead of this brute. We'll be prepared in case he tries anything."

"Like what?" I asked, wondering what she imagined.

"Like anything," she said.

Once we've rescued her pooch from the churchyard, I thought for the eighth or ninth time, we could shut the Chinese Whatsis in the living room and retire to the boudoir.

I nodded my head. "Maybe we'll have dessert later."

—

We crossed the Anacostia River after dark. The radium-painted hands of my army watch said 9:46. Dunley Street had no streetlights, nor any need for them. The sparse, sickly swamp's trees, as we drove down toward the soupy flats, choked off hardly any of the patches of half moon, so I shut off the lights and let my Nash crawl toward the blackened stump of a steeple.

I expected Mrs. Ellendale to lose her dinner over the rotting smell of the Anacostia's sewage, but she proved a trouper as we came to a short stretch where I could park thirty yards away from Dunley Street's crumbling pavements and amid a clump of weeping willows. I racked a slug into my .45 and eased the hammer forward. She made no complaint as I slipped out of the car and told her to stay put, save for glaring at my presumption. Glad my pre-war Nash had no frills such as doors that opened to turn my ceiling lights on, I softly shut the door. Somewhere ahead of me, a distant owl hooted an alarm. Who, I asked my brain, is that bird warning?

Now the lusty wind swayed the highest branches, and the tatterdemalion clouds all but covered the half moon high over my head. Now the voices of two or three men grumbling in German became steadily more audible ahead of me. Now, though the night remained warm, I heard a match strike and saw it ignite something small, maybe a signal fire. I could barely make out a station wagon behind them. If we hadn't blundered into an ambush, the blaze might be meant to help my client find the pick-up point for the Princess. Yeah, and if only Bastogne had been a Hitler Youth cook-out, I'd have had more fun.

Walking in woods calls for skills not easily developed. I stepped silently beside the road, the moonlight and the glowing rags of clouds showing me the crackly branches waiting to snap an alarm. Still, no woods at night is ever dead silent, even around a churchyard. Even between verses of the Horst Wessel song from up front, I picked out three, maybe four, cracks or footsteps off to my right—what, a deer?— that might help with any clumsy moves of mine.

—

At length I stepped between two twisted and mossy trees, standing taller than the shrubbery, just as the raggedy clouds bared the half-clad moon. The valise with the ransom hung limply in my left hand, and my automatic waited for instructions in the other. I'd caught them more ready than I was.

"ACHTUNG!" The fat man's loudspeaker voice, brutal from archiving years of ersatz coffee, stale cigarettes and ill-will, no doubt, blasted the birds from the trees and snapped the second guy to full alert. Both of them held pistols. If they had a third oaf, I saw no sign of him.

Take charge.

"Hey," I called out, "I've got the money in my bag." I shook it. "Where's the lady's dog?"

"Hund?" the second yodeler called out, his accent heavy, "who in Scheiss you call ein Hund?" I heard him ram a round into his luger, a sound I knew too well. I held still, hoping not to thrust two Nazi bozos into starting a gunfight.

That fat man, already aiming at me, yelled in a less heavy accent for me to toss the valise to him.

"Uh-uh." I yelled, "not till I get the dog." My voice covered easing the hammer back. They exchanged fast glances, stupefied as movie fascists.

"Hund," I tried.

I heard the German for "Shoot him." As they cocked their pistols in the fetid night, I lunged to my left, my .45 roaring. Not aimed—no time. Just a fast point-and-shoot. Both of them fired, both of them missed, neither by much.

In that moment, another shot cracked the night, and a colorless cloud erupted from Hund's head. Calling hoarsely, "Hold your fire," another figure rushed in from my right, jamming the muzzle of a small automatic against Hund's temple and firing it. As she stood, I recognized my client, her face spattered and snarling, the lioness who hunts to feed her young.

Jeez!

I glanced at the body near my feet, and the shrinking tongues of their signal fire showed the big lug with a .45 caliber hole just below his right eye. I heard my client chuckle, gesturing toward the corpse at me feet. "Again you're better than I expected, Mr. Griffin."

—

No third Nazi bastard materialized, and my employer said she didn't think there'd be one. Nor had there ever been a dog. "Before we report anything to the police," she said, "let's go get a drink and make sure our stories match."

"Fine," I told her. "There's a lot of crap in what you told me, sweetie."

She shrugged.

I drove us to her apartment and parked the Nash out front. Inside once more, she made a pot of coffee so we'd be sharp. We sat across a maple table and drank it black. "Yes," she said, smiling. "I did get several of the facts wrong this morning. The dog? I've had various dogs in my life, but not recently. The hostage plot? Well, no dog, no hostage."

"Wait." She seemed to be on a roll, but I wanted to ask the questions. "We shot two men who tried to kill me in that old ruined churchyard. They were Nazis, right?"

Her grin died as if I'd unplugged a lamp. "Yes, they—"

"German Nazis."

"Yes, Mr. Griffin."

"And they were after you, not me."

"Well, no. Let me tell you about them. The obese one, Sturmscharführer Klaus Bauer, the SS sergeant major, served as a senior flunkey in a death squad in Poland. His boss, Standartenführer Karl Sachs, an SS colonel, ran the death squad."

"But what—?"

The lady cut me off. "The Nazi escape mechanism—the acronym in German is ODESSA—ordered Sachs and Bauer to set up a terrorist operation in New York. They reached Washington before we found out about them."

"We—?"

She stood up and walked to her kitchen, returning with a jar of Toll House cookies, and offered me one. I took it.

"Years before Israel achieved statehood, early in World War II, the Jewish organization, created a number of specialized agencies to rescue Jews from death camps and provide intelligence, among other tasks. As a moderately prominent correspondent for an American newspaper, I asked for and received the opportunity to serve as an agent. I'll not name the agency, nor give you my real name."

The cookies tasted sweet and musky, and damned good. I took a third. "So when you found out about Sachs and Bauer—"

"We set in place a scheme to intercept them." Whatever her name, she had a canny smile. "Their operation was penetrated. Others among my colleagues reached Sachs with counterfeit orders, and they expected tonight to be met by a single ODESSA agent with money and instructions. I live within reach, and the agency sent me."

Her eyes looked tired. "That's a lot to expect of a journalist," I commented, wishing as the words came out that they hadn't.

Now the eyes sparkled. "Yes, Mr. Griffin, it's a lot to expect. It always was. But during the war I assassinated five senior Nazi officers—panzer division commanders and death camp swaggerers. You see, in 1942, the Nazis took my daughter and her husband in Paris and sent them to the Treblinka death camp, where the SS murdered them."

—

I led the lady to her couch and held her gently for quite some time, as she sobbed quietly into my right shoulder. At length, she released my shoulders and gave me a kiss without passion. "Do you have any remaining questions, my dear detective?" She scooted a foot or so away from me.

"One," I told her. "Why did you hire me?"

Whatever her age, the years hadn't ruined her smile. "I'd seen you, as well as your office, from the sidewalk. You truly are a good-looking man."

"Nice try, sweetie. What else? You told me a pack of lies and involved me in a deadly scheme. What was your purpose for conning me into it?"

She flushed and the lines of her face became straight ones. "I'll be bluntly honest. I needed a focus for the Nazis' attention, so they weren't shooting at me while I was shooting at them."

I turned my chin toward the door, my gaze still locked on hers. "A clay pigeon."

"But an armed and active one with sharp reflexes. You're no

store-window dummy, Mr. Griffin."

I snorted. "I think by now you can call me Jack."

She laughed. "And you can call me Gwen, though it's not my name. And only if you'll walk me into my bedroom so we can help each other out of these filthy clothes."

—

Birds sang merrily when I woke up the next morning in her bed. I lay there naked and Gwen had gone. The closets stood empty. My handkerchief had been spread on the little maple table, a vivid lipstick kiss in its center.

After phoning my office to say I'd be late, I drove to Dunley Street again. The ashes of the Nazis' little fire still littered a small circle of sod, but the dead men were not visible. Tossed into the Anacostia, buried in the muck or carted away? I found neither the pistols Gwen had left on the ground nor the car I'd glimpsed the night before. Washington's best hotels couldn't rival Gwen's cleaning service.

I headed back to my apartment, passing the building where I'd slept with her, showered and reached the office that bore my name in gilt on our "bizarre little mock turret." You don't report invisible killings, so I didn't, ignoring my bullet's role in two deaths I would never regret.

I would regret never seeing the spy in the midnight black hose and garter belt again, though. I knew I'd regret not seeing her out of the hose and garter belt ever again, too.

The Lissome Liquidator
James Donzella

"YOU HAVE YOUR mother's eyes," said Derick Crowne. "Let's walk."

Crowne, codename "The Salesman" a long-time friend and colleague of Cassie's Uncle Victor moved along a path next to Hans Christian Anderson's statue in New York's Central Park. Cassie, hands in pockets; marched along, step for step. A thin white mist gently rose above damp grass that early morning like steam off a fresh cup of hot coffee.

"Your Uncle told me about Tenev. He's trained you well."

"There's more left to do. And expenses…"

"Your skills demand a high price. I can get you…work…" Letting the word trail off he turned to her. Cassie nodded. "Be careful, always. Move only when you are sure of your target. That Russian! Poisoned in England—very sloppy. He survived. Where's that assassin? At the bottom of the sea, I expect. Price of failure."

"Understood."

"There's a woman in Bangkok. Sex slave trafficker," he said handing her an envelope. "Read. Then decide. Your code name—Enigma."

Following Derick's instructions, Cassie committed every detail in Isabella Morantez's report to memory. Her habits—hobbies—allergies, the report looked like a detailed medical chart. Morantez owned a nightclub where trafficking in under-aged girls operated. Influential contacts insulated her from legal troubles, but she had become a liability to an important international figure. Morantez needed to be… liquidated.

Cassie set up a numbered Swiss Bank account for money transfers and once the initial deposit received, onto Bangkok to establish a residence in the Phrom Phong area. Setting herself up as a business investor, relationships with local contacts were formed. It didn't take long for her to tap into the underworld of human trafficking, letting a select few of her new contacts know that she was recruiting a stable of young girls for clients who were rich and well known. Two weeks into her mission, Cassie received an invitation to a party from Isabella Morantez' business associate Irv Borge. The party would take place at Isabella's club in Nana Plaza, heart of the Red Light District.

Mimosa Club is one of those joints that had a reputation for catering to an upper-class clientele. Liquor—top shelf and over-priced, but none cared about price because you didn't go the Mimosa for the drinks, you went for entertainment—entertainment for any orientation. Cassie presented her invitation to a three-hundred-pound-plus bouncer and he handed her off to a young Asian man, dressed in a formal tuxedo who escorted her through a marble appointed lobby reminiscent of the Royal Palace with tall gold pillars, walls lined with stone-carved ancient warriors. Thunderous pounding of disco-music assaulted your ears immediately upon entering the club. The scene would have made Hugh Hefner blush as a mass of party goers were parading around completely naked, as men were cavorting with women—women cavorting with woman—men with men. If Cassie had arrived in a string bikini, she'd been over dressed. They weaved their way through the throng up a flight of stairs where they entered the VIP area. Once the door closed, only the pounding bass rhythm vibrated through the floor. A wall of glass allowed VIP occupants to observe the orgy below. Irv Borge rushed up to Cassie, flashing a broad smile. The mere sight of him knotted up her gut like a hangman's noose around a fat man's neck.

"Miss Lenox, so glad you came."

"Mr. Borge, thank you for inviting me. Please call me Maria," she said her stomach churning like a washing machine on the heavy-duty cycle.

Hand on chest. "Maria. Irv," he said. Cassie nodded. "Let me get you a drink," he placed a hand on her elbow, escorted her to one of the three bars that were located around the room. "What's your pleasure?"

"Scotch, rocks."

"Scotch, rocks and vodka tonic," he called out. "I mentioned you to Isabel."

"Thank you, but I may have not expressed myself clearly. I'm not interested in a…club such as this. My clientele…"

"I understand," Borge said as he collected their drinks. With a nod, they moved to an empty café table in a corner of the room. "You have specific needs. What's the term…bubblegum set?"

Her stomach flip-flopped again, as if she discovered a used Band-Aid in her mashed potatoes. But Borge took the bait. Now she would set the hook.

"That's part of it, but let's be clear. I'm not trying to setup here Irv. My clients are—"

"Scattered?"

Cassie raised her glass and smiled. Reel you in, nice and easy. She thought. You'll never see the gaff coming.

Irv and Cassie continued to chat and surfed the buffet table as they watched revelers on the floor below degenerate into orgy that would have made Emperor Caligula proud. At one point Irv excused himself, returning ten-minutes later taking her aside to meet Isabella. Isabella Morantez was stunning. Beautiful combination of Asian and European features, gave her a captivating mysterious and exotic look. Cassie was impressed. Pleasantries exchanged and plans made to meet the following week to discuss business. Phase two of her plan initiated.

Isabella lived in the Bang Rak district in a penthouse apartment. The same young man from the club, Isabella's "houseboy", greeted Cassie at the door dressed in skin-tight athletic wear. As he motioned her in, muscles rippled across his chest like a bowling ball dropped into a pond. Cassie followed him to the terrace where luncheon awaited. A door opened and Isabella entered the living room. Bright sunlight revealed eyes, hazel in color with a feline shape. Crossing the room with cat-like sleekness, every move had a purpose, like a stalking panther. Every nerve in Cassie's body signaled, this woman was dangerous.

"Nice to see you again Miss Lenox," Isabella said as the houseboy held her chair. "You may serve now."

"I see your butler also works at your club."

"Jeremy? He does many things for me, if you know what I mean."

Cassie took a glance as he walked away noticing the taut rump that looked like it was carved out of polished marble. "Seems very qualified."

"Have you enjoyed your stay in Bangkok Miss Lenox?" Isabella inquired.

"It's Maria. And I have. I spent yesterday at Pattaya Beach, scuba diving."

"You scuba? It's a passion of mine."

"Really?" Cassie responded feigning surprise. "We should make a dive together."

"I'm going to hold you to that… Maria," she said with a smile. "My friends call me Isabel." Cassie nodded. "Irv tells me you're not planning on setting up business here?"

"Not quite. My clients have frequented the clubs, but are interested in more of a private arrangement."

"It can be expensive."

"Not a concern."

"I see," Isabella said. "How can I help you?"

"You must see plenty of prospects too young for your club. Instead of passing them by, you could recruit them for me."

"For a fee."

"A generous fee."

They continued their conversation for most of an hour. Isabella's people would recruit under-aged boys and girls for Maria Lenox and her clients. When the meeting concluded, Cassie promised to schedule a dive date with Isabella. Cassie had wormed her way into her confidence. It was now a matter of getting Isabel to let her guard down.

———

About a week later, Isabel garnered several recruits. Cassie presented herself as a representative of an anti-human trafficking organization and set up a halfway house to care for exploited children until the authorities could return them to their families or find a safe place to care for them. She paid Isabel a hefty "finder's fee" for the rapid response. They scheduled a diving date for the following week. Isabel was in with both feet. Once Isabel was up to her neck in the scheme Cassie would spring the trap.

After an intensive course in scuba techniques Cassie scheduled an outing with Isabel. They met at the marina in Pattaya where Isabel kept her boat. A man named Vayson, captained the vessel. They made several dives around a coral reef for a couple of hours and had lunch at one of the restaurants. Later that week, Isabel invited Cassie for dinner. Jeremy was working the club that night and Isabel prepared the meal. They had a long discussion about her business. Isabel revealed that she could provide police protection if needed. Isabel had high-ranking officials on her payroll, as well as evidence that would keep them in line.

"I could use help," Cassie said.

"How so?"

"I'd like to get a gun."

"It's illegal for a foreigner to own."

"I know. I don't want to carry illegally. I don't need that kind of trouble."

Isabel rose from the table and went to the bedroom. Quietly Cassie followed. She was able to observe Isabel remove a 25" x 30" painting from the wall. Behind the painting was a wall safe. Isabel removed a keychain from her pocket and opened the safe. Cassie silently made her way back to the dining room and sipped coffee as Isabel returned.

"Let me see," she said opening a black leather organizer. "You're in the Phrom Phong Area. That would be Captain Malee. I will arrange it."

Cassie's meeting with Captain Malee was cordial and fruitful, leaving with a permit to own and carry a handgun. A package arrived at Isabel's apartment containing an expensive hand carved jade figurine as a thank you. As the next few weeks passed, Cassie's collection of rescued children grew. Isabel had suggested another diving party and they agreed on a date. Cassie put the final stage of her plan in motion. Cassie suggested a two-day diving excursion to Ko Phai Island for the upcoming weekend. Isabel planned arriving on Friday as Cassie had an important meeting and would meet on Saturday

Cassie arrived mid-morning on Saturday. After an hour of reef exploring, the two women returned to the boat for fresh air tanks.

"I'm bushed!" Cassie said as she removed her air tank.

"Bushed?"

"Yeah! Tired. It was a late night. No reason to head back so soon. Vayson can use my gear and dive with you."

"You're very kind," Isabel replied.

———

Once the two were submerged, Cassie went to work. Cassie attached a hose to the exhaust pipe of the gas compressor before she started it. Once the compressor was running, she attached the fill hose to Isabel's empty aqualung. Holding the hose attached to the exhaust close to the compressor intake, she pumped air mixed with carbon monoxide into the tank. Breathing through a regulator, the diver would never suspect they were taking in deadly carbon monoxide. Cassie had just finished filling her own tank with air when Isabel and Vayson returned to the surface. Cassie assisted Isabel into the boat.

"How was the dive?"

"Very nice," Isabel said. "But I've had enough for today."

———

Before they met for dinner, Cassie did some shopping in the village. At dinner an excited Cassie showed Isabel a waterproof camera she purchased. The evening was filled with food, wine and laughter as the two women were forming a strong bond.

"Can't wait till tomorrow. Wanna' get some pictures."

"This is what I would imagine it's like to have a sister," Isabel said.

"I agree," said Cassie. "It's so good to be with someone you feel comfortable with and trust." Cassie reached across the table and took Isabel's hand. "I hope this friendship lasts an eternity."

Isabel and Vayson were on the boat when Cassie, in a state of distress, arrived.

"Best laid plans," she said as she climbed onto the boat. "Just got a call. Problems. Need to head back to Bangkok."

"Sounds serious."

"Yes," Cassie responded with a nod toward Vayson. "Some important equipment has been damaged."

Isabel understood not to inquire any further with other ears close by.

"I'll leave my gear," Cassie said. "Try to be back this afternoon."

From the balcony of the Bay View Hotel, Cassie focused her binoculars on the harbor area and watched as Isabel's boat headed out to sea toward Ko Phai Island. Cassie headed for Bangkok.

———

Cassie arrived at her apartment two and a half hours later, had lunch and settled in for the rest of the day. Once evening came, she swung by the Mimosa Club and just as she had hoped Jeremy was working that night. Fifteen minutes later Cassie was inside Isabel's apartment making quick work of the lock on the wall safe. She found Isabel's client book filled with names, dates, preferences, bribes and evidence of murders and kidnappings. Isabel had the goods on everyone from police officers to politicians, bishops to bankers. As she was leafing through the pages the front door of the apartment opened and the living room lights came on. Cassie heard male voices, one in particular she recognized as Irv's. Ten floors above the street, she only had one option. Cassie slipped out to the bedroom balcony.

"She's been missing for hours," Irv cried. "The harbor police think she's been swept out to sea."

"Have you talked to Vayson?" Jeremy asked as the bedroom lamp came to life.

"They were diving and were separated. She just disappeared. Oh no! The safe."

Jeremy rushed to the open safe. "Isabel's book! It's gone!"

"Lenox," Irv grumbled between gritted teeth.

Cassie made her way across the ledge until she was able to drop down to the balcony of the apartment below. The place dark, she jimmied the balcony door, slipped through the apartment, made her way down the stairwell to the street and hailed a cab. She arrived at the Paragon Hotel thirty-five minutes later where she had rented a room the previous day under the name Mrs. Emily Rathman.

—

The following morning, the grey haired, bespectacled Mrs. Rathman waited to board her flight to Sydney Australia. She occupied herself reading the morning Bangkok Post. She was most interested in the article about executive and club owner Isabella Morantez who had gone missing after a morning of scuba diving off Ko Phai Island. Authorities believe Morantez became disoriented and drowned when the air in her tank was exhausted. When an announcement called passengers to board the flight to Sydney, Rathman rose and casually walked to the gate, dropping the Post into the conveniently placed trash bin next to the ticket counter.

Leaving
Alberto Ambard

I WANT TO TALK ABOUT a boy with a storm in his eyes. He's pressing a long knife against my pregnant belly. He's willing to kill us for a cheap Casio watch, few small bills, a cell phone, and a credit card that's over the limit, although he doesn't know this. He's fifteen, but has killed before; violence is all he knows.

It's a cool midnight. Just moments ago I was walking back from the movies; the salty Caribbean wind blowing on my cheeks. The street was quiet; so quiet the sound of my neighbor's cello came loud and clear as she played a horrendous version of the Ode to Joy.

Cursing the day she decided to take lessons, I began searching for the keys inside the darkness of my purse when a hand grabbed my shoulder and pushed me against the wall. He didn't give me time to react.

Now his knife is on the verge of cutting my skin open. A brief gaze between us seems like an eternity.

"Make a sound and I kill you, whore," he hushes.

A piercing scream formed in my lungs and climbed up my vocal cords, where, miraculously, I'm able to stop it. Now I have a giant apple stuck in my throat.

Without thinking I bring my hands over my belly and around the knife. I want Giovanni to feel their warmth over that sharp, cold something he has never felt.

"Give me your watch, your phone, and your wallet, now!" the robber says, louder.

I'm tempted to let the scream out, but the knife presses harder. I'm pulling my belly as far away from it as I can; I can't breathe well. What's more, the instant I intend to beg for my life I can't emit a sound.

I can't feel my muscles at all. My existence consists of nothing but the feeling of the knife, the boy, and my baby. Everything else around me has disappeared, including the terrible sound from the cello.

In the absence of words, my eyes, floating in an ocean, are imploring for my life and the life of my Giovanni when the boy's chilling, high-pitched voice erupts.

"Are you going to hand me everything, bitch, or should I kill you?"

His eyes are going in all directions. He's sweating and sniffing repeatedly. His stench is a combination of body odor, something metallic, something sweet, and something pungent; the smell of the streets. He too feels fear, but in the way an aggressive poisonous snake feels fear.

The screaming ball of air in my throat is dissipating. I take a short breath and manage to speak, just in time before the impatient boy loses it.

"A baby is two centimeters beneath the skin, please don't hurt us. I'll give you everything," I stutter.

Shaking like a frail flower, I hand everything to the boy and even take my favorite scarf off and give it to him. This wasn't any scarf; my father had given it to me as a present during his very last Christmas with us.

"Why would I want this?!" the boy yells and throws the scarf back at me, then runs away, leaving me with nothing but the sound of the cello, now loud and clear, the scarf, and a profound sense of relief.

—

That same night I decided I had to leave this hell. Two years later the day had come. I was in a hotel room next to the airport. The scarf had set off the stormy memory. I could see it folded inside of one my three pieces of opened luggage. They were my greatest problem at that moment.

My flight was departing the next day at nine in the morning. That I decided to spend the night before the journey at a hotel was a decision based on survival, not on convenience. The airport is less than an hour from the city, but I wanted to arrive at least at four in the morning, and driving through just about any street in Caracas at that time is plain suicide.

I wanted to be the first passenger to get to the counter so I could beg the airline worker to bend their stupid rule. They only allowed a maximum of two pieces of luggage per family; and offered no option to pay for additional pieces. For God's sake, we were a family of three leaving the country forever!

Besides the luggage, there were other reasons to get to the airport that early. Did I want somebody to pay under the table and take away my seats? Or have a security guy pulling me aside to check my luggage, as if I was carrying a nuclear weapon? Asking me endless stupid questions, knowing that the clock is his best friend and that I'd give up and pay him a well-deserved commission? In Venezuela, one has to be at the airport as many hours before flight departure as humanly tolerable.

It was a nice hotel room. We had a balcony facing the Caribbean. Doubt had barely bothered me. A childhood friend already leaving in Portland was waiting for us. I only knew what she had told me about the city, but I had created my version of it; a version I believed. My friend said it was going to be tough at the beginning, from being professor D'Nunzio, an attorney, to cleaning houses. I felt ready. Not even my useless ex, who left me after Giovanni was conceived, resisted the idea of us leaving Venezuela. Who could?

My only worry was Eugenia. Would she adapt? Would she make friends? I turned my eyes toward her. She was having fun watching movies and eating candy she picked up from the vending machine, while playing with her curly brown hair. Noticing I was watching her, she turned and with a smile erased all of my concerns away, like when she was just born and with that same smile erased all the pain and suffering from the harsh delivery.

Giovanni, the survivor of the knife, was just over two; a fly in a jar. It took a while to get him to sleep, but as soon as he did I began working on the luggage. My goal was to fit the content of the three pieces we had into two, to avoid the ordeal of the airline rule.

The first two pieces of luggage had the bare minimum amount of clothing and shoes for the three of us, although most of it was mine. I figured Eugenia and Giovanni were growing. There was no point wasting valuable space on clothing that wasn't going to be useful in a year or two. I could only remove the scarf, which I put aside to wear to the airport and gain some space. Of course I was bringing the scarf with me.

The third luggage had extra jackets, some of my jewelry, and Eugenia's ballet shoes, which I swear smelled like cat piss. I wrapped them inside three plastic bags before packing them. We're also bringing her school transcripts, and a bottle of rum for my friend and her husband—I had to bring them something. Eugenia wanted to bring her PlayStation, I couldn't say no to that. I could've left some of this stuff behind, but I couldn't bear to leave certain sentimental things.

There was one of those decorative plates people hang on walls; a present from my mom. It had her hometown in Italy painted on it. She gave it to me as a joke. Some of my best memories are about my family gathering during Christmas to make hallacas and struffoli at my parent's. For whatever reason, I always managed to sit in front of the wall where that plate hung, and when I got bored of greasing plantain leaves, or filling the hallacas with the meat, raisins, the red pepper and the green olives on top of the spread masa, I'd look at the plate and imagine how life would've been in Gaeta. I could daydream forever, but I had to pass the hallaca to my mom so she could wrap it to bring it to the steamer. She would always shake my shoulder; wake up, Vita!

And there was a river rock my grandma used to smash garlic. She was an encyclopedia of Venezuelan traditional recipes. A hundred and one years living with us and nobody took note of the recipes; a real shame. In that rock I was bringing her with me; the smell of her hands smashing green plantain and garlic to make tostones, a tradition I had little idea would be lost in just years.

I must have packed and repacked each suitcase four or five times, a futile effort that exhausted me. I was also hungover from the wine I drank and the tears I cried during the farewell parrillada earlier that day. Tired and defeated I decided to leave the luggage alone and headed to take a shower.

The hot water transported me to a nostalgic dimension, or maybe I just fell sleep right there, I'm not sure. I remembered a concert I attended with my parents as a child. I couldn't believe my eyes. The singer had even milked a cow right there while singing a "milking" tonada. He closed the show with a song about a farmer leaving the countryside to find riches in the city. Right before jumping onto the bus, the farmer turns to look at his beloved savannah, and sings to it. Deep inside my dreamy state, I began singing the song:

"I stay right here with you, even if I'm going far,
Like a turtledove flying away, leaving its nest on the ground."

After a sleepless night, we got to the airport at three thirty in the morning. We were third in a line that didn't move until five forty. The smell of rancid, recycled frying oil coming from the nearby coffee joint was intolerable. Two young kids right behind me kept running around the small space while their father talked on his phone, oblivious to their behavior. They knocked over my luggage at least twice, but the worst was the screeching screaming of the youngest. I was about to strangle somebody; I would've killed that young boy and his father if Giovanni, who luckily was sleeping like a rock, had been woken. Just then, the airline attendants arrived.

A few minutes later one of them signaled me to approach the counter. Her name was Yasandra. She had a nose this and set of eyes that... Why bother with details? Let's just say nature wasn't kind to her.

As soon as she spotted me struggling with the three pieces of luggage, she said, cold like a hailstorm,

"Ma'am, you know we only allow two pieces of luggage per family."

I didn't want her to know we were leaving for good. I'd heard too many stories of airline workers connected with the regime, who, out of political resentment and sadistic enjoyment made the life of those leaving the country impossible. So, instead of telling the true, I denied the undeniable.

"What are you talking about? I didn't read that anywhere," I said.

Yasandra sighed.

"Ma'am, it's in big letters right on the front page of our website, and when you make the reservation you must click that you've read the rule and agreed with it before you can purchase the ticket."

"Well, I wouldn't know that; my travel agent got my tickets," I said, defiant.

"Can I see your reservation?" Yasandra said and extended her hand. I handed her the papers.

"You see, ma'am, it's even printed here. I'm sorry, whether you knew the rule or not is irrelevant at this point, we can't have you check three pieces of luggage."

Next, I used the "I have a baby" tactic. I even shook poor Giovanni so he would wake up and cry. Oh gosh, what kind of mother am I? That didn't work either. I got angry, yelled at Yasandra, coursed humanity, then begged and offered to pay her whatever fees the airline wanted, and ultimately cried in desperation, confessing I was leaving for good.

"Okay, ma'am, let me see what I can do," Yasandra said, surrendering to my tears and Eugenia's pleading eyes.

She looked to her right, and then to her left two or three times.

"Since you're here so early, I'm going to try to assign your third bag to a random passenger," she hushed, as if giving the name of a winning horse on the tracks.

She exposed a simple plan. A plan that only exists in the chaotic collective imagination of Venezuelan society. 1) She asked that I leave the luggage with her, she was going to put it under her desk. She would make a story if someone ask. She asked that I waited away from the desk, so no supervisor could see what was going on; 2) she would wait until a party showed up with either no luggage or just one piece; 3) she would assign my third luggage to such party without their knowledge and send it away, but instead of giving them the ticket, she was going to meet me away from the counter and give me the ticket; 4) I would use the ticket to pick up the luggage in Miami.

Upon hearing this, a strong desire to hug her took possession of me. Yet, I controlled myself, knowing that a gesture like that could alert a supervisor. Doing my best to get it together I grabbed the passports back and put them in the inside pocket of my purse, but did so in such excitement; a second later, I'd forgotten I'd done this.

The children were starving, so I brought them to the source of the oil stink. I bought two empanadas and passion fruit juice for them; coffee for me.

The smell of the coffee under my nose was making love to me. Too bad I finished it in less than five minutes. I spent the rest of my waiting time looking around a pathetic scene. I had to recourse to my memory so I could avoid seeing reality; the rotten, decomposed, and pillaged airport. Even the floor, which once was a giant art piece designed by a famous artist was no more; the colors were faded, pieces were broken or stolen, a major scale disaster.

Puff! Anger disintegrated when I spotted Yasandra telling something to her coworker, then walking toward the counter's door. I grabbed my purse, put little Giovanni in his stroller; and told Eugenia to follow me to a spot where Yasandra could see me. She walked toward me with a smile.

Before she arrived, I rushed to find my wallet inside my purse. I began counting dollar bills. I hoped she would accept the sixty—a fortune—and not the hundred or two hundred dollars I suspected she was going to ask for.

"No ma'am, you don't have to do that, it's okay," she said, to my surprise.

I stayed motionless for a moment; my mouth half opened. I was about to insist, but my phone rang; It was my mom. I rejected the call and turned the phone off before adding,

"Please, accept this, you have no idea how thankful I am."

I handed her the sixty dollars, but she waved a no.

"Are you sure?" I said, and touched her shoulder.

Yasandra hesitated before pointing at a small souvenir store next to the coffee shop, saying almost in a confessional tone,

"You know? Today is my daughter's birthday. She's six, and well, she always wanted a lunch bag with a Disney princess they sell at that store. If you could buy that for her you would make my day."

—

Sitting at the gate, I remembered my mom's phone call.

I turned the phone on, and sure enough, she's called over ten times.

Oh God, something happened! I thought. Everybody knows a victim of an armed robbery in Caracas.

I dialed her number; she picked up immediately.

"Oh, dear God, thank you, thank you!" she yelled.

"Mom, what's going on?"

"Vita, you don't know what happened at the hotel?"

The hotel got attacked by the usual "commando." Meaning, nine to ten heavily armed men or boys, like the boy with the knife on my belly. They enter buildings, and going floor by floor, starting from the top floor, rob as much as they can while killing whoever tries to fight back.

The 6:00 a.m. news radio show had broken the news. My mom was listening to it while making her usual morning coffee. Three dead victims, over twenty families robbed of everything they had, including passports.

I took my scarf off and held her in front of me. My shoulders were shaking, my heart was pumping joy; we've made it. I thanked Jesus and Santa Rita for taking me out of that hotel in time.

I thought about the boy with the knife. I wondered if he was still alive, or in prison, mastering his skills.

I thought about my mom. *I'll bring her with me as soon as I can; I'll convince her this time around*—I convinced myself of this.

I looked at Eugenia. She was playing, and sharing a chocolate with her little brother. I interrupted her with a comforting hug. When I let her go, I sighted and exhaled it all out; and relaxed for just a second, when a sudden thought made me jump out the chair:

"The passports?!" I yelled out loud.

Eugenia looked at me, surprised. I rushed to my purse wishing the passports were there. And they were.

Get On Home
Dena Linn

IT WAS SNOWING big, wet clumps of white that slammed into the picture windows of the Colorado bound bus. Beto startled, hearing distant sloshing, snow slipping under the bus's wheels, his forehead damp, his pits and palms in a sticky sweat. His focus zoomed in and out, a kaleidoscopic dream. His head rested against the frozen window, slick glass, like a cell wall and his hooded gaze caught snow sliding, falling, then it was sucked under; he sensed the same pressure in his gut, under and under and again, boots trampling his stomach. He might have called out, but no one cared. Further on, the nightmare continued, shuffling men, grey men, grey walls, grey food, grey metal. He'd been one, shit-kicking rough and fists proud, only an extra twenty-eight months, no one cared less. And that "time on top" landed Beto ass first, not in license plate stamping but home economics. It all floated, the sounds, the men, mixed in the dream.

Everything turned quiet, except for the start-stop whine of the sewing machines' balance wheel. Eventually, Beto'd made Lilly a doll, in his spare time, named it Lillytwo. Sewn and stuffed, with black buttons for eyes, full red-painted lips, pink and white ribbons for striped socks, wearing a blue pinafore. Meticulous, calloused fingers, Beto had sewn each quarter-inch of lace, patting and blowing the glued parts till they dried. Little sister Lilly was probably twenty now.

Stiff, his neck twisted; the side of his face, its skin frozen, the nightmare memory washed over like the wool-cycle. Between the yard and infinity fence, the guy wasn't dead, and anyway, good riddance. Beto wanted to yell, *Get up, lazy fuck, fight!* But guards swarmed, clubbed and shackled him, his stomach felt the hit, tight pressure, the prison yard blazed, and he was gone, gone, and falling.

Another image, a brain locked in a ringing tower, was he dreaming? Beto had lost count, but he knew he had Lilly's doll in the sack

A sudden gruff voice. "Your stop!"

Beto gathered his bag, nerves on pins, suddenly surrounded by supposedly sleeping strangers. He pulled his beanie hat tight, chanting silently: Keep cool, walk on past. They don't know you. The bus door slammed, a hiss of brakes. It drove off and left him in the road's frozen slush. Now he was just cold.

He piece stepped, somehow knowing to stay off the balls of his feet. Jabbing, always recruiting, that high school boxing coach's voice toned clear: "Maintain lightness in your heels Beto-boy, you'll run faster." Beto whipped around, eyes scanning his heart in his throat. No one there. The bus station was in pitch except for the dim glow of an LED display. 1:15am. Beto made it to the station's corner and all the memories flooded back under the streetlamps' glow, his youth, other boys, all pussies, bad decisions—women, bricks, and blood, nothing petty. All in fun. Shiny black asphalt peeked through white tracks, indicating where caffeinated taxi drivers usually waited.

Everything was quiet. Icicles hung like fireplace pokers from low roofs; there was a slight wind and nothing moved. The town looked forlorn. There was the seen-better-days general store he'd started his career in, stealing candy. Its curtains were drawn tight in fear. Next door, a closed sign hung from a string dangled behind the salon's glass front. Beto took his hand up, leaned close, and then was looking far back into the darkest of recesses. Dust mites swirled around his mother, face pinched, up to her neck in a black cape, hiding hands that stroked the family Bible, that space-age plastic drying bucket over her head, and at the very base of that leatherette chair, sat little sis Lilly in blue, her eyes matching, wide legged and ever diligent working her own dolly's hair. His hand dropped with his gaze to the dusty window frame. Then they weren't there at all.

Beto let his head turn slowly, the view closed around him, the streetlights glowing, the cold, dirty glass, metal chains dragging. No chance to breath, the sound of metal sliding, the buzzer, the *slam*, his shoes licking his side of the cell door, then it was his shoes wet with snow. He shouldered his carry-home sack and turned, blinking, looking up. A vertical sign flashed above a corner cut door. The bar was still there. And it had that same busted neon: *rink here, Eat here.*

Some things, even if you want them to, never change.

Beto, my son, alcohol's the Devil's drink. It'll take you from those who love you.

His mother's voice rose behind his head. A sharp intake of air, he spun around, gripped, tense, sweating. No one. He panted, stomped his feet; his mind weak, traumatized, chilled. He yanked open the bar's outside door and then pulled it closed against the night. A heater gurgled above, belching hot, dry air.

Then he opened the inside door and stepped into its darkness.

His eyes took their time to adjust, widening and closing, years and memories flew by. They'd installed diffuse colored spotlights into the wood ceiling that now winked like so many scattered stars. He let his eyelids close softly, his knees alternately bending just enough to raise and lower his state-issued rubber heels, thinking lightness, contemplating the safest escape route. His fingers tightened white around the neck of his sack.

The backs of a neat-looking couple faced him. A man, the hem of his smoking jacket, hiding the barstool, hat on the bar to the side of his drink. His hands were hidden. There was a trim female, fidgeting for balance on the stool at his side. Beto's eyes shifted to another man, sitting undisturbed at a square table. He had a thick neck visible at the top of a black turtleneck, monster hands swallowing a dime-store soft cover, and a nasty scar, even more gruesome in the diffused blue spotlight; he had a bottle of beer neat on a coaster. Beto held his body tight, head still, eyes shifting, saw the worn briefcase at the man's feet. Beto sensed the man's eyes move from his book to Beto's sack and back down. Straight ahead, Beto focused, the delicate cream neck and large, hooped earrings, back narrowed down to tiny buttocks that perched. He saw a long pale arm raise, the hand disappeared at her face then dropped to tap the side of a martini glass. Her hair was white and punky and bobbed short, strands feathered around those hoops. She suddenly seemed familiar, like from high school.

The barman nicked his head as Beto approached. "Long time! How's your mom?"

"Wouldn't know." Beto shook his head darkly and let the sack plop between the barstool's feet—a five-stool separation from the couple. Beto arched his back and looked down. His naked wrists on the bar top, *he was free.*

"This here is Arturo. Everyone knows Art." The barman raised an empty wineglass, tipped it in the direction of the man with his hat on the bar, sitting next to the woman. Then he brought the glass back into the light, squinted, stuck his rag in and rubbed, slung the rag over his shoulder, inspected his work.

Neither the man nor familiar-faced woman looked in Beto's direction. The man, long lean fingers, was picking his cuticles; rings of various stones, shined. Beto thought the woman could have been in history class, what, fifteen years ago.

"No, nope. Don't think I do." Beto's ears heard the beer taps' siren song, saliva building at the sides of his mouth, then metal and glass collided, and Beto flinched. "Uh, can I get a coffee?"

"Sure. Let me just"—Barman was picking up pieces, his gaze never leaving Beto, his words toned upward toward the bar rail— "Hey, your mom would want you to call, Beto-Boy."

Beto bowed his head, hiding his wince. His peripheral vision caught the woman with the bobbed hair laugh, her private joke. She shivered, starting at shoulders and slinking down to her rump. The man with the hat blocked most of his view, bigger than Beto'd thought, and a pocket square sticking out from his right breast. For a second Beto wished for the color of that square, for anything lush, calming, clean. From the corner of his eye, all he saw was the curve of the lady. Familiar, nice looking, her shoulders rose out of the loose sweater top. They were rice white and smooth. With a languid arm, she drew those lacquered nails around the bar clicking a beat. Beto followed the line of her shoulders up to that blond hairdo, then her pointed chin. The man, Art, shifted, hiked the sleeve of his shirt, his watch was enormous. Then loosened his tie, his thumb and forefinger pinched at his pocket scarf, further cutting Beto's view, then set his lean hand on top of the woman's fidgeting fingers, fixing his gaze on the bar's back wall mirror.

The barman swooped over with a burnt coffee carafe, filled Beto's cup full of black, and in one move, returned the stained flask to a Bunn burner, his hand posed then plucked up another glass. He held it vertical, by its base, then angled, a water drop at its bottom glinted off a spotlight. The barman's lips furrowed down as he tipped the glass rim and retrieved his rag from his shoulder. That drop of water caught on his forearm sleeve. His affiliation tat menaced through the dampened fabric. Elbow up, he shoved the rag inside, rubbing vigorously. He turned to the bar's back mirror, having a clear view of his patrons and the front door.

Beto's eyes widened, a minatory thought, He's inked? He watched the barman flex his glutes with each twist of his rag.

The glass sparkled as the barman set it silently on its appropriate shelf. Then he took the rag, folded it twice, and ran it in a tight sine curve from one side of the bar, past the neat couple and up to Beto. He leaned in, lips closed. "Watch yourself."—Held the damp rag up to a spot light, then crushed it in his palm.—"What else can I get ya?"

Eyes forward, Beto worked to contemplate tapioca pudding versus a slice of pie. The pastry pedestal was on the back bar. He could see the pie from all sides reflected in the mirror and also follow Arturo's scowl, intent between his fingernails, the woman's hand, and the mirror. His shoulders were near his ears.

Looking down, Beto picked up the teaspoon, and stirred his coffee. Arturo's eyes shifted, and when Beto looked again, there was the dark stare of that black turtle-neck wearing man, that bluish scar, sitting at that small table with his limp-paged book. That man broke eye contact, looked unperturbed, stretched his thick neck, left, right, and then returned to the book's pages.

"More coffee?" The barman came carrying the burned carafe and let the hot stream flow into the cup. Beto nodded, slightly turning as if to blow on the hot liquid. He watched the woman wiggle her skirt-covered butt back and forth on the barstool, shiver, starting at her hips and ending with her white bobbed crown and the man paternally took her hand and squeezed around it. Beto had not seen a lady dressed up pretty-like in a long time.

"Glass a water if you don't mind."

The barman picked up a squat water glass, wiped it with vigor, threw the rag onto a pile of other rags, then stood wide-legged before the fountain. "Would the lady like still or sparkling?

"She'll take the bubbles, and here." A ringed finger tapped the bar. "Jack Daniels, neat."

Beto's eyes tightened. Art's hand slipped into a pocket, then flashed, low, a hint of rolled green.

"I'm going to the little girls' room."

Her lithe body slide from the stool. It took a couple beats before she had a tiny evening bag untangled and set on her shoulder, then she adjusted her skirt. Beto watched her hand smooth along her rump, but his mind saw the rolled cash, then focused back on her tight walk down the hall toward the phones and toilets. He watched her for as long as he dared before it became too obvious. He picked up his teaspoon and rammed it into the coffee cup, seeing greenbacks, all the plans, hearing the clink and slide of metal, seeing, again, a mangled kid, a dead guard. All the images vibrated.

"You'd do good to ring your mother." The barman was turning a whisky glass he held between his thumb and pointer, the other hand reaching for the top folded rag on the clean pile under the mirror.

"She's asleep and not expecting."

Arturo suddenly straightened, pushing his chest toward the bar, toward his hat, then swiveled his head. "We've been expecting you, Beto, right?"

The blond bob glided into view at the edge of the bar's back mirror and Beto was distracted. Her delicate fingertips pushed at each nostril. Beto leaned toward the reflection of her smile. It was glistening pink, and her top and bottom lips reminded him of his mother's tea roses that came faithfully, mustering through spring's slush and snow to blossom like it was their first time ever seeing the sun.

"We're expecting? Darling?" A high pitch and giggly, the woman's ankles unsteady as she slid back onto the stool. Then she popped up, standing tall on the rung to speak over Arturo's head. "Such a bore; we've been waiting for so long."

"Bus was stuck; snow, pile-ups." Beto nodded to the barman and then let his forehead angle indicating the pie on the pedestal, trapped under a plastic lid.

Art turned on his stool, his back to the woman, and looked directly at Beto. "Well, you got your ass here now. You carrying?"

The barman's moves quickened as he tightened his grip on the rag, holding the plate with a slice of pie in his other hand. His eyes flittered between Arturo and the plate. The scoop of a-la-mode was slipping. In a drawn-out movement, he set the pie in front of Beto and then moved back and stood, planting his feet wide between Beto and the couple. He snapped his rag between his two fists. A long minute passed, and he finally turned and grabbed another tumbler to inspect.

Beto saw the mirror reflected the man with the book. He took his beer coaster and placed it between the pages, looked at his wrist, and then leaned toward the briefcase at his feet, fussing with something solid in its depths. In the mirror, Beto saw Arturo's shoulder twist back facing the room behind. His whole arm went straight down past that pocket of wadded cash to his side, and his hand gently patted the air. In the reflection, the ceiling, tiny colored shafts of light, and the man at the table slowly reopening his book, sliding out the coaster and replacing it under the beer. Beto's eyes were caught between the man with the book, whose neck arched, forehead rolling up to the spotlights, and the bob, whose eyes rolled down, disdainful at her glass of bubble water, nails incessant, clicking the rim of the empty martini glass.

"I want another one!" Her voice petulant.

"We've been waiting—and we don't like to wait." Art spoke to the back mirror, his eyes drilling. Beto adverted them, feigning contemplation of a fork full of pie. The flaky crust, the goo, the slippery ice cream, and a thought slide into his mind and grabbed, then shook him. It wasn't the woman who looked familiar, it was something with this guy, Arturo. The thought made him gulp and rub his hands on his pants. His fork clattered to the floor like so many keys.

The barman's hand descended with grace and placed another fork in front of Beto and then returned with two white napkins sliding then pressing down firm along the bar top. Beto observed the blue veins popping on the back of the barman's hand and heard his closed mouth hiss, "Them's bad news, eat your pie, Beto-boy." Beto scrunched the napkin in his lap. The barman stepped back, grabbed the damp rag from his shoulder, spun facing the back mirror, and held the rag tight, searching Beto's eyes. He then said, "Lilly. She's gone."

The sack was safe on the floor. Beto's boot could feel the resistance of Lillytwo. "Gone? Far?" Beto's head tilted to the side and up. Wasn't little Lilly too young? Beto crimped, a dark memory, his mother white fisted as she yanked off his sister's doll's head with a sneer that said, "Aren't you a little too old for this?" Mother held the head, a trophy, and laughed. Lilly ran for cover into Beto's arms. Then he'd been sent away, his arms locked away, and Beto learned to fear the worst. He searched the barman's face

The corner of the rag was sticking up from a Collins glass, and the barman drew it out softly, holding the glass to the light, rotating it to the left, to the right. His profile to the bar's back mirror, his voice soft like a-la-mode. "Buried, closed coffin—almost put your mother in the next grave—Beto-boy."

His gut crammed, intestines twisted. "Huh?"

Taking up a delicate glass, bulbed for rich cognac, the barman held it in front of his eyes and regarded Beto through it. Beto saw a resignation through that warped curve. The glass, aloft, in front of the barman's squint, in front of Beto's eyes, started to fill, drop by precious drop, not with a golden liquor but a burgundy blood.

Then the bobbed hair leaned far forward over the bar, turned, ignoring Arturo, and faced Beto. "We were waiting, Art's waiting. Me too." She giggled, rubbing her nose. A tickle of blood leaked over her top lip. "But you're here now"—Holding a thin bar napkin to her nose—"That's obvious."

Beto looked at her pouty face and reassessed. It looked hollow and tinted yellow. The pink of her lips, like a paint streak, her nose, twitching, misshapen like a boxer he'd known. The decision: not attractive. He hadn't seen a female outside of in a guard uniform in ages, but he still had his senses. He ate his pie, controlled, slow, sensing each bite of sweetness slip down, only the pie, not the lady. And, today a free man. Time done, lessons learned, all different, all new. And Lilly, dead? Painful to picture any different than dolls and bows; an ache was rising.

"That's obvious." She said again.

Beto's body shuddered, his head jerked hearing the smack of a hand hitting a cheek.

Arturo! That was Art, Art Betancourt, failing school, dragging classes behind, forever the wiseass, a whole different kind of trouble. He saw the woman touch her blossoming-red cheek and Art's fingers bullying her other hand into the bar top. "That was not necessary, dear."

"You're hurting." Her nose dripped; her voice squeaked.

Beto sat back from a stinging memory, one of thousands. In the mirror, he could no longer see the man with the book. The book was alone, holding the table, but the briefcase was gone. The thick-necked man was gone too and the bar door closed. Not there for whatever Art was leaning into.

The barman caught the house phone on the first ring and handed it across the bar. Arturo had to remove his hand from the woman's, taking the call. Beto, in the mirror, could see his eyes widen and then cross down.

The barman leaned into his drip rail, leveling with Beto's eyes, "You should go now Beto, get on home."

Beto took the cue, placed a couple bills on the bar, leaned over between his legs and grabbed his sack. He turned a soft smile to the barman. Crossed with quick steps to the first door. Stepping in between the two doors, the dry air blew from the heater and choked. He steeled himself, then opened the outside door.

Big, wet clumps of white slammed into the grated windows; the bus took a sharp curve on two wheels. A lurch and a seat belt bit into Beto's gut. A sudden heaviness around his wrists proved to be double locked handcuffs. Vision dry, heat belching from the bus's floor heaters up along the window into Beto's hazy eyes that saw the barman, standing wide-legged, bullet-proof vest tight, smiling at the confusion on Beto's face. Smiled while Beto wondered if he was still dreaming.

A Dark Place
Quintin Peterson

HE COULD WATCH little girls all day long. Oh, how he loved tweenagers! Sweet. Juicy. Tender. Mmmmm.

As usual, no one paid any attention to his white late model Ford panel van, which on this occasion was parked across the street from Our Lady of Victory School. Obscured by the nondescript vehicle's dark tinted windows, the driver was afforded the opportunity to take his time and make his selection carefully, which was the way he liked it. Experience had taught him that nothing good ever comes of hasty decisions.

Intently, he studied the prepubescent females cavorting on the playground, looking for a new girl to thrill.

Who would be the lucky one; who would be his new bride? The luscious brunette with the ponytails? The delightful, leggy redhead whose skirt was a bit too short? The curvaceous caramel colored black girl with cornrows and the high, round rump? Wait a second, stop the presses. Bingo! The scrumptious blonde who filled out her Catholic school uniform oh-so-nicely. Yes. He raised his binoculars to his bloodshot eyes and adjusted the focus to make sure that she indeed was the girl du jour. Yes. Goldilocks would do nicely. She would make a perfect addition to his celestial harem.

The comely girl's golden, shoulder-length hair bounced, and her plaid skirt rose and fell as she played jump rope. Ogling her through the binoculars, he licked his lips as he caught glimpses of her white panties. An overwhelming desire for her gripped him and his burgeoning arousal made him uncomfortable in his already too snug-fitting jeans.

He smiled broadly, exposing his nicotine and coffee-stained teeth. Today was going to be another great day, and the nights to come, another great Honeymoon.

—

Three days after she went missing from Our Lady of Victory, a health nut out for his early morning jog found the body of twelve-year-old Melissa Glass on Glover Road in Rock Creek Park, just off Military Road, NW. Naked, her wrists and ankles raw with rope-burns from course restraints, her neck blackened by bruises sustained as the result of manual strangulation by powerful hands, she was propped against a tree, her legs spread as far apart as they would go, a note safety-pinned to her chest...just like the others. Just like the others, her hair was neatly combed in place and her eyes were scotch-taped open. Her blonde mane, which was draped across her slender shoulders, gleamed in the sunlight that pierced the leaf-filled branches above her.

DC Homicide Detective Sergeant Winston Henderson had noticed that she had the prettiest hazel eyes in the photos of her smiling at family affairs and in school portraits, but they were a grotesque milky color now.

The detective knelt and read the killer's message, some sort of sick poem fashioned from words and letters clipped from magazines and newspapers, like a ransom note. It read exactly as the other three notes he'd seen pinned to dead girls' chests in the last month:

"Bushmen choose their brides from
The newly born and the very young
And allow
Mother Nature time enough
To endow
Their choices with enough
To make them resemble women
Before making them women.
I am a bushman,
And I'll have you now."

It was official: Melissa Glass, daughter of the ultra-rich developer Solomon Glass, was the Bushman's fourth victim...that authorities knew of. Only God and the Devil and this demon knew how many victims there truly were, how many this monster had killed in other places around the country, using a different Modus Operandi maybe—

they hadn't gotten any similar MO hits to the DC murders using the FBI's Violent Criminals Apprehension Program database—or how many he had violated and left alive before he'd acquired the compulsion to kill.

A few reporters had learned of the killer's signature, and knew the poem verbatim, but to their credit and the news agencies they worked for had agreed not to publicize it to make sure kooks didn't waste investigators' time by coming forward and "confessing" to the murders. The compromise between the department and the news media was that they could openly refer to the killer by his nom de plume.

Henderson stared at the murdered girl and shook his head. "Christ," he muttered.

That dirty bastard had raped and killed a big wig's daughter now. High- profile cases don't get any higher than this. They were in deep shit now. The media was going to crucify them, and Mayor Donner and Chief Barkley were going to be all over them like a cheap suit until they caught this son of a bitch. And the task force didn't have anything to go on.

Outside of the park, a pack of ravenous news hounds outside the park eagerly awaiting confirmation of the identity of the latest victim were encamped one block away on 27th Street NW behind yellow crime scene tape where police officers were posted to keep them at bay. As they waited, TV and radio reporters speculated on air that the body in Rock Creek Park could in fact be that of Melissa Glass— Henderson had heard one of them on WTOP radio on his drive to the crime scene. It was only a matter of time before Mister and Missus Glass showed up at the scene to find out for themselves…and he would have to face them and give them the god-awful news.

The detective saw a white van, the morgue wagon, enter the park and drive toward the crime scene.

Winston looked at Melissa. He suppressed a shudder as he saw a fly saunter across the dead girl's left eyeball. Quickly, he waved away the insect with a latex gloved hand.

Discreetly, he made the sign of the cross. Solemnly, as he had done several times a day since the Bushman had made his horrific debut, Henderson prayed within himself to a god he no longer was sure existed.

"Ms. Glass, I presume."

Winston Henderson looked over his left shoulder, up at the ever-dapper "Hollywood" Frank Medarac, Chief Medical Examiner for the District of Columbia.

"Glad you could make it, doc," said Henderson.

"Wouldn't miss it for the world," Hollywood Frank replied. He stooped next to the detective and read the note pinned to the girl's chest. "It's our boy alright." The ME paused briefly, looking the girl over and then added, "He's got good taste."

The doctor noticed something and directed the detective's attention to it.

"Did you see here, these marks?" Medarac asked. Without waiting for a reply, he continued. "Stun gun, same as the rest. Based on the distance between the contact marks, he's still using his trusty Stun Master 775."

Henderson nodded. "How long's she been dead?"

Hollywood Frank, his hands sheathed in latex, performed a cursory examination, and guesstimated, "Two, maybe three or four hours."

Just like the others.

"The evidence technicians are finished with her," he told the M.E. "What say we get her out of here?"

Medarac nodded. He caught the attention of his two assistants standing by the morgue wagon and motioned them over. "Tag her and bag her," he told them.

Henderson stood, turned and walked away. Maintaining his best poker face, he concealed the turmoil beneath his seemingly calm exterior, just as the calm surface of the murky Potomac River masks its turbulent undertow. He could not allow his colleagues even a glimpse of the angst that gripped him...or to suspect that he was scared. This maniac frightened him, not simply because of his heinous acts, but also because the killer made Henderson doubt that he was good enough to apprehend him.

During the course of this investigation, the armor of the special kind of callousness, the requisite emotional detachment police officers develop early in their careers in order to protect their psyches, had lost its integrity, in much the same way Kevlar body armor deteriorates over time, leaving him vulnerable and insecure. Emotional detachment not only allowed him to think clearly and methodically track down suspects, but also to bear witness to the most terrible things and make death notifications to the grief stricken relatives of murder victims, yet still go on with his own life and sleep at night. But now, the emotions he had learned to suppress were upon him and, for lack of a better definition, he was now emotionally disturbed. Now constantly assailed by an odd mixture of anger, melancholy, outrage, and hopelessness, he was drinking too much and sleeping too little. The Bushman slayings had taken him to a dark place, and he longed to come out into the light.

Henderson was forty-two, nine years away from being eligible for retirement with twenty-five years of public service, but he looked older…as old as he felt. Furthermore, the job had scarred him not only mentally, but also physically. In the performance of duty, he had been shot once and stabbed twice, but the scars of the flesh paled by comparison to the wounds no one could see, the ones that would never heal.

Several independent studies have revealed that police work prematurely ages people and shortens their lifespan due to the stresses of the job of dealing with the dark side of humanity on a regular basis. His sixteen years of service had definitely aged him. His neatly cut hair was graying, but he wasn't balding, thank God! There were slightly dark circles under his eyes, but at least bags weren't yet present; the eyes themselves were bloodshot and tired-looking, partly due to lack of sleep and partly because of the new extended wear contacts he was still trying to become accustomed to—wearing eyeglasses at this point would only add to the perception that he was over the hill. It was true, of course, but there was no need for everybody to know it.

The detective also was plagued by guilt. The survivors of the victims were counting on them, on him, to give them justice; the people of this city were depending on him to protect them from this brute, and he wasn't up to it. He was letting them down.

Henderson had worked many murders during his twelve years as a homicide detective, some of the toughest in fact, but he wasn't cut out for this; how detectives who investigated Special Victims cases involving murders of young children and babies on a regular basis, he'd never know. Murdered kids and baby killers gave him the creeps…and nightmares, even when he was awake. He understood the motives behind murders involving gang bangers, drug dealers, and the like, and homicide as the result of passion, but he had never dealt with this kind of murderer, who apparently killed for the joy of it. Henderson was convinced that this killer was truly evil, fueled by motivations he could not fathom. He was ill prepared for this battle against good and evil, felt outmatched. His arms were too short to box with the Devil.

Detective Henderson was certain that he shouldn't be part of this task force, that the search for this beast was better suited to those with thicker skins and abundant familiarity with the demented minds of violent sociopaths and psychopaths. It had simply been his misfortune almost four weeks ago to the day to catch the first Bushman murder case, eleven-year-old Shayana Spencer. She'd been abducted from the vicinity of Barnard Elementary three days before her naked, ravaged body was found in Fort DuPont Park. Consequently, when the second victim turned up–ten-year-old Annette Lohan, found in Anacostia Park, three days after she went missing on her way home from Whittier Elementary and five days after Shayana was found—he had been assigned to the Metropolitan Police Department/FBI task force put in place to investigate these serial murders.

He knew that Shayana Spencer was the first of many such killings, that her murder was only the beginning, so the very day her body was found, Henderson had adamantly, and perhaps a bit too forcefully, pressed several of his superior officers to form a task force of professionals trained in tracking serial killers to handle the Spencer murder case, and the cases he knew would surely follow. "I'll assign one of my people to the task force, of course," he'd offered. Therefore, he also couldn't overlook the high probability that he had been assigned to the task force because the officials he'd locked horns with realized that he didn't want any part of this investigation, and this was their revenge. Damn them. In hindsight, he probably would have fared better had he used the Brer Rabbit "please don't fling me in that briar patch" reverse psychology tactic.

The third victim, eleven-year-old Juanita Lopez, was found in Meridian Park three days after she went missing from Truesdell Elementary, four days after the task force was formed.

The rest of the task force, which was now scattered about the crime scene along with evidence technicians, consisted of Detective Carl Anderson, who normally worked along with Henderson out of the Major Case Squad; luscious and curvaceous Detective Lourdes Rojas of the Special Victims Unit, with whom who shared a mutual attraction; FBI Special Agent James Roman of the Washington Field Office; and "legendary" profiler FBI Special Agent Darwin Roselle of the Behavioral Sciences Unit out of Quantico, Virginia, who in

Henderson's opinion was their weakest link...and he didn't mind letting him know what he thought of him in all of the group's discussions regarding the unsub.

As far as Henderson was concerned, Roselle's "profile" of the unsub was a bunch of the same old, rehashed gobbledy gook: white male, twenty-five to forty-five years of age; clean shaven, small to medium build, possibly sexually abused as a child, probably self-employed, drives a van, lives alone in a house with an attached garage or in a rural area, blah, blah, blah.

Equally useless in the Bushman murders was the notion that serial killers kill people within their race—the Bushman had killed a black girl, a Hispanic girl and two white girls. Besides being in the same age group, the only thing the victims had in common was that they were remarkably good-looking.

As for the parts about the suspect's transportation and residence, sure he drives a van, because he needs to be able to hide his abductees from prying eyes, and sure he lives alone in a house with a garage or in a rural area, so he can get his victims into and out of his house without being seen and have privacy to take his time and have his way with them. Shit, it didn't take a genius criminologist to figure that out, it's just common sense. Duh.

No, Roselle didn't impress him, and wouldn't unless he came up with some insight that would actually help them catch the Bushman.

Though they were more suited to this kind of work, Henderson was certain the other members of the task force shared his consternation, if not his despair. Apparently as disturbed as he, not one of them had used gallows humor, the pressure safety valve for public safety workers, who joke abundantly at scenes of horror to defuse their distress. Hell, they couldn't think of anything funny to say. Many of the people working these scenes had daughters within the age group targeted by this murderous sexual predator, and though his daughters were grown now, Shayana Spencer reminded Henderson of his daughter Mariah when she was Shayana's age. And he had two nieces attending DC private schools who fell within that age group.

Certainly, the frustration he felt also gripped the others who had made it their life's mission to speak for the dead. If the killer were true to form, which Henderson didn't doubt, no physical evidence would be found on Melissa's body or at this "crime scene."

In the previous cases, the girls were murdered in the killer's lair or possibly inside of his van just before they were dumped—no, not dumped, put on display—in locations where they could be found quickly.

The maniac violated his victims for three days before he killed them and had the wherewithal to shampoo and bathe them to eliminate hair, skin and fiber samples, and to douche every desecrated orifice of the victims with a bleach and disinfectant solution to make it impossible to gather DNA samples via his vile secretions.

Whether he was a cunning criminal mastermind or simply a devoted viewer of CSI, the killer had them over a barrel. The consensus was that the only hard evidence linking the psycho to these murders would be found in his lair and in his vehicle. He undoubtedly kept souvenirs, such as clothing and personal items of the victims, and his van must contain physical evidence linking him to one or more of the murders, so prosecuting him would be a snap...if he made it to trial. More than likely, he'd spend the rest of his miserable life in an institution for the criminally insane, a darling of the psychiatric community, practitioners, and academicians alike.

Whatever the case might be they had to catch him before he killed again. But how?

As soon as the second victim turned up, in conjunction with forming the task force and initiating in-depth background checks of current and former employees of District of Columbia public and private elementary and middle schools, and scrutinizing all registered sex offenders in the Washington, DC metropolitan area, high ranking police officials had made it a point to warn the public, and to direct public and private elementary and middle school teachers and administrators to advise their students to avoid strangers, keep a watchful eye, and report any suspicious characters near or on school grounds, all to no avail.

Police department personnel made sure at every opportunity during news interviews to let the public know that the department was offering a reward of twenty-five thousand dollars per victim to anyone who provided information that led to the arrest and conviction of the Bushman, but not one individual had called the hotline with good information.

Officers dressed in plainclothes and operating their own personal vehicles had been assigned to patrol the vicinities of schools attended by pre-teens and watch for suspicious characters, but not one viable suspect had surfaced.

Nothing they had attempted had made a difference; the Bushman had managed to claim more victims.

Reporters seemed to feel it was their duty to, in every report, give the impression that the police department and the Donner Administration were incompetent. Perhaps they were right, Henderson thought. The Bushman was out there somewhere, perhaps even now searching for his next victim. And there was nothing they could do to stop him.

His Nextel signaled that someone was calling him via the walkie-talkie function. He removed his cell phone from its belt clip and answered, "Henderson."

"Captain Braxton here." It was his boss, the commander of the Violent Crimes Branch, Captain Zack Braxton, better known as "Blackjack Zack" because of his penchant for using his blackjack on handcuffed prisoners back in the good ol' days.

"The victim's parents are at 27th and Military Road making a ruckus," Blackjack Zack said. "We need you to get over here right now."

Henderson closed his eyes and sighed. "Copy that," he said. "I'll be right there."

He returned his phone to its holder, then snapped off his latex gloves and stuffed them into a pants pocket.

Detective Rojas intercepted him as he strode toward Military Road.

"Where are you going in such a hurry?" she wanted to know.

"Her parents are here," he told her.

"Damn," she said. "You know, the best thing would be is if when we find out who the Bushman is, we just hire a hitman, take out a contract on his sorry ass, and that would be that. You know he's just going to be put in a nut house if we take him in. He'll get to take it easy for the rest of his miserable…"

"Contract," Henderson said. "Lourdes, you just gave me an idea. Get the whole team in on it and pull whatever personnel together you can to assist you. First, get a list of every privately owned company that has maintenance or repair contracts with DC public schools and get the same from Our Lady of Victory. Then contact these companies and obtain lists of all of their employees, and all of their work orders in the last couple of months, see if any one person has done work at all the schools the victims attended. And subcontractors, too. And if you don't find anything, go back a couple of months at a time until you do…"

Rojas smiled. "I get it! That's good thinking, Sarge. Repairmen, technicians, what have you, have access to schools, don't attract attention, and can move about freely…"

"And," he added, "May even have had innocent contact with the victims, you know, 'Hey, how are you?'"

"Then later," Rojas said, "when he was ready to make his move, he could get close enough to strike, without setting off any alarms. After all, he wasn't a complete stranger, right? He was just the kindly maintenance man, or whatever, who was always so pleasant."

Henderson nodded. "Whoever you come up with, do a background check, find out where he lives, what he drives, and pull his ID photo from DMV. Clue our people in and get on it ASAP. I'll hook up with you back at the command center as soon as I make this death notification and can get away."

They nodded at each other and then strode off in opposite directions, like people with a purpose.

—

The task of pulling together all of the needed information from the Comptroller of the District of Columbia, then compiling employee lists from contractors and subcontractors authorized to do repair work and maintenance at DC schools, as well as obtaining the same information from Our Lady of Victory, and then identifying suspects by cross-referencing work orders for the last couple of months at the schools the victims attended had been a huge undertaking. Working out of the Metropolitan Police Department's high-tech Command Information Center, located on the fifth floor of the Henry J. Daly Municipal Center, just down the hall from the Office of the Chief of Police, the task force had used every available computer and data retrieval geek and every Criminal Justice Information System certified employee they could muster. Still, the project had taken a full day and a half before they got results. Immediately, Detective Henderson called for a briefing in the CIC with Chief of Police Melvin Barkley, Executive Assistant Chief Caryn Jackson, and Commander Hilton "Bad

News" Hughes, Superintendent of Detectives.

When the top brass was seated, Henderson nodded at Detective Rojas. She pushed a button on a console and the suspect's Maryland driver's license photo was displayed on a huge plasma screen TV.

"His name," Henderson informed the brass, "is Robert Lawrence Harvey, age thirty-five. He's a subcontractor for G & G Maintenance and Repairs, Inc., which has a contract with the DC Public School System and several private schools in DC The name of Harvey's small business is 'Mr. Fixit.' And a Mr. Fixit he is indeed. Harvey is a multifaceted handyman. He's a certified electrician, a plumber, heating/cooling systems repairman, does painting and drywall work, you name it. And, out of all of the people who have done work in the past three months at the schools the victims attended, only Harvey has worked at all four. In fact, in two of the cases, he worked at the schools on the very days the girls were abducted."

"Consistent with my profile," Special Agent Roselle added, "he's self-employed and owns a van and a house. He resides in an old farmhouse in a very rural area out on 301 in Waldorf. He gets lots of privacy there. Nearest neighbor is two miles away."

"I looked into his background," Detective Anderson said. "Through IRS, credit bureau, and phone and utility billing records, I found out every place he's lived in the past ten years." He referred to his notebook. "He's lived in Dallas, Texas; Atlanta, Georgia; Winston-Salem, South Carolina; Richmond, Virginia; Baltimore, Maryland..."

"And with that information," Rojas added, "I contacted the sex offender branches of the police departments in the cities he lived to determine if they had any unsolved sexual assault cases involving little girls during the time periods he lived in their jurisdictions that we could possibly match up to him. Each police department came up with several cases with similar suspect descriptions, where the suspect told each victim that she was his wife or that he was her husband. I suspect that Harvey is a viable suspect in hundreds of such cases."

Roselle nodded. "If this is our suspect, the chances are good that he upped the stakes to murder because he had to—simply raping the girls no longer thrilled him. He had to start killing to achieve the rush. It's quite common, actually."

"Sounds like we've got our man," said Superintendent of Detectives Hughes.

"Good work, all of you," Chief Barkley said. "How far along are we on obtaining arrest and search warrants?"

"That's going to be a problem," Roman chimed in. "The U.S. Attorney's Office says we don't have enough for warrants...and I agree. We have no probable cause. Harvey having worked at the schools, even on the days girls were abducted, isn't enough. It's circumstantial; we have no hard evidence linking him to the crimes."

"The hard evidence we need," EAC Jackson said as she rubbed a hand along her cornrows, "is in his van and his house, no doubt."

"Any chance," said Chief Barkley, "that we can link him to one of these sexual assaults in another jurisdiction? Get them to issue an arrest warrant so that we can pick him up and hold him as a fugitive from justice? It'll give us a shot at searching his van."

Rojas shook her head. "No DNA. The suspect used a condom in each case. He also hid his face, either with a ski mask, or a handkerchief over the lower part of his face."

Chief Barkley rubbed his chin. "Any ideas as to how we can get search warrants so we can put this psycho away?"

Henderson looked Chief Barkley in the eye. "Leave that to me, sir. Tomorrow, Harvey has work orders at three public schools. We'll assign plainclothes tactical officers in unmarked cars to watch the three schools and assign patrol cars to stay in the areas of the schools, but out of sight. They'll have Harvey's driver's license photo and the description and tag number of his van. I'll be notified when he shows up at one of the schools and the task force will converge there.

"If Harvey should commit a traffic violation when he leaves the school, we can pull him over ... and if he should be suspected of being under the influence of drugs or alcohol, we can arrest him and impound his vehicle ... for safekeeping."

Special Agent Roman and Special Agent Roselle frowned, Chief Barkley—and every other cop in the room—smiled.

"Or we may even catch him in the act," Detective Lourdes Rojas added. "The act of abducting a girl, I mean. If we're lucky." She looked around the room and then continued. "What? I'm just saying what we're all thinking. Catching him red handed with a little girl would solve our warrant problem. The U.S. Attorney won't deny us search warrants then."

Chief Barkley nodded and took his feet. "Carry on," he said before he walked from the room, the EAC and the superintendent of detectives on his heels.

—

The dimly lit basement of the Bushman's home had two special rooms, each with a hand-made wooden sign posted above the door. One sign read "Chapel" and the other "Honeymoon Suite."

The "Chapel" room actually appeared to be a small chapel, with wood paneled walls and two backlit, stained-glass windows behind and on each side of the pulpit, where a bespectacled mannequin dressed as a pastor stood before it holding an opened book in its hands; and wooden pews filled with mannequins dressed in Sunday best, witnesses to each blessed event. Inside of a compartment in front of the pulpit, hidden behind a small door, was a cassette tape player containing a recording of a minister performing a marriage ceremony. The Bushman played it when he wed each bride. And just outside the chapel was another cassette deck, inside of a compartment next to the door. On that tape were two tunes, "Here Comes the Bride," preceded by the Dixie Cups' hit, "Chapel of Love."

—

The bride and groom always waited just outside the chapel and listened to the entire song. When the girls finished singing and "Here Comes the Bride" began to play, arm-in-arm the Bushman and his betrothed entered the chapel.

The Honeymoon Suite, which was laid out like a master bedroom with a full bath, is where he took each bride immediately following the wedding ceremony and consummated the marriage. It contained only a cherry wood dresser, and a matching king size Four Poster Bed dressed in white satin sheets, with lengths of heavy rope to secure the bride's wrists and ankles attached to each post. This was his favorite room in the house.

Adjacent to the Honeymoon Suite and the laundry room was a small room, which contained a sewing machine, an Empire Dress Form, and everything else a seamstress or tailor needed. There, the Bushman looked over the tiny white wedding gown, which he made alterations to, as needed, to afford each of his young brides a perfect fit. The gown was in great shape, as was the veil. Carefully, he re-hung the wedding outfit in the closet next to his tux, directly above an assortment of tiny white patent leather shoes of various sizes and closed the door.

He left the sewing room, closing the door behind him, and went to the Honeymoon Suite. The Bushman opened the closet that contained the clothing and shoes of all his brides. He reached to the shelf above and picked up his last bride's underwear, which would soon take their place with the underwear of the other brides in a special box at the rear of the shelf.

The Bushman walked over to the king size bed and stretched out. He unzipped his pants and fondled himself as he sniffed Melissa's tiny white panties. He closed his eyes and sighed, then grinned broadly as he reminisced about the inexorable pleasure, he had derived from having her, over and over again. And suddenly, the sensation was gone; he could not recapture the high.

It was always the same: Three days of bliss with each bride, a couple more days of joy reliving the experience and then poof! The thrill was gone.

He sat bolt upright, threw her panties across the room, into the closet. More. He needed more. And soon. No, he needed it now.

The Bushman got up from the bed, strode to the door and exited the room.

It was time to find that next special young lady.

—

Seventh District Plainclothes Tactical Officer Steven Freeburn waited until the heavy pedestrian and vehicular traffic died down before he approached Robert Lawrence Harvey's van, which was parked near the playground of Leckie Elementary, located in the 4200 block of Martin Luther King, Jr., Avenue, SW. His actions obstructed by the van itself and the car it was parked in front of, he stooped near the rear of the van and pretended to tie his right shoe, but then adeptly pulled an ASP expandable metal baton from his rear pocket, extended it to its full length with a flip of the wrist, and shattered the right taillight with a single blow. Afterward he slammed the tip of the ASP hard once against the asphalt to collapse it and returned the metal baton to his rear pocket. Officer Freeburn then casually returned to his unmarked police car, a seized-for-forfeiture late model red Chevy Camaro, which was parked on the opposite side of the street.

As soon as he squeezed his burly frame into the Camaro, he keyed his radio, which was tuned to the 7D tactical channel, and announced, "We have probable cause for a traffic stop. Broken taillight, passenger side."

"Copy that," Detective Henderson replied. He smiled. The old broken taillight tactic. Beautiful. He keyed his radio and said, "All units, stand by."

The task force had responded to the vicinity of Leckie Elementary as soon as the 7D surveillance team notified them at nine that morning that the suspect was on the scene.

Henderson and Lourdes had been sitting in the cruiser, which was parked next to a wooded area on Second Street, SW, one street over from and parallel to MLK Avenue, for about an hour. The other members of the task force were parked behind them, Detective Anderson alone in his unmarked cruiser, and the feds together in theirs. One plainclothes tactical unit was parked on Darrington Street, SW, and the two scout cars on nearby streets, one on Danbury and the other on Galveston.

"It won't be long now," Rojas said.

"It can't be soon enough, Lourdes."

As if on cue, Officer Freeburn announced over the air, "The suspect is exiting the school."

Officer Freeburn watched Harvey push a large, metal tool cart across the playground, onto the sidewalk, and toward his van.

The officer spoke into his radio, "The suspect is approaching his vehicle. He has his tool cart, so his work at the school must be completed. He should be on his way shortly."

Harvey pushed the cart to the side of the van next to the sidewalk, left it there, and walked around to the driver's side. He unlocked it with his remote control, reached in and turned on the ignition, and then returned to the cart. The van was handicap accessible, so he lowered the ramp, pushed the cart onto it, stood beside it, and raised the ramp. He then pushed the tool cart into the van, locked its wheels, and secured the cart with vinyl straps bolted to the floor of the cargo hold. Afterwards, he closed the door, stepped through into the passenger cabin, and sat behind the wheel. He pulled off.

"The suspect's in motion," Freeburn said into the radio.

"Mark units, make the traffic stop," Detective Henderson said into the radio.

"Unmarked units, move in, but hang back until the stop." He turned to Detective Rojas. "Here we go, Lourdes."

A block away from where Harvey had been parked, the officer in the scout car that had been parked on Danbury Street pulled up behind the van and activated his vehicle's light bar. Panic struck Harvey when he saw the police car in his side mirrors. He pulled over just the same.

Maintaining a calm exterior, he waited patiently for the officer to walk to the van. He noticed that the officer seemed uncharacteristically apprehensive as he approached the driver side of the van. Harvey sensed that the officer was prepared to draw down on him at the first sign of trouble. The police must be on to him. He didn't know how, but they were. He rolled down the driver's side window and readied himself.

Officer Leo Swanson cautiously approached the suspect vehicle. Once he was alongside of the van, not standing directly in front of the driver's window, Harvey put on a big grin and turned up the charm.

"What's the problem, officer?"

"You have a broken taillight," Officer Swanson told him.

"What?" Harvey said. "Let me see…"

Harvey opened the door and jumped out of the van.

The officer placed his hand on the butt of his service weapon. "Please, get back in the vehicle, sir…"

Before he could draw his weapon, Harvey pressed his Stun Master 775 into Swanson's throat, sending 775,000 volts into the officer, instantly incapacitating him. Swanson collapsed, hitting the roadway like a sack of potatoes.

Harvey jumped into the van and sped away. He traveled only a short distance before the second scout car, the one that had been parked on Galveston, came from the opposite direction and blocked his path. Harvey collided with the scout car in front of Hadley Memorial Hospital, setting off his airbag in the process. The impact of the airbag striking his face bloodied his nose and the nitrogen vapor escaping from the bag made him wheeze. He tried to get out of the van, but the collision had jammed his door. He heard sirens and screeching tires and then nothing. Abruptly, uniformed and plainclothes officers converged on the van. All of them were pointing guns at him.

"Show me your hands," a uniformed officer yelled at him. "Let me see your hands!"

Harvey raised his trembling hands and kept them in plain sight. And then he began to weep.

"Please, don't hurt me," Harvey pleaded through the open driver's window. "Please. Please don't hurt me."

As gawkers gathered, a burly man dressed in civvies and wearing a badge suspended from a chain around his neck yanked forcefully on the driver's door several times until it finally opened with the grinding sound of metal against metal. The man then yanked him from the vehicle.

"On your knees," the burly man commanded as he forced Harvey to his knees.

The man then ordered him down on his belly and then helped him get there with a shove. Afterwards, he directed Harvey to put his hands behind his back, but also helped him do that too. In the blink of an eye, he was handcuffed.

Harvey sobbed into the asphalt, saying over and over again, "Please, don't hurt me."

Henderson holstered his Glock. "Somebody check on the officer who made the traffic stop and the one in the scout car and get an ambulance here ASAP," he said.

"Read him his rights," he told Officer Freeburn. "Come on Rojas, let's check out the van."

"You need a search warrant," Special Agent Roman reminded them.

"The vehicle was in an accident," said Rojas. "We're just making sure there are no passengers who need medical attention."

As soon as they boarded the van, they heard muffled noises.

Stooped, Rojas and Henderson walked over to the tool cart secured to the floor of the cargo area, the source of the muffled sounds. Henderson opened it. Inside, they found a bound and gagged little girl. Her frightened eyes were overflowing with tears.

"Everything's okay, now," Rojas soothed her.

Henderson and Rojas gently lifted her from the cart. Rojas removed the gag while Henderson untied her.

As the girl wept and hugged Rojas tightly, Detective Henderson patted her on the back and reassured her, "Everything is alright now."

—

The upper level of Harvey's farmhouse was bright in the mid-day sun, but the lower level was dark and shadowy, cut off from the sunshine and only dimly lit by low-wattage bulbs. His confession had been chilling enough but seeing his madness first-hand during the execution of the search warrant was something that would haunt Winston Henderson for the rest of his life. The Bushman's confession had shed light on the workings of his sick mind, but not as startlingly so as the descent into this dark place.

To Henderson, it seemed that this tour of the madman's world had lasted an eternity. The "Chapel," the Honeymoon Suite, the music, and his journal. It was all so diabolical.

Detective Anderson and Rojas, and Special Agent Roman, who had been too disturbed to remain, had gone upstairs long ago. The only member of the task force who didn't seem to mind being in the killer's lair was Special Agent Roselle, who was still in the "Chapel". Conversely, Roselle seemed as happy as a kid in a candy store.

In his confession, Harvey had explained how he believed that the girls he had "married" were his forever. They were waiting for him in the afterlife…just as seventy-two virgins per martyred Muslim suicide bomber await them in heaven, Detective Henderson supposed. He had sent the girls to a better life and ensured that they would not be sullied by other, unworthy men.

Henderson looked at the poster bed and the ropes attached to each post. He didn't want to imagine the suffering that had been inflicted in this gilded torture chamber, but he did. The terror. The torment. The agony. The screaming and the tears.

He felt a twinge of guilt. Had he been at the top of his game, maybe he could have saved Juanita Lopez and Melissa Glass. Maybe.

The detective let the Bushman's journal drop from his latex sheathed hand back into the dresser drawer where one of the FBI evidence technicians had found it. It would be bagged and tagged along with everything else.

He left the Honeymoon Suite and stayed out of the way of the FBI and MPD criminalists who were documenting Harvey's insanity, vigilantly photographing his lair and collecting and hauling out the physical evidence needed to help put the Bushman away for the rest of his days. Undoubtedly, Harvey would be declared mentally incompetent to stand trial and be remanded to an institution for the criminally insane, but at least he wouldn't kill again. That was something the detective consoled himself. But was it enough, he wondered?

Detective Henderson walked up the stairs, out of the darkness, and into the light.

Alphabetic Karma
Scott Archer Jones

THE SECOND TIME my parents threw me out, I already knew the streets couldn't work for me. I'd learned enough the first time. I needed to stay with a relative somewhere.

My moments of revelation in my first journey into the badlands still burned. My father went so far as to drive me downtown to a park and force me out of the car. I cried and screamed, but he had locked the doors, and my jerking on the door handle did nothing except make him smile. If he could be that cold, so could I. I wiped my tears and snot into my sleeve and stared back at him. He eased away from the curb, in no hurry at all to leave his only child on the pavement. Little Kimmie, fifteen years old, cut off and dumped. He'd said, "When they call us to report you're in the morgue, we'll claim you ran away."

I didn't have a coin in my pocket. That night I slept on the ground inside a clump of bushes gone gray from city pollution. No way would I want to lay out there on a park bench in full view while I closed my eyes. But Zoe found me on a bench the next day, around noon. I picked her up on my threat radar, a hundred feet away staring at me. When she caught my gaze, she clumped over—clumped because her trainers swallowed her feet, maybe three sizes two big. She slumped on the other end of the bench, stared out over the park, and asked, "Are you in some kind of trouble?"

"You could say that."

She was in her mid-twenties going on forty, maybe twenty pounds underweight, her face smudged in dirt. "Runaway?"

I could hardly get the words out. "More like throwaway."

She pivoted to face me. "Name's Zoe. First day?"

I glanced down to see my hands clasped together, knuckles white. "You might say that."

"Know what you're doing?"

"Not at all."

"Got a buck or two?"

I shook my head.

"Okay. I'll loan you five. The first thing you need is a blanket and a day bag. Let's hike over to the thrift store."

Zoe fairy-godmothered me for four days. She had money from somewhere and we panhandled all day. Mostly she scored dope with her funds, but each night we would settle somewhere in a corner, huddle under our blankets, and sleep on the concrete. My bones ached so deeply in the morning, only an hour in the sun could iron me out. At first, Zoe didn't want me to watch her injecting, but soon she had an episode where she was desperate to punch the drug into her vein. I saw the pop, right there, on the sidewalk with people walking by not ten feet away.

I remember squatting in a downtown parking garage on the stairs where they exited to the roof, taking a pee. Five steps up from me, Zoe told Levon, "Hit me up here, baby." She swept her hair off to the side and pointed to the scabby pinpricks on her neck that rode her jugular. He jabbed in the needle and shoved in the plunger. Levon acted as her regular hit doc, but I believed he should at least have provided a new syringe and needle for the cost of the dose.

I watched Zoe shudder as the drug rushed home. Is smack trying to rush home to me? Is this me in three months? That night Levon offered to trade four days of dope to Zoe. Zoe's side of the deal? Kimmie, that's what. I left Zoe in the stairwell, struggling with her decision.

I hitched back across town. For a half hour, I begged my father to forgive and forget, there on the front step's Italian stones. Gave it my best shot. "My best friend out here is an addict. Do you want me to end up like her?" Trouble is, it's true, I could end up that way.

They let me back into the house. And they laid down the law. Rules on attending school. Rules on staying in at night. Requirements for my grades.

Returning home gave me an uneasy grace period. I liked the therapy and the circle sessions. I held power—I could shock. I would sum up the mishmash of patients in my circle as pathetic in their own ways. They thought they had problems working through grief, anxiety, alcoholism. Booze isn't even a good high.

I could see myself reflected in the glass window of the group session room, my own stage. I propped an elbow over my thigh and leaned forward in my best butch pose. Like Alia Shawkat. A pale white face, hair cut flat on one side, spiked on top, dyed pink on the other side. That mirror of me opened her mouth. "What the crap do you know?"

The woman speaking, Doreen, stopped with a jerk. Her face folded up like a small cereal box. She began to cry.

I said, "That's right. Cry. You've been sober, what, two months? You have a house, a family. You got it easy."

Doreen's therapy bond-mate Chris stabbed a finger at me and said, "Shut up. Leave her alone."

"I'll tell you what tough is. Tough is when they lock you up in a shrink ward for four days because they say you pose a danger to yourself. Tough is eating out of dumpsters and getting used to the smell."

Doreen continued to sniffle. Chris draped an arm across Doreen's shoulder. He pivoted to authority—turning to the counselor, he said, "We're all of us here as patients, not just her."

Dressed in his blue leadership blazer, the counselor grinned faintly and leaned back. I stared at him, my best hard-slitted eyes measuring him up. Maybe he thought it good to let the confrontation play out. Maybe he was bored. Maybe he was incompetent.

I twitched up my sleeve, showed the tattoo, a spray of lilies that ran up my left forearm. "See this? I picked up this tattoo to remind me every day. Every day, of how they raped me in the park."

This was total fabrication. My joy in life had narrowed down to hard-core bone-bruise lying.

———

Family reentry didn't work well—I iced my way through the escalation, the shouting, the ultimatums, my mother Margy's guilt. She acted like some bird that had torn its wing, thin and crumpled. Her perfect face dissolved and ran under leaky tears. They actually dripped onto the coffee bar, puddles of high-priced makeup. I had carried her for two years after Dad went all pervy. I even got her to quit drinking—ironic, right.

Why should I do what they want? Because Dad threw me away

like an old snotty tissue?

My father had made things really complicated in the family, if complicated meant poisonous. He had betrayed my basket-case mother when he slept with a flesh accessory named Benjy. Dear old Dad betrayed me when he let Benjy feel me up, and the Benjy after him. Dad liked to watch, but he didn't like my mouth much by the time I turned fourteen. Go to the cops? Who believes a kid?

When he threw me out again, I had twenty bucks and a one-month metro bus pass. I knew my best option was Uncle Zach.

I journeyed out of suburbia into the city, to a trailer park that overlooked what had once been the stock yards and slaughterhouse and was now a wasteland. The park was packed as tight as I imagined the cows had been in the chutes a hundred years before. The trailers six feet apart, the narrow lane clogged with cars. I marched through, stared left and right at the Chicano families, at the sad old women who had outlived everyone, at the slackers who had given up on having jobs. Uncle Zach's trailer squatted in the back, close to the fence. On the other side, the freeway sprawled in all its noisy glory.

Zach's trailer dated back decades. As a younger man, he'd strewn a dozen tires across its roof to hold it down, proof of the power of our winter storms. The trailer's metal sheeting had surrendered most of its color, leaving turquoise smudges like an old lady's eyeshadow. A wooden ramp gave access from the street to the door—as I climbed up it, my hand caused the rail to quiver with a promise of collapse. A small manufacturer's ornament riveted by the door told me this trailer was a Valkyrie.

I leaned in and heard the coughing inside. On the fourth knock, I picked up on the voice, "Coming, coming. I'm putting on my goddamn pants."

He threw the door open—worse than I remembered. Uncle Zach must have gained another fifty pounds. He overflowed the wheelchair like an abundance of pudding. His jowls had developed new wrinkles; his chin couldn't decide if it was a double or a triple. The beard had coarse hairs like porcupine quills, set apart far enough to display Zach's pink-flushed skin.

"Uncle Zach, it's me."

"Me? Me who? Wait a minute, I can't see a thing without my glasses." He donned a pair of aviator-type glasses, with a light-brown tint. "Jesus, Kimmie, what are you doing here? Does your old lady

84

know you're out here?"

"All I can say is, both me and Dad know I'm not at home. They're probably having the locks changed right now."

Zach peered at my face, dropped his gaze and brought it back up. "Huh. So that's how it is. You better come in." He rolled backwards into the scant living room and gave me the space to slip past him into the kitchen.

I glanced around. The air was tainted with the death of a hundred cigarettes. Stuff was heaped all over the kitchen counters. The floor was clear—it had to be for the chair to roll around. A living room with one chair—a rocker recliner. A small TV was bolted to the wall, covering the window by the door, its cable connection stapled to the oak veneer and leading down to the floor. A giant can of popcorn waited in the chair. "Nice place, Uncle Zach."

"Fits me like an old shoe. The old girl and I will probably finish about the same time. Now what's this about your folks?" He gestured to the easy chair in the postage-stamp living room. "Sit. Sit."

I heard a tock-tocking sound in the trailer and gazed down at a metal-wrapped hose on the floor. Uncle Zach held a mask in his lap; it pumped out a breathy ooze. O2, and a compressor somewhere in there.

I waited for him to tug at the joystick on his electric chair and spin it around. I squeezed past to dump down in the recliner and settled the popcorn on the floor. A handful of cigarette ash sprang up, drifted across the room to settle on other flecks of gray. A full ashtray lurked on the chair's fold-out shelf. "Uncle Zach. You promised them you'd quit smoking."

"Yeah, well, what are they going to do? Kill me for breaking my promise?" He leaned forward, a slight gesture, but like moving a mountain toward the valley. "You're here because?"

"You know Dad."

"I used to think so—he is my brother. Thought I knew you too, but you've grown up a lot. What're you, fifteen?"

"Hm."

"I know your old man is a stickler. I know he don't like me. And I know I left home at fifteen—and look how well it's working out for me."

I gave him the narration, didn't even lie about what was my doing as compared to my father's. But not the deep truth. "That's why I need a place to stay."

"Stay. That's tough. I'm living here on Social Security—pretty tight. And there's not much room in the trailer."

"Please, Uncle Zach. I'll do nearly anything."

"This the first time they've kicked you out?"

I wiggled in the chair, a fish suddenly caught in the shallows. "Not exactly."

Zach scratched his rough, ugly beard. "That's bad. The more practice they get, the more serious they get about it." He held the mask to his nose and mouth and took a hard drag on it. A rumbling cough, full of desperate phlegm. "I gotta go pee. You stay here, and I'll think about it while I'm in the back."

I studied his back as he rolled away and the chair hummed in a high whine. Mom's sister is in Wisconsin. How would I get there?

When he rolled back, I saw he had forgotten to zip his pants, but I was okay with it. The oxygen mask covered most of his lap and his belly rolls pressed down on any explicit evidence.

He rested his forearms on his knees and even took off his ball cap. "Okay. Okay. See, we'll try it for a couple of days. You can sleep on that foldout bench, under the front window."

I felt the world open like a bright new place. I shocked myself— the salt of tears scorched my eyes.

At the sight of my crying, he looked away, clear to heaven through the tin roof, and said, "Maybe it'll work, maybe it won't. Maybe your dad will come around to regret it and come around to a love for his kid in a couple of days."

Right.

———

I watched Zach jerk the chair over the threshold onto the platform outside. He dragged the door mostly shut, but the hose trailed after him. With the mask strapped to his face, he fished out a silver whip, the antenna off a car. The button at the far end had been snapped off. Lighting a cigarette, he wriggled the filter into the antenna's butt end and extended it. Huffing on the oxygen mask, he inserted the skinny end into the corner of his mouth and sucked.

"Whatcha doing, Uncle Zach?"

His voice was muffled by the mask riding his face and the tube stuck under it into his mouth. "Smoking out here. This shit is no good for a kid."

"No, I meant with the shiny cigarette holder."

He shook his head. "I gotta keep the butt away from the oxygen. Started a small fire last year, burned myself under the ear. Still can't grow a beard on that patch."

"Really clever." About as clever as living with a time bomb.

"Thanks. I thought so myself."

"You have a vacuum cleaner? I might sweep up, some." I couldn't see his mouth, but his forehead wrinkled and his chins quivered. Uncle Zach was laughing. At me.

"Knock yourself out. It's one of those stick kinds—in between the refrigerator and the wall."

—

Uncle Zach joggled my foot as I lay in the rocker-recliner scrolling my phone. "Hey, I'm gonna roll on down to the corner market. Want to come?"

I jammed the phone into my back pocket; my friends were cutting me dead now I wasn't hanging in their school. I walked beside him to the 7-Eleven. Once there, and it took awhile, he wouldn't let me get the door. On the way in, he shouted, "Hey there Angela, how's it going? Harry, are they still hanging between your legs, or are you wearing a size smaller in pants?" He bought a frozen pizza, beer, and cigarettes. And a half dozen car fresheners, those green trees on a string. Zach lit up outside, whip antenna extended like a magic wand.

"I thought you used that to avoid getting blown up."

"It's kind of my style now. There goes Zach, looking like Franklin Delano Roosevelt. Besides, I can keep the smoke away from you."

"Thanks." We rolled back down the block, him up on the sidewalk working the joystick on his buggy, me off the curb in the street. I stepped around the dog poo and over a used rubber.

He said again, "This shit isn't good for kids."

I thought about how much better this was than sleeping on a cold concrete step curled up against Zoe. "I'm not so much a kid anymore."

"Don't knock it. Being underage gets you a break with the system. It did for me."

We split apart because of some cars bunched against the curb. I peered in them as I scuffed down the line—two had mounds of sleeping bags and blankets in the backseat. This isn't Daddy's gated community. We came back together at the fire hydrant. "So you're going to smoke on the porch all the time?"

"Maybe not at night. It's a pain to get out of bed into the chair. Maybe I'll cut back."

———

Zach and I coasted along for a while. Finances were ugly as I tried to find work at one place or another. Once I tracked down something serious, things eased up at the trailer. We brought in enough money for food, and I could even pay to turn the cable back on.

I stumbled on my new job at Raven's, a five-bay car repair shop. A jumpy guy in olive coveralls escorted me into the office in the back along with my paperwork—most of it was blank, showing how little life I'd had. The office enjoyed a large window out to the garage floor, a wall of manuals and three-ring binders, and a desk piled with paperwork in white, pink, and yellow. But that's not what I saw first. I fixed on the tough old woman in a black webbed office chair, gray hair, crepey arms hanging out of a sleeveless T-shirt, and a ball point stuck behind her ear. That wasn't what rocked me back—it was the scar on her face. It began a half inch above her eyebrow and ran clear down to her chin. It was bad-ass. I guess she was lucky she hadn't been blinded. But I wasn't asking.

She glanced up, coughed, and slid on a pair of glasses. A sweep up and down, those eyes behind the gogglers. Not a word.

I launched into it. "I'm looking for a job. I'll do anything, no matter how shitty. And I'm a quick learner."

"You don't look so menial. Pink hair, expensive jeans, three diamond chips stuck in your ears."

"I dressed up for the interview. My name is Kim. I can work off the books. School won't get in the way."

Raven leaned forward. "Gimme your hands."

I leaned over the desk, stuck my fingers out.

Raven rolled them over, to scrutinize the palms. "Not a mark, not a callus on these."

I snatched my hands back. "I think that's going to change, one way or another."

"Huh. Here's the deal. You sweep up, do the toilets, maybe inventory the tires. It's part time, no benefits. Seven dollars an hour, on the books, and you'll pay taxes."

Just before closing, Raven set me to spreading out degreaser and hosing down the concrete. After a week of this, her number-two, Chaki, handed me a filter wrench and taught me how to do oil changes. They handed out washed coveralls twice a week. My big chance in life, to crouch under cars and bust my knuckles. Changing spark plugs turned out easy if I picked the wrench with the long handle and laid across the fender. Twice that first month we had to pull a radiator, flush it, and check for leaks. The jumpy guy I met first, name of Twitch, hit on me once. He groped my butt and whispered in my ear, but I whanged his knuckles with a wrench I had in my hand—no one else bugged me after that. Raven gave me a full thirty-three hours a week and a bump to twelve bucks. It was sweet, sweeter than life with Dad and Mom.

—

Zach cradled the bowl in his lap, the O2 mask hung off his ear. "This is not so bad. What do you call it?"

"Green mac 'n cheese. I saw it on the cooking channel."

"You're sneaking in vegetables on me, aren't you?"

"Spinach. I won't tell, if you won't."

There wasn't much to say for a while, just the clicking of spoons in the bowls. Nevertheless, Uncle Zach couldn't leave it alone. "I worry, you know. Are you going back to school in September?"

"Why would I do that? I have a good job. You quit school at fifteen and here you are, doing okay on Social Security."

"Listen, Kimmie, things weren't all that great. The only time things were easy, for about a ten-year stretch, I ended up doing a nickel." He shifted in his wheelchair; it squeaked underneath him.

"A nickel?"

"A five-year prison stretch. But I put some money aside and that's what we're living on, as much as the Social Security."

That snapped my head around. "You have retirement?"

"Dow Jones 500, kid. Bringing in four hundred a month."

"You're kidding. You know about investing?"

"Mutual funds. High dividend, low risk. What else do you need to know?"

I peered around the trailer—it was shaping up. You could detect the counter tops now and see through the windows. Uncle Zach kept buying those tree fresheners, and we did the laundry together at a washateria about two blocks away. I got a hoot, watching him roll with that big basket in his lap, waving at all his friends, and some not-so-friends.

The macaroni had put him in a good mood. I decided to deliver the announcement. "I'm thinking about dyeing my hair."

"Why? You look okay as a blonde, now that the pink grew out."

The woman next door, as old as the mummies, cut my hair. Mrs. Cisneros gave me a tough shag, all kind of brutal and punk—she was pretty cool for a sixty-year-old. "Mrs. C, she and me are agreed. I'd look better in midnight black."

"What if I say no?"

"You want me cooking for you or not?" Real food cost less than the junk, but I had to trudge ten blocks to the nearest real grocery store. Nobody bugged me if I wore Raven's coveralls and tucked my hair up under a ball cap.

"Well, yes, I guess I do want you to keep cooking. But no more tattoos."

That's when I decided to have my nose pierced.

———

The first summer was killer and not in a good way. On Sundays, I'd sit outside with Uncle Zach as he smoked and told me lies about his glamor crime days. We baked in the heat, like sweet potatoes in the oven. The September rains brought a huge relief, and we'd hang in the living room and kill the time like it was just something to get through.

From the depths of his recliner, he asked me, "They're showing a marathon of Bewitched. Want to watch, eat popcorn?"

"Whatever." I perched in the folding chair, by his arm rest in the lounger, within reach of the popcorn bucket.

"Don't hurt yourself with all that enthusiasm." He flipped the tube on and we soaked up the fifty-percent magical mayhem and fifty-percent commercials—Zach had cancelled the cable. Falling back on old habits. He flapped a pudgy paw at the screen. "You could be one of those three witches. Maybe find you a waitress job in Hollywood, start auditioning some, look for an agent."

"Huh. Who would fix you chicken salad and Frito pie?"

"Who would spend my Social Security?"

—

The day my mom came to visit, about a year in on my arrival, I pulled my first transmission. Chaki and the boys, they figured out how to catch the tranny in a modified engine stand and showed me how to use a couple of jacks to ease it down. The grease on my forehead and my cheekbone scrubbed off with the orange goo in the garage sink, but the pumice did rough my skin some. Even with coveralls, I had greased up my flannel shirt cuffs and the bottom inch of my jeans.

I should have known something was up when I discovered a Lincoln Town Car parked by Zach's trailer blocking the aisle. A man leaned against the car in a wrinkled blazer; he dipped his head but said nothing. I trooped in the trailer door like a oily zombie. Inside, I discovered my mother, in a pearl-colored pantsuit, her hair three carefully-sculpted shades of blonde, like shadowing in a painting. Dad would have to pay to fix the wattle developing under her chin.

I was pleased with how shocked Mom appeared. No grease in her world. She rose out of the recliner with a fragile lurch. Took two steps forward and brought her arms up. She wanted a hug and leaned forward to claim it.

I rocked back and retreated to the wall near the door. She appeared a lot older, tense, drawn thin. Living with Dad could do that to you.

"Kimmie."

"I go by Kim now. So you found me."

She gave me this miniature grin, all rueful. "Don't be silly. We've known all along. Zachary called us."

I shot my best steely, threatening stare at my uncle. "You."

He looked truly woeful, like a puppy who got caught peeing on the rug.

Mom said, "He did the right thing, and it's for the best."

"There's a phrase I don't miss. 'It's for the best.'"

—

Three years into this life, and the whole time I stayed clean—Zoe and the drug ghosted in the back of my mind. My mom texted once a week and I texted back, but she never dropped by again. Maybe too painful.

Uncle Zach seemed the same, all roly-poly in his chair, even though I had slowly melted forty pounds off him. But his breathing worried me—those short gasps with a dollop of mucus. His lungs worked hard, but he didn't benefit much from it. And all this was after he had quit smoking, the biggest damn struggle I'd ever seen. He wore patches like parks have trees. Even so, the whip antenna stood by the side of the door.

In two months I would be eighteen. I'd had two boyfriends, and that worked out so great I was thinking about trying out women. And soon Zach might be in the hospital, with the bills piling in. I kept thinking how the system was stacked against us, me working a second job behind the counter of a convenience store, him sliding toward shaky old age. No way to front any serious medical, besides the halfway house of Medicare. I decided I'd step outside the system.

It began with Tony Dabrowski, out of the blue. He sauntered up to me in the third bay. "You're damn tough, near as brutal as Raven."

I lay on my back on a creeper, under a Winnebago that wouldn't fit the lift. I stared up at him standing there with a cup of coffee. He had unzipped his coveralls and exposed his colossal chest masked by a T shirt. He showed off that roll of fat just above the zipper. Upside down from my point of view, it appeared ludicrous, like a Polack being squeezed out of a sausage casing. "Why thank you, Tony. You say the nicest things."

"But the black lipstick, that's kind of sucky."

"Stick with the part about me being tough, Tony."

"No, I mean it." He crouched by my shoulder. "I'd talk to the other guys, but they got commitments. Family and shit."

"Talk to them about what?"

"I got a sideline, but my boy, my driver, he quit."

I sniffed deep, to catch a whiff of what this was about. The only thing I picked up was a nose full of rotting undercarriage from the Winnebago.

"I...liberate, that's what. I 'liberate' contents of trucks from their trailers and find a market for those contents. Cigarettes, computers, office furniture, once a load of canned crab meat. You name it and I've moved it."

He was offering what I was searching for, an alternative path to money. Tony was steady, quiet, and dependable, at least in the garage. "Tell me more, oh great liberator."

"I cut you in for a regular percent of the take. I do the heavy work, 'securing' the truck and driving it off. You follow me in our own semi or meet me and we unload and abandon the truck. Then I get to work selling the haul."

"I don't know how to drive a semi."

"I seen you do it, pulling one forward to unblock a bay. You just have to learn to back up and to swing wide at the corners."

Tony wasn't dumb. He's giving me the sales job. I asked, "Don't trucks have GPS trackers now?"

"I pull over in a couple of blocks and short it out."

"What about drivers?"

"Prefer not to come up against them. Maybe. Sometimes." Tony appeared bashful, for someone who had just confessed to armed truck-jacking.

———

This new career worked pretty well for a while. Uncle Zach never heard me coming or going at night, as he lay in the back of the trailer exhausted from breathing. To celebrate my hidden illegal wealth, I had my left eyebrow pierced twice, for two gold dumbbells. Outside of that, I didn't splash out—the money was reserved for emergencies. I hid the rubber-banded rolls up under the trailer in a waterproof bag. Tony was as good a human turning over trucks as his garage persona, and I didn't mind collecting only an eighth of the take.

By the fourth jack, I was in the zone. For this one, Tony had located a yard with six trucks behind chain link and a padlock. He cut the chain and eased himself inside; he looped the whole thing back up so the gate appeared locked. He picked out the truck facing out, checked the back to confirm the trailer held a load, then jimmied into the cab. I waited, leaning against a wall at the end of the fence, thanking God no dogs showed. But I could make out security cameras, so Tony had left his image behind—a bear-shaped figure in coveralls and a black ball cap tugged down real low, collar turned up.

In about ten minutes, Tony had broken the column lock, bypassed the kill switch, and hot-wired the rig. The diesel fired up, Tony flicked the lights, and I ran to open the gate. He cruised out of the lot and turned to the right as I swung onto the step and crawled into the cab. Six blocks later, minus the GPS, he dropped me off and

I trailed behind in our vehicle.

We parked near a junkyard, back to back, door to door. I crawled into the liberated trailer and shoved a steady progression of boxes toward Tony on the ground. He grunted them up into our trailer, and, when the doorway was jam-packed, we both swung up to re-stow the load deep in our own rig. We had boosted a mixed load, maybe on its way to a hardware store. The last things off nearly killed me—100 five-gallon buckets of paint. We kindly left their pallets. One thing for sure—my upper-body strength was way better and I was into Ibuprofen.

The unload and load took us about an hour, and that's when we were sitting ducks. Tony shifted location each time, searching out parking lots or graveled areas with no cameras. He insisted we work in the dark, but chose nights with a moon. He allowed, "Cameras ain't no big deal. They can figure out weight and height, but that's about it. Still, when you can avoid them . . . "

Tony also insisted I drive back, to hone my trucker skills. We'd park in his warehouse and unload—afterwards his wife Helen would feed us breakfast in the apartment upstairs while the kids got ready for school, slapping together their own PB&Js.

—

Tony and I finally cracked a tractor trailer that was too tough. We stumbled across a driver sleeping in his rig to save money on a motel. We turned sloppy, I guess.

The truck had been slotted against the curb outside of the transport yard. Tony said, "Guess he showed up here after they locked up."

Scanning the fence, I spotted a camera covering the street. "We're on tape, Tony." We both hauled our caps down and our turtlenecks up over our mouths.

He broke the seal on the trailer door and cut the padlock off with his bolt cutters. The doors swung open—he flashed a light around. "Looks like Samsung appliances. Need a dishwasher?"

I banged the doors shut and latched them down. "Time to move."

Tony ran down the side of the truck and swung up on the step. The door burst open. Tony flew away from the truck. He landed on his shoulders in the street. As I sprinted toward him to haul him to his feet, I heard a flat crack, like concentrated thunder banging into my ears. "I'm hit! The sumbitch shot me."

Stupid me. I ran forward to heave Tony up on his feet. I glanced up at the truck door to spot the driver, phone in one hand, a silver revolver in the other. I believe luck turned my way—he was dialing with his thumb even as he threw off a couple of shots at me. Like a red hot iron, the first bullet tore across the front of my thigh, banged the street, and sang off into the blackness. The second ripped off the first joint of my ring finger.

I jerked Tony onto his feet. "Run! Run, you Polack." The driver ignored us as he shouted into his phone.

Our parked truck waited a half block away. By the time we staggered up to it, Tony knew he had been hit through and through. "Candy ass gun. The entry isn't as big as my finger."

Tony, the bastard, had taken a round into the shoulder and out his back, and was reporting on the bullet size. Maybe shock. Probably showing off. He grunted like a weightlifter as he tried to scale the steps into the passenger seat, and all the time I'm shoving on his ass, trying to boost him up.

Ten miles to Tony's warehouse, with the crease across my thigh red-hot and throbbing. It let me know the gun wasn't that small. As the streetlights trolled by and rained pallid blue or amber into the cab, I could detect the puddle of black across my jeans. Not bad—I didn't see any gouts of blood spurting out. I had jammed my bleeding hand into a work glove, so I didn't have to gaze at that.

Tony jumped on his mobile and called ahead—"Helen, I been shot. Call Doc Murchison and have him get to the warehouse as quick as he can. Tell him we'll pay double. Get Donnie to open the doors."

Big man, balls like brass—but he had passed out by the time I rumbled us into the building and jerked to a stop.

From there it was an anticlimax. Doc Murchison showed up from his vet clinic within a half hour. Helen told me, "I think we're out of business for a while."

"You think?"

"We'll patch you up down here. I don't want the kids to see." Doc replumbed Tony's shoulder and quick-glued my bullet crease together. He gave me four stitches in the end of my finger and a lecture about the dressing. It took both Helen and me to carry Tony up the stairs. Panting like exhausted horses, we poured him into the bed. She asked, "You okay to get home?"

Tony made it back to Raven's within a month. He claimed it had been a hernia and laid off heavy tires and crap for a while. He may have gone back to truck-jacking later, but it wasn't with me. My crime run didn't last as long as Uncle Zach's, but then, I didn't have to do the nickel.

———

When I turned twenty Uncle Zach and I had to tap into our hard-way gains. I hired a woman in the trailer park to watch over Zach while I worked at the garage. He was on his own in the evenings while I held down a job as a cashier at the market. I knew the end was near when we decided on a hospital bed. I had to disassemble it to wiggle it into the bedroom—I leaned the old box and mattress against the trailer on the freeway side. We both knew there was no going back. But oh, how he hung on the monkey bars and straps I rigged overhead. He levitated back and forth between the radio and the miniature TV and the stacks of magazines—like the slowest pendulum in the world. His regrets came with weirdness. "I tell you, Kim, I wish I had taken up knitting. Too late now."

Making withdrawals from under the trailer, I paid for upgraded hospice and the nurse to come in, better than flat Medicare. They turned out to be stingy with the drugs, sizing them out for hundred-pound chemo victims, so I made a deal with Emilio, Mrs. Cisneros' nephew's son four trailers down. Emilio carried a bit of everything. "I run the Honk N Holler of recreational merchandise."

It wasn't so bad until the last week. Zach ate less and less and wheezed more and more. I fed him mostly beef broth and emptied the bedpan after it had run through him. The BMs smelled, but they arrived further and further apart, and drier and drier. The last week, like I said, Zach and I agreed privacy was a thing of the past and I attended to all his functions. He told me on Monday, "I'm through. No more food, just enough water to swallow the pills." His lips cracked like an old parking lot.

With no food to buffer the drugs, Zach slipped off to La-La Land. I sat watch over him as much as possible, and called Raven to tell her I wasn't coming in. I don't know what was dream and what was memory, but we circulated through seventy years of work and play, of bitter disappointment and some happiness.

On Friday, lying on his back like a great mound of waiting, he flipped and thought I was someone else. He said, "Margy, don't dump me. Not for that shit brother of mine. I'll get us some money."

It felt like he had hit me in the forehead with a tire iron, not just my mother's name. Uncle Zach passed that Saturday night. Neighbors helped me lug him out of the trailer to the gurney outside, where the funeral home van waited, saving me a hundred bucks. Those funeral home assholes didn't have to struggle with Zach down the narrow hallway past the closet and the bathroom, but they didn't lay any gratitude on us, just the discount.

—

The trailer has been handed down to me. I pooled the left-over money stashed in the bag and the last of Zach's mutual funds and bought a small share of the garage. No idea where that's going.

It's been seven years since Dad dumped me out on the street, and Zoe's probably dead by now, but if not—I thought I might find her and bring her home. I can nearly afford her dope. She'd have a safe place to fix and it might stretch her days out some. She saved me, those first weeks on the street. Uncle Zach saved me, those years in the trailer park. Strange they both had names with capital Z's. Alphabetic karma.

It should be my turn to pay back. And I don't want to live alone.

Chump Change
Susan Walsh

"AND SO, DEAR DAUGHTER," Marty Wentz typed with a vengeance, "I have completed another thrilling day here at Mariner Family Retirement Community," the M-F Retirement Community, he thought, then continued. "I can feel my synapses slowing as we speak—so to speak—and I can hear cells dying off one by one. Words cannot express my gratitude for your generosity in sending me here to protect your inheritance dear old dad. With all the love you deserve, Det. Martin J. Wentz, (Ret.)" With his hand a bit shaky on the mouse, Marty teetered dangerously close to hitting "send" before deleting the email.

Christ, Marty thought. I can't keep playing Russian Roulette. One of these nights I'm gonna send the damn thing. Then what? As much as he blamed his daughter for incarcerating him in the retirement home, he knew, but tried mightily to avoid thinking about it, that he bore some responsibility. Yeah, he could have been a bit nicer to her mother. Could have been more careful with the bucks. And the late night cruises to the local pub. Marty sighed. As Windows shut down and his screen blinked to black, Marty caught a glimpse of his reflection, stunned as always by the sight of his heavy-jowled, sixty-nine year old reflection so at odds with the man in his prime he knew himself to be. As the computer continued its shutdown, old Jake leaped up with one emphatic woof, and pranced to the apartment door. At 11:00 p.m. Marty smiled his first genuine smile of the day. He remembered the first time the dog had done that. He thought Jake must have been startled out of a bad dream or had a seizure. By the third night, Marty got it. Jake learned to recognize the sound of

Windows shutting down and knew that meant it was time for their late night walk.

"You're the smartest one in the place, Jake," Marty said. *Including me*, he added silently, a sentiment he couldn't bear to say out loud, even to the dog.

Marty walked Jake across the parking lot to a spot just outside the reach of the flood lights, and lit up a contraband stogie. He had come to relish these nightly walks with Jake, cigar or no. They had gotten later and later, because only then could Marty seem to avoid the OBs, as he thought of them, the old biddies who seemed to make up ninety per cent of the M-F population. With a decent head of hair, no walker and most of his teeth and hearing, Marty was a catch, and he could avoid their attention and inane chatter only by going out late at night. Ironic. He would have killed for that kind of popularity in high school. Now, he just wanted to be left alone to brood about the turns his life had taken and the unfairness of a cop in his prime being put out to pasture. If all that wasn't bad enough, it was Monday night, meaning tomorrow was shopping day.

Tuesday mornings, the residents were herded into buses and mini-vans. It was way too much togetherness for Marty and the OBs but without a car he had little choice. As he trudged toward the common area, he became aware of an insistent, high pitched whisper.

"Officer Wentz! Psst! Officer Wentz!?"

He stopped and turned, and a tiny, white haired woman, traveling at a good clip, barreled right into him. She was flustered and took a bit to gather herself.

Finally, "Officer Wentz? Do you remember me?"

When he looked closer at the woman, he was surprised, and pleased with himself, to realize that he did. After nearly thirty years, he recalled her name, and all the details of the case that had brought them together: neat, logical, well-organized. Proof positive he wasn't ready to be retired.

"Mrs. Otis. Of course I do."

But ix-nay on the "officer" business, he thought. He didn't like people knowing his line of work. It made the drop in status all the more embarrassing. Meanwhile, Mrs. Otis looked like Jake at walk time, beaming and all but dancing with excitement.

"Officer Wentz. He's here. I know it. James Etherton is here. I can't say any more right now. Is there somewhere we can talk later?"

Out of habit and conditioning and years as a detective, Martin Wentz, (Ret.) suddenly came fully alert. The sound of that name—a perp who'd gotten away—snapped him to. He had ignored the OBs from his first day at Mariner Family, but this old gal had his full attention.

"Of course, Mrs. Otis. Why don't you call me tomorrow? I'm extension 307. You can come over for tea."

Mrs. Otis seemed to blush a bit at the suggestion of coming to his apartment. *For god's sake*, Marty thought. *The dame can't think I'm making a pass at her.* He was annoyed at her coyness, but desperate to hear what she had to say about Jimmy Etherton. For once, he'd be willing to put up with the old biddie nonsense. *For once*, as he thought with mounting relish of bringing a cold case to a close, *it would be worth it.*

Marty turned abruptly, opting to skip the shopping trip, suddenly having more important work to do. He returned to his apartment, went rummaging into the back of his "spacious walk-in closet," one of the amenities promised by the M-Fs, and pulled out a large cardboard box. Marty had kept his own records and details on some of his most interesting, or in this instance, most elusive cases.

James Etherton was an accountant, worked for a local bank back when there'd still been such things. He was detail-oriented, meticulous, and above all, patient. He was believed, after the fact, to have been embezzling from the bank, in amounts so small they would be almost impossible to detect. Eventually though, a new computer system was introduced, this was back in the early 80s, which would put an end to Jimmy's scheme. Jimmy left the bank, still on good terms, his theft undetected, purportedly for a new job and promotion out of state. He was gone by the time the new system was fully up and running. Then the bank was robbed. Based on information provided by an accounting clerk, one Mrs. Ruth Otis, Wentz came to believe the robbery was committed by an accomplice to cover up Etherton's embezzlement. Marty's first thought when she'd told him her story was to wonder why Etherton would be back in the area. But why not? Etherton never knew the police had made a connection between him and the robbery. To Marty's frustration, they were never able to piece together enough information to go after him.

Tuesday night, for the first time since he arrived at Mariner Family, Marty did not draft a nasty email to his daughter. Instead, he spent the time online, contacting the department. He would need some access, as a retired detective that shouldn't be a problem, to the station, and to the official files and documents from the case. He outlined what he knew with the promise of more information to come after his meeting on Wednesday. And instead of sinking into the fitful sleep of the terminally gloomy, he dropped off that night and slept soundly, looking forward to the day ahead.

When his phone didn't ring first thing Wednesday, Marty was annoyed. He knew the biddies were usually up at the crack of dawn, but he was nevertheless reluctant to call Mrs. Otis too early. He could visualize her puttering around her apartment in robe, slippers, and hair curlers and imagine her jumping out of her skin at the sound of the phone shattering her early morning routine. He was impatient to hear what she had to say, but there was other business to be done, so he got Jake out for his morning walk. As he opened his apartment door, he realized someone had stuck a note part way under. He opened it and read "Off. Wentz: Important. Will arrive promptly at 2:00 p.m." The note was signed R.O. He smiled a bit at the cloak and dagger of it, and went about his morning routine, taking care to be back in 307 well before 2:00 p.m. He knew the OBs were always early.

Sure enough, at 1:50 p.m. he heard a knock. He opened the door to see Mrs. Otis, looking nervous as a cat. All of ninety-eight pounds dripping wet, she nevertheless almost knocked Marty backward as she pushed her way in the door. He wasn't certain whether she was just excited about Etherton, or worried about the other biddies seeing her enter a divorced man's apartment for an assignation, the word she would have used, no doubt. He offered her tea, which she accepted, and offered to keep the apartment door open if that made her more comfortable.

"Not necessary, Officer Wentz," she giggled. "I believe we are both over twenty-one."

Again the blush, and Marty swallowed his impatience. Lapsing as if it had been only yesterday into his detective role, he began.

"Now, Mrs. Otis. Why don't you tell me what you know?"

"He's here. Etherton. He's here. And he's doing it again. Exactly the same as before." Mrs. Otis spoke with emphasis and determination. "He is running errands for the residents. He drives one of the shuttles, too. When he brings their groceries or whatever, he shorts their change. Maybe only a few cents, sometimes a dollar or so. Not enough so anyone ever notices or gets suspicious. But, Officer

Wentz. There are over eight hundred residents here. If he took just fifty cents from everybody that's four hundred dollars a week! Twenty thousand dollars a year..." *The dame, always good with numbers, had a point,* Wentz thought. *It was exactly the kind of scam Etherton ran at the bank. Amounts so small no one would consider them stolen—just lost or miscounted.*

To Mrs. Otis he said, "You say you got a good look at him. Did he seem to recognize you?"

"No," she continued. "Remember, Officer Wentz, James was gone by the time you talked to me. He would have had no reason to remember me."

Right again, he thought. *She was pretty sharp for a dame.* Marty went off on a tangent for a moment, thinking about the women rising to the ranks of detective about the time it was "suggested" he retire, when Mrs. Otis brought him back.

"Officer Wentz? Did you hear me? Tomorrow morning. He drives the shuttle to the Golden Basket."

It was an eating place popular with the residents. Buffet. All you can eat and a senior discount on Thursdays to boot. Marty, of course, would never have been caught dead going, but this time he'd be there.

"I don't think we should both go," Marty said. Did Mrs. Otis seem a bit regretful? "It would be better if he didn't see us together." Etherton might not have known what part Mrs. Otis had played in the robbery investigation, but he might still recall her as a bank employee. Marty had been on television after the robbery. If Etherton saw them together, it might spark a recollection. So it was arranged. Mrs. Otis, regretfully, would skip the trip to Golden Basket this week. Marty would board the shuttle to check Etherton out. Once again, he thought about the satisfaction of closing the case: the grudging respect of the youngsters at the department turning into genuine recognition of his skill. He'd checked earlier. No one from the department had bothered to return his emails yet. But with hard evidence. He smiled to himself at the way that would all change.

Wednesday Marty felt more alive than he had in years. He visited the in-house barber shop, splurged on a haircut and shave, got his shoes shined. After checking out Etherton next morning, he intended to head directly to the station, and wanted to look great for his triumphant return. That night he emailed his daughter, a message he actually sent, giving her some detail about the case, as he had come to think of it, and once again slept soundly, after giving Jake the peppiest late night walk he'd enjoyed in quite a while.

On Thursday, Det. Martin Wentz, he now omitted the "retired" part of his moniker, was up early, spit polished and ready for action. He reviewed some of his notes from the case. He called the concierge to verify the departure time of the Golden Basket shuttle. The old coots were always asking things like that. No one at the desk would think it was the least bit odd. By the time Marty was at the shuttle shop he was humming with energy and pent up excitement. He let several residents move ahead of him in line, on the pretext of waiting for someone. It would give him more time to observe Etherton from the sidewalk. Finally the shuttle appeared across the parking lot. Marty strained to catch his first glimpse of Etherton, while feigning a lack of interest, as the van pulled to the curb. Then the doors opened. As Marty got his first good look at the driver, something died a little in him.

The dame was right. The driver looked like James Etherton alright. Too much like James Etherton. And that was the problem. Etherton would be pushing sixty. This kid was maybe thirty, tops. Marty's mind replayed every detail of his conversations with Mrs. Otis. Her giddiness, the flushed, excited face. *The dame was as mad as a hatter*, he realized. *Probably had no idea what year it was, let alone how old James Etherton, the real James Etherton, would be now.* He snapped out of his thoughts as he realized the driver was speaking to him.

"Sir? Sir? Are you alright? Are you getting aboard? Do you need some help?" asked the purported Etherton driving the van.

Marty backed away from the bus, muttering something about forgetting his billfold. Suddenly he had an out of body view of himself, just another one of those old M-F coots. *He was no different from the rest of them. No different from Mrs. Otis herself.* He thought of the emails he'd sent. To his daughter, to the precinct, to his old partner.

Back in his room, for the second time in two days, Marty dug deep into his meager reserve of cash. He splurged on a cab to the Discount Liquor Emporium, then made a stop, while the damn cabby kept the meter running, at Joey's Pizza Shop. Not caring. About the money, his liver, his cholesterol numbers. He just kept replaying the last two days "on the case," his shame at his gullible stupidity deepening by the second. He couldn't pin this on anybody but himself.

By that night his apartment looked—and smelled - like the aftermath of a frat party. Pizza boxes, beer bottles and whiskey stink everywhere. Marty lurched up from his desk, and Jake got up, looking plaintively with a slow wag of his tail toward the door.

"Forget it, Jake," Marty mumbled. Then swaying and sagging slowly back down, he snorted a mirthless laugh and muttered, "It's Chinatown," just before he passed out in the remnants of an anchovy pizza.

Three days later, a resurrected Marty Wentz gazed in his bathroom mirror, looking far better than he had a right to. He'd given in to a couple days of alcohol fueled self-pity. Then, from some still functioning part of his brain, he realized he had to get a grip. He had lost his fight when he arrived at Mariner Family. If he didn't want to finish out his days here, then by god, it was up to him to do something about it. He had to create a nest egg his daughter didn't have her hands on. Even as he had slammed into rock bottom, a plan had started to form in his mind. As he had after rough weekends in the old days on the beat, Marty had drunk copious amounts of water and fruit juice, downed quantities of aspirin and vitamins. Spent hours in a hot shower letting the steam sweat the toxins out of his pores. He emerged after the lost weekend with a zip in his step and a new resolve to take charge of his future. He started down the hall early on Monday morning, knowing he wouldn't have to wait long to find a small flock of the biddy hens. Sure enough there was a group outside 326. He swallowed his reflexive annoyance and pasted on his most charming smile. It was not without effect. There was a reason Marty had once excelled at wheedling information out of reluctant witnesses, especially of the female persuasion.

"Good morning, ladies," he beamed at the group. "I was just on my way to the Mariner store downstairs. Can I pick anything up for anyone?" Sure enough he found an eager taker.

Less than fifteen minutes later, Marty was on his way back up in the elevator carrying a bag containing bobby pins and witch hazel. He fingered the receipt just enough to crease and slightly smudge it. He tapped lightly on the door of 328, a number he now knew to be the residence of one Mrs. Harold Sadler—Hattie to her friends. It would be important to remember these names and numbers for the future, a piece of cake for *this* retired detective. Marty gallantly handed Mrs. Sadler her package and her change.

Most of it, anyway. As he strode back to his apartment, he fingered the two quarters and the dime in his pocket. He was almost giddy with delight. He couldn't believe how that small windfall made him feel. It was only chump change, but just like twenty lawyers at the bottom of the ocean, it was a good start.

Her Eyes Were Open
Benjamin Fine

I SERVED THREE YEARS on a ten to fifteen stretch for armed robbery when the Governor of Ohio decided, for monetary reasons, to pardon a big group of nonviolent offenders. Somehow my shyster lawyer got me on the list and I have no idea how he convinced them that I was non-violent. Suddenly I was a free bird; back out in the civilian world with no parole and no supervision.

I thought that Ohio, me having a record there, wasn't the best place for me to stay. I kept in touch with Joe Johnson, a con I met in the joint when I was doing a stretch in Nevada. He lived in Connecticut so I decided to head there. In Akron I picked up all the cash I had stashed away from the jobs I had done and hopped a bus to Bridgeport. Joe found me a room in a boarding house in Stratford, the next town over, and helped me find a job installing electric generators. I figured I'd work at that a bit till I found something more to my liking and background. Joe helped me pick up an old car from a friend of his so I had wheels in my new location. Joe himself had found God and was constantly trying to get me to see the light in Jesus so after a while I steered clear of him. I don't like to think a lot about the right or wrong of what I'm doing. I follow my gut instincts and the money. I'm the kind of guy though that always finds people to hang out with and get me where the action is.

After settling in, I started to drink each evening in a nearby tavern. That's where I met Dejean Bramble, a thin black guy with a big smile and a gold tooth in the front of his mouth. He was always joking and jiving and we struck up a conversation. He was a small-time grifter and pimp and when he found out I had done hard time he looked at me in awe. Being a con was impressive to him. Dejean and I started palling around together. Coming from prison this was odd since in the joint there was no integration. The gangs ruled and even guys that tried to steer clear of trouble had to ally somewhat with one of the gangs. I'm big, I can handle myself and I look the part. I did some tough man contests back in Nevada and it left me a bit of a beat up face. The Aryan brotherhood, they wanted me. They're a bunch of wackos but I fought alongside them once or twice in the yard so they watched my back. The Crips and the Bloods were for the black guys and the Latin Kings for the Spanish. In the shower once, some black guy touched my ass. He was one of the toughest Bloods and I beat the shit out of him so the black guys steered clear of me.

Dejean came into the bar one night with a hot blonde girl about twenty and a guy, tall and skinny, about my height and probably the same age as the girl. Dejean waved me over and introduced me.

"Hey Roddie, I want you to meet these kids. I told them you're a good guy and a good friend of mine."

The girl came toward me and held out her hand. In a soft, flirty voice she said, "Hi Roddie, I'm Jessie." Up close she was a stunner, with a body to die for, long wavy white blonde hair and big blue eyes that sparkled. Her girlish voice, out of place in a tough bar like this, made me melt. She shook my hand formally like she was meeting someone in authority and it seemed odd. "This is my boyfriend Matt," and she pointed to the guy behind her. The boyfriend was a skinny prick with acne and he had the look of a junkie. She probably was a junkie also, but she was such a knockout, I ignored that.

Those big blues of hers looked right into my eyes and she said in that sweet voice, "Dejean says you're good people Roddie, and we should know you." The twinkle in her eyes made everything else fade away and I just smiled and stared. I'm usually smooth with broads but with her I was shy and blurted out "Jessie you're a honey and a half."

"Roddie, you're real good looking in a tough sort of way." Her gaze seemed to be fixed onto my face. She was hot and I wanted her, but she was way too young for me, although my brains were still located between my legs.

I was flattered and surprised. "Jessie, you're blowing up my ego. These days I'm mostly invisible to any woman under thirty." I laughed.

She shook her head. "No Roddie you look good to me," and she seemed like she meant it.

The boyfriend seemed angry and pulled her away. They walked onto the little dance floor the bar had and Dejean sat down next to me. "Pretty nice, eh Roddie?" he said and smiled. "I think she likes you. You can thank me later if you get anything." He looked over at her dancing. "Great ass" he said and snickered. "She and that skinny-assed boyfriend has themselves an H-problem. I gives them little jobs to get them cash."

I sat back to drink some more and the boyfriend left the dance floor and walked over to me. He was rail thin, wearing a long sleeved shirt that hid the tracks on his beanstalk arms. He looked at me eye level. "You want her?" he asked, "She likes you, so I'll make it cheaper than normal; a hundred bucks. Take her to your place, bring her back here and I'll pick her up later. "

I should have turned it down. Getting mixed up with a hot hooker is always trouble, but I glanced over and saw her looking at me. She was smiling the same as when we were talking and all I saw were sweet young blue eyes and that hot body. She was younger and better looking than I had been with in a very long time. I nodded yes at her and she walked over. "Give me the hundred now," the boyfriend said.

"I'll pay her," I told him curtly, and then led Jessie out to my car.

On the short ride to my place she chattered away like a schoolgirl. I knew she was a junkie but there seemed to be no hard edge to her. Jessie was either one of the world's greatest actresses or just a sweetheart in a bad situation. I've been around the block more than once but I couldn't tell or maybe I didn't want to know. There was an innocence about her that I liked immediately.

She was wearing tight jeans and a lacy shirt that showed off her magnificent young chest and while she studied my face, I had trouble keeping my eyes off of her. "You'll see the whole package soon enough" she laughed, "keep your eyes on the road."

At the rooming house I parked in the driveway and took her upstairs. I was supposed to tell the landlady if I had guests, but usually she was asleep, and if she wasn't, she just looked the other away if you brought someone in.

Jessie was upbeat and talking away in that sweet girlish voice as I took her into my bedroom. I knew it was a fake situation because I knew I was paying her, but that didn't change the fact that it felt good having her by my side. The warm feeling felt real as she held my hand.

The guy who rented the room next to mine was a pill head and I saw him take guys into his room all the time. We heard him coughing and Jessie said "That's McCann in there, right?"

"You know him?" I asked. I was surprised. McCann was definitely gay so I couldn't see him with Jessie.

"Yes," she answered. "He comes to the bowling alley in Milford and buys pills from Dejean. I brought him some stuff here once. I think he's gay. He turned down a girl Dejean got for him."

She said everything matter-of-factly; buying pills, McCann gay, DeJean trying to set him up. Her manner and her sweet voice were endearing and I was getting hooked.

Once inside my tiny room, she started to unbutton her blouse. I didn't want it like that, just sex and nothing else; I liked her and I wanted it to be something. I put my hand on her arm to stop her from getting undressed, then pulled her over to me and kissed her. I could feel her body melting into my large frame. At first she was surprised, but then she kissed me back and I felt something special inside; perhaps a long forgotten memory from before my life got fucked up. Her mouth was soft and warm and her kisses seemed real. We stood kissing for quite a while and then, still dressed, I lay down with her on my bed. Then we made love like lovers, slowly and passionately.

When we finished, she cuddled next to my side in the space left on the bed. She put her head in the crook of my neck and it felt right; like she belonged there. The small bed was uncomfortable even with Jessie next to me, yet for those few moments it felt wonderful and natural having her beside me.

She hugged me like it had all meant something. "It was really nice Roddie" she told me in an almost whisper.

"You don't have to say that Jessie. I enjoyed it though."

"No I really mean it. You're a nice man." She kissed my neck.

We lay there for a while and then I stood up and looked at her. Her naked body was amazing, tight and alluring. "Jessie you are beautiful," was all I could say to her.

She smiled a sweet schoolgirl smile and then said again "Roddie you are really a nice man. Did you really do hard time like Dejean said?"

"I done a couple of stretches," I told her, "It's no big deal. You do the crime you have to do the time." I laughed.

"Wow, I know it's tough in prison." She seemed as awed by my record as Dejean. "My old boyfriend Tony is in Niatic. He got two years for dealing and he's a mess."

"I hope he survives the joint. It's no picnic," I told her, playing up the menace to impress her more.

She stood up and dressed and I stared at her like a teenager after his first piece of ass. It was stupid; she was just a hooker. I've had many women over the years, but I watched her like a young boy in love. I have a daughter out in Reno, haven't seen her in ten years, but she's probably older than Jessie. Of everything in my fucked up life my biggest regret is that I don't really know my own daughter .

Jessie smiled at me the whole time she was dressing. I wanted to do something to show her that it had been special. I handed her a hundred and fifty dollars and she looked at it and shook her head.

"No Roddie" she said trying to hand the cash back to me," Matt said it was only a hundred."

I pushed it back at her. "It was special Jessie. Keep the extra fifty. Don't give it to Matt."

She put the whole wad in her purse and we left. Back at the tavern she kissed me goodbye and drove off with the boyfriend. Dejean was sitting at the bar sipping a scotch and when I walked over he had a big grin, his gold tooth gleaming. "She wonderful ain't she," he laughed. "You jus' been to heaven." I couldn't disagree.

Jessie started to hang out with us in the tavern and she and I talked almost every night. She was complicated and the other guys in the bar shied away from her. Her clients must have been from elsewhere; I never saw her leave with anyone but me. I took her twice more over the next two weeks.

She controlled her boyfriend like he was a dog. He tried to act tough but she was in charge and dragged that prick around like he was on a leash. Yet they weren't hurting for cash so she must have been taking care of him.

A couple of weeks went by and then she said to me "I want you to meet somebody. I think he could use you and you'd be in with a hot crew." From the bar she had me drive her and Matt to an office on North Avenue in Bridgeport. We walked in together. The sign on the door said "Costas Giannis, Attorney at Law." I recognized the name; Dejean had tried to get me to meet Costas also, but I had never gotten around to it.

There was a waiting area with no secretary and Jessie led me right into the main office. She didn't knock. The boyfriend slinked away and stayed off to the side in the foyer. Costas was a fat guy with slicked down black hair, a puffy face and wearing a thousand dollar suit that he had sweated through. He sat behind a big desk and another guy, short haired, muscular and hard- looking sat next to him. Costas at first ignored me and looked at Jessie with big goo-goo eyes. She walked over, sat down on his lap and kissed him. "Hi honey," she cooed and then said, "This is the guy I mentioned Costas. I think he'd be perfect." The fat man had his hand on Jessie's delicious bubble butt and it was clear his mind wasn't on meeting me. Jessie had him in her palms, just like the boyfriend, and just like me, whenever I was with her. Eventually Costas asked Jessie to step aside and turned in my direction and smiled. "I'm Costas Giannis," he said to me, holding out his hand. I shook it and he continued. "Jessie says that you'd like to work with me." The other guy nodded silently. "She says you're called Roddie. Where you from and what's your last name?"

"Roddie Grant. I'm from here, there and everywhere; originally Nevada, but I done some time in Ohio."

Costas nodded and turned toward the hard guy sitting next to him. "Well Roddie from here there and everywhere, this is Eddie Bratsenis, you'd be working with him. We need help from time to time; lost a crew member recently."

I knew what he wanted and my rep as an ex-con was my in. "I may be available," I told him. "Depends on what the job is."

"Nothing too hard," Costas told me. "We don't believe in trouble and the money is good. You're not on parole or anything?"

"No I got a complete release in Ohio." I liked the idea of new action and I enjoy working crews like this, so I told the fat man I'd work with them.

"Eddie, show him the club upstairs," Costas told Bratsenis. "You guys get to know each other."

Bratsenis stood up and he was a bit shorter than I was. He led me up a back staircase and showed me into an upstairs office that had some couches, a refrigerator and a pool table. "If you want you can hang out here," he told me. "When we have some work I'll let you know. Keep your regular job, its better cover." He didn't say much and after ten minutes or so I left and went back to the bar. Jessie stayed behind. Costas had it bad for her.

Dejean told me that Costas was connected and tied into all the local Greek wise guys. He was also tight with Angelo Barberi, who was in the Patriarca family from Providence, and ran most of the gambling in Stratford. "Man you get in with Costas, Roddie boy," Dejean said, "you be in fat city. I do some selling for him occasionally."

I stayed with the electric generator company but only went in occasionally; told them my back hurt. After a few days Bratsenis called me. The first job we did was easy but it was typical of the types of things we pulled off. We followed a truck into the Fairfield rest stop on 95 and watched as the trucker went into McDonalds. Bratsenis got into the truck, the keys were conveniently left there and drove off. We took the truck to the back of a closed used car lot in Milford and two guys off loaded it into a second truck. It had a shipment of computer tablets. Bratsenis then drove the original truck to another rest stop twenty miles north and left it there. I followed him and we drove back together. "Roddie" he said to me, "a piece a cake. No trouble." He laughed. Before we heisted the rig he handed me a thirty-eight. "Just in case of trouble." Three days later, Bratsenis handed me a thousand bucks cash.

Costas put money out on the street and Eddie and I did some collecting for him. My size and beat up face came in handy in the collecting business. Eddie drove us to a jewelry shop in a nice strip mall in Westport. The jeweler was with two customers when we walked in but turned white as a ghost when he spotted Bratsenis. Eddie silently motioned him to a back work area and he left the couple he was waiting on. I followed.

"Things didn't work out too well this week at the track, eh Solly?" Bratsenis said to the man, who was shivering and nodded his head. "You owe Costas four large and I want it now," he said to the frightened jeweler who shrugged and pleaded.

"I'll get it to him."

Eddie pushed him against the wall. "Not good enough Solly. Maybe Costas will take a Christmas gift to tide him over." He picked up a nice watch that sat on a workbench. "This a Rolex Solly?"

"That's worth more than I owe," the man stammered.

"Good," Bratsenis said, "Costas will take it as payment." We left the jeweler sitting there.

Some weeks after I started with Costas's crew Jessie called me and her voice seemed scared over the cell phone. I really liked her but now I didn't want to get too close. Costas could turn on me over her in a heartbeat and Bratsenis was dangerous. Dejean told me that he was a suspect in several local hits.

"You have to come out here quick, there's some trouble," she said.

She gave me an address in Greenfield Hills, a posh area in Fairfield, and I pulled through an iron gate into the driveway of a brick mansion. Jessie answered the front door and led me inside. She was dressed like a million bucks but was agitated and took me quickly into a huge living room. An older man, well into his sixties, sat on a couch. His head was down and he was shaking. He didn't look at me. "What happened?" I asked her. She shrugged and said, "He thinks he's having a heart attack. He couldn't get it up so I gave him a Viagra and then we smoked a joint. Then he started to freak out. He won't let me call the hospital."

I shook my head at her. "Gave an old man a joint and a Viagra; Jessie you should know better." I walked over to the man and calmed him down. "You'll be all right Mister, just lie down for a while, then call an ambulance." He nodded his head and I took Jessie and left.

On the ride back as usual she chattered away. The old man's condition didn't faze her and was forgotten. "Nice place eh Roddie?" She said, "That old guy's a judge, a big-timer. He calls me whenever the wife is away. She travels a lot and he lets his servants go so we're alone."

Two days later Costas called a meeting with Eddie and myself in the office. Jessie sat with the fat man and she spoke. "The judge has a safe with a lot of cash and jewels. It's a pushover. I know the security codes. He likes taking me out, but we go far away cause he's afraid of being seen. He only calls when the wife is away and then he wants to be alone in the house. He's a freak; likes to jack off watching me dance. He gives the servants the evening off so we're alone. I told Costas that if I take him away you guys can get into that safe easy. You'll have plenty of time. That safe is fucking loaded."

Everything seemed so easy. Bratsenis could handle a small safe, I could go in with him just for protection, and we got Louie Vacca to drive. A week later Jessie said that it was a go; the judge was taking her to a restaurant in Mystic and we had the whole evening to do the job. We watched from the street as he and Jessie rode off. It was as easy as she said. Knowing the security codes we just walked in. I stood guard in the bedroom while Bratsenis went into a big walk-in closet and cracked the safe. The haul was amazing. The judge had a huge wad of cash, we counted it later at a hundred twenty-five large. I wondered why a judge had so much cash lying around but it was ours now. There was also a collection of jewelry; diamond cocktail rings, necklaces, broaches. We gave it to Costas. I bet it was worth more than the cash. We reset the security codes and were out of the place in an hour and a half and back at Costas's office by ten-thirty. He met with Bratsenis in the office and then Eddie handed me an envelope with ten large in it, a big haul for such an easy job.

A few days later Costas held a small celebration in his office. Jessie and Matt were there along with Bratsenis, Vacca and myself. Costas sent out for Chinese food. "Gentlemen", Costas told us with a big smile across his fat face, "we've had a hell of a week. Let's enjoy it." He held out his glass and we all drank up; top of the line Chivas. "I haven't heard from any of my contacts," he told us next. "I don't think that Jessie's judge even reported anything. He must have insurance." He took another sip of the scotch then held up his glass again, "That's his problem. Let's drink to Jessie, she's our hero."

During the party the heat in the office was blasting and Costas was sweating through his fancy suit. He had Jessie glued to his side, his hands roaming all over her body. Matt had his skinny ass off to one side and Jessie ordered him around like he was the hired help. "Hey Matt get me and Costas another drink. Hey Matt, a plate of food for us." He snapped to it, doing everything she asked, but he was sulking. I might do anything for her also but I'd never be a dog for no broad. That skinny prick took it though.

Costas had us take it easy for a few weeks after the heist and I put in a several days at the generator company. There was no heat on us. I was drinking with Dejean when Bratsenis called my cell. "You better get your ass over here right away. It's important."

At the Greek's office Matt sat face down in the entryway and I walked past him into the main office. Costas sat behind his desk with Bratsenis to the side in a chair. Costas was crying and Bratsenis spoke up, "That scumbag strangled Jessie," pointing to the outer foyer. Costas wept some more and I was stunned. "She must have pushed him too far." Eddie said. "She's in a motel room in Milford."

Jessie had charmed me and just like the boyfriend and just like Costas I liked her a lot. Thinking of her lying dead in a motel room was like a kick in my gut. Still I stayed cool while Costas wept; only way to act in my world.

"What's he doing here then?" I asked, pointing at the outer office.

"Prick thinks we have to protect him", Bratsenis told me. "Says he knows too much. He'll talk if he's caught."

Costas stopped weeping and his face took on a look of pure hatred; only a woman can bring on something like that. "You have to take care of him Eddie." The menace in the fat man's voice was clear.

Bratsenis walked to a closet behind Costas's desk and took out a shoulder holster and a berretta. He put the holster on and turned to me. "Roddie you drive."

I've never wacked anyone, although in Reno I watched Joe Murrell take out a snitch and helped him get rid of the body. In my world killing someone at some time is expected so except for the danger of being caught I wasn't scared of it. I was uneasy walking out with Bratsenis but what could I do. I worked for Costas and something had to be done about Jessie's death.

"Come on" Eddie said to Matt who was shaking.

"Where are we going" Matt asked, his voice trembling.

"Costas has a safe place up near Hartford. Keep you there till this blows over. First you're going to show me where you left her."

"I'm not going back there." Matt said terrified, "what if someone found her?"

"You'll go where I tell you," Bratsenis told him as he dragged him to his feet and walked the skinny prick to the car. Eddie sat with him in the back and I drove to the motel in Milford. We cased the place and everything seemed clear. Matt took us into the room. Jessie lay on the bed, her neck purple where the scumbag choked her. Her skin was pasty white. Eddie checked the pulse in her neck and nodded that she was dead. I felt like throwing up. I've seen dead bodies but she was special to me. Her eyes were wide open and I leaned over and closed them. The least I could for her. Eddie took a bracelet off of her wrist and a diamond necklace from her neck. They were gifts from Costas. Eddie put the jewelry in his pocket and walked into the bathroom while Matt stood there sobbing, staring at the body. Before I knew what was happening, Eddie had a cloth over Matt's face and the berretta, with a silencer, at his temple. A single shot, just a dull click from the berretta, and Matt fell to the floor. Eddie waited a few seconds then felt his pulse. He was dead. Eddie wiped the gun clean, took off the silencer and placed the piece in Matt's hand. He left the light on and singled me to look outside. There was no one around and the two of us left. In the car he said "Murder suicide, that's what they'll see." I thought it wouldn't work but what could I say.

Back at Costas's, Eddie handed the fat man the bracelet and necklace. Costas shook Bratsenis's hand, started to cry and asked. "That douchebag is taken care of, right?" Eddie nodded.

I was freaked by taking Matt out. If Costas's operation fell apart or if the Judge did some more checking I was looking at murder as well as robbery. But I was also upset over Jessie. I banged her only four times but we had talked so much that I felt real close to her. It started me thinking about my daughter Robin back in Nevada. There was never much between her mom Candy and me even though I knocked her up. We just palled around together and when I did a stretch for assault in Carson City, Candy pulled up roots and went to Reno. Robin had to be twenty-five now.

I called the last number I had for Candy and she answered. "It's Roddie," I told her. "How you been?"

She wasn't pleasant. "What the fuck do you want; need some cash you deadbeat?"

"No" I told her "I been east the last few years and I'm coming back to Nevada. Was thinking about looking up Robin. How's she doing?"

"She's doing fine, no thanks to you."

"Do you think she'll see me?"

"What the fuck for?"

"I'm her dad. I just want to."

"Well if you get here, call again and I'll let her decide." Candy then hung up.

I couldn't tell Costas and Eddie that I was leaving. They wouldn't let me go, maybe even take me out because I knew too much. I just had to run; there was little chance they'd track me down.

I packed what I could in a single suitcase and cleared out my bank account. Left the car at the rooming house took a cab to the train station and caught a train to New York. At Penn Station I jumped on a bus to Chicago. From there I'll find my way to Reno. Bus travel is underrated, it's comfortable, cheap and best of all pretty much anonymous. When the bus eventually got on Route 80 West I took out my one photo of Robin as a little girl and looked at it. She had big blue eyes and they stared out of the picture. Over the years I hardly ever thought of her but I stared at the picture and it kept changing from Robin as a little girl to Jessie and then back to Robin.

The Lady With Emerald Green Eyes

James Donzella

THE WORST KIND of trouble always looks good from the start. I found that out Friday afternoon. I had taken a couple of aspirins to ease the pounding in my head from Thursday's all-night party. Truman had declared victory in Japan and the two-day riot had finally subsided early Friday morning. Wednesday's Chronicle, with its one word headline, *PEACE*, still rested on my desk staring me in the face when she walked in.

"Are you James Wolf?"

"Guilty," I said. "Come in please." I rose from my chair. "Have a seat."

She looked about 22 or 23 years old and stunning. A real traffic stopper but I could tell she'd brush you off as easy as a flake of dandruff on a navy blue blazer.

The woman assessed my tiny office with a cursory glance.

I shrugged. "It's small, but I call it home."

Gliding to the only chair in the office with an air of sophistication, she sat down. Those emerald green eyes were mesmerizing. They made quite a dent. Long red hair flowing out from under a stylish feathered hat reminded me of the bright orange and red hues of a wildfire illuminating a night sky. I opened the polished wood cigarette box on the desk and offered a smoke.

"Cigarette?"

After choosing one from the box, I moved around the desk and brought my Zippo to life, getting a better look at a pair of eyes, greener than a field of shamrocks. The tip of the smoke glowed red. An exhaled stream of blue smoke poured out from the side of a perfectly formed rose shaped mouth.

"Thank you Mr. Wolf. You'll have to forgive me. I'm a little nervous."

"Relax," I said as I returned to my seat. "First things, first. What's your name?"

"Dorothy Adams."

I lit myself a smoke. "Okay, Miss Adams. What can I do for you?"

"It's a rather delicate situation Mr. Wolf. I need help desperately. I'll pay whatever you ask."

I reached for a pad and began to take notes. "Take your time; tell me what's goin' on."

"I made a terrible mistake awhile back."

Dorothy looked down at her lap, hands lay there, palms up.

"We all make mistakes Miss Adams."

"Adams is my maiden name. I'm married now to a very important person. Several years ago I…"

"Someone blackmailing you?"

A lower lip quivered followed by a nod. "I received a letter," Dorothy said opening a black leather handbag and removing a folded sheet of paper. She offered the note with trembling hand. I could tell she was wound up tighter than a girdle on a fat lady at Thanksgiving.

The note demanded ten-thousand dollars in cash or the husband would be informed of the indiscretion.

"What's he shakin' you down for?"

"Some photos."

"Blackmail's a crime. Have you contacted the police?"

"No! I don't want the police involved. This is the last payment," a brown envelope appeared from her bag. "You give him this and he'll give you a package."

"Is that it?"

"Yes, but… I… I want this to be the end of it. I want you to make sure he won't come back for more."

"I see. Put a scare into him," a nod as she looked down at her hands again. "I can't guarantee that a scare will work. Blackmailers often do come back for more when the money runs out. They can be trouble. You're sure you don't want to get the police involved."

"I'm sure," Dorothy said probing inside the handbag.

"Have you made any arrangements with…?"

"Mr. Gendel is his name. Yes, I have a meeting arranged for eight o'clock tonight. Here's the address," she said handing me a slip of paper and two crisp 100-dollar bills. "Will this be enough for your services?"

"That'll be fine," I said as I put the money in the desk drawer.

———

I stopped by Clooney's on Broadway to grab a bite and a drink around six o'clock. At the bar, I found my old friend Dr. Percy Haladae pontificating on the invention of the potato chip by an African chef, George Crum, in 1853. Two bar buzz saws, a blonde and a brunette hung on his every word.

"Commodore Vanderbilt complained that the fried potatoes were too thick. The cunning and crafty chef cut potatoes paper thin and fried them to a crisp delighting the difficult to please Vanderbilt. Thus presenting to the world this enchanting salty snack," Doc said, and with aristocratic flair. He daintily plucked a chip from a bowl and chomped on it with pronounced gratification, generating laughter and applause from the two women.

"I see you're up to no good Doc," I said as I took a stool next to his and dropped my hat on the bar.

"Giaco!" he yelled. Doc's volume tended to increase a few decibels with each ensuing cocktail. Doc, an ex-dentist who decided that gambling and alcohol held more interest than filling teeth, when in need of money, made dental molds in his tiny lab in the basement of an old building in the Tenderloin.

"Ladies, may I introduce my good friend Giacomo Lupo."

"It's James. James Wolf. Nice to know you."

"Yes, James changed his name when he decided to join the local constabulary."

"You're a police detective?" the brunette slurred, reeking of gin.

"Private these days."

"We should keep him in mind if we need someone to keep an eye on our husbands," the blonde said as they clinked glasses and laughed.

We moved to a table. Doc and I chatted while I ate the meatloaf special and drank a beer. Just after 7:30 I paid my tab and left. Jefferson Gandel had an office on Polk Street, a few blocks away from Clooney's. I parked my car across the street from the building around

7:45. I lit myself a smoke and sat back to wait for eight o'clock to roll around. I was feeling good. This was my second case in a month. I had been at this P.I. racket for only three months after getting kicked off the San Francisco Police Department on a police brutality charge. I couldn't count on any work from the D.A.'s office. Mahoney hated my guts. He had it out for me since the Watson Jewelry Store robbery. In a shootout with the robbery suspects, I accidentally shot and killed my best friend and partner Sully Sullivan. It was the worst day of my life. The brutality charge was the coup de grâce.

"Damn it!" I yelled as I tossed my smoke on the pavement. The curse of the human mind to recall the past and react to it like it happened yesterday. I know Sully would never have blamed me.

You still brooding over that Jimmy?

I looked into the rearview mirror. There was Sully, his signature brown fedora pulled down to the eyebrows.

"More often than not," I said.

He pushed his hat up with a thumb and smiled. *The past is the past. You can't get back a past moment or capture a future moment and save it for a time when you need it.*

"You have turned into quite the… what am I lookin for…"

Philosopher. It comes with the territory.

"There's a term for what's happening to me right now. Probably from all the concussions. It's where you hallucinate?"

You're not hallucinating. When you graduated from the academy, your mother prayed a Guardian Angel'd protect you. She prayed every single day. You have to trust"

"If I only have one person… ah… angel I can trust, I'm glad it's you."

I've told you before. Get that thick Italian head out of the past pal. You can only die once. You live every day. Don't waste today by dwelling in the past.

"I can't seem to help it—"

In that instant Sully vanished and when I glanced at my watch, it was eight o'clock. I got out of the car and crossed the street to the building that housed Gandel's office. Yellow light shone through several of the office windows. I entered the building and started down a long hall. The deeper I got into the building the darker the hall became. About halfway along the hall I stopped. The remaining ten feet of the hall was as black as a cup of truck-stop coffee. I turned back and took a step toward the entrance when I felt something hit me hard on the back of my head. I went to the floor and tried to push myself up when a rag covered my face, held there by a strong hand. A sweet smell filled my nostrils. I struggled to get free, but another blow struck me on the right side of my head just above the ear. A black void encircled me as I plummeted down a deep shaft. As I started to swirl deeper into the blackness, the pleasant sweet vanished, a bitter taste invaded my mouth.

—

I opened my eyes a bit and could only make out shadows of light and dark as if staring into a thick Tule Fog. My head felt like a basketball dribbled up and down the court for a couple of hours. As the fog began to clear, I could see a face. It wasn't pretty either. It was enormous and round, but what stood out through the haze, a large Fuller Brush moustache covering its upper lip.

"He's coming round," a voice in the distance said.

"Can you hear me Wolf?" the man said as he flashed his shinny buzzer in my face "It's Lieutenant March."

Lieutenant Ray March's ugly mug came into clear view. "Oh it's you March. For a second there I thought it was Halloween. So they finally made you Lieutenant, huh?"

"Thanks for reminding me why I never liked you Wolf."

"Where the hell am I?"

"Hospital. Found you slumped over your steering wheel on Jackson. Your car on the sidewalk."

"Hospital? The last thing I remember I went into a building on Polk and somebody slugged me. They put a rag over my mouth. Smelled sweet."

"Did you notice a bitter taste?" a male voice asked.

I looked to my left and behind March stood a white coated doctor. "Yeah."

"Trichloromethane. You were hit and drugged," the doctor said.

"Christ!"

"What were you doing at the Polk Street address?" March questioned.

"I have a client. I was to pay off a blackmailer."

March turned to Inspector McNabb and said, "Bring him in."

"Hey McNabb, how's tricks?" I said, but McNabb didn't react, he just left the room. "You want to tell me what the hell's going on here?"

McNabb and another gentleman came into the room. The man, in his mid-fifties, stood about five-feet six, balding on the top of his head and a white bandage on the left side of his forehead.

"Is this the man who robbed you?" March asked.

"I couldn't say. I really didn't see him."

"This is Mr. Gandel, Wolf."

"Jefferson Gandel? He's the guy who's blackmailing my client."

"Blackmail!" Gandel shouted. "I've never blackmailed anyone in my life, this is preposterous."

"We found this in your jacket pocket," March said as he took a brown envelope from McNabb. "It has $1,000 in it. It appears it's some of the money that Gandel had in his deposit pouch."

"Let me see that," I demanded. March handed me the envelope. "You've got a problem here March. This isn't the envelope my client gave me. The envelope I had to pay off Gandel had his office address written on it in pencil. Must have been too dark to notice when the punk who blackjacked me made the switch."

"Who's your client? We can call 'em and straighten this whole thing out."

"Dorothy Adams. She's stayin' at the Saint Francis," I said. March nodded to McNabb and he left the room. "Listen, all I was supposed to do was deliver an envelope to a Mr. Gandel and he was to give me an envelope to return to Miss Adams."

"Something doesn't sound right about this," March replied.

"You know March. A lot of people think you're dumb, but I think you're a real genius. What time were you mugged Mr. Gandel?"

"About seven-fifteen."

"I was having a drink at Clooney's from six to seven-thirty. You can check that."

"No one registered by that name Lieutenant," McNabb said as he returned.

I sat up and peered around March's round body. "Any reason why I can't get out of here Doc?"

"You have had a concussion and—"

"I'm feeling a lot better. I need to get on this before I get framed for the Lindbergh kidnapping!" I barked as I threw off the bed covers.

"Just leave this up to us Wolf," March said sternly.

"You couldn't find an elephant in a mailbox, March, even if I gave you the street corner."

———

It was nearly eight o'clock in the morning by the time I checked out of the hospital. I'd been out, because of the chloroform treatment, for close to 10 hours. I drove across town to the St. Francis on Union Square to see if I could stir up any leads.

Things just got interesting. You've been framed, Sully said from the back seat of the car.

"I've been matted, mounted and hung. I look like the mamaluke of the year over here."

I can't figure a motive.

"Here I thought this was going to be easy money and I get a robbery pinned on me."

Easy money always comes with a hook.

"That's good; you should set it to music," I said

Sully shook his head and vanished as I pulled up to the hotel.

———

"You're the second party to ask about a Miss Adams," the desk clerk said. "I had a phone call—"

"Yeah I know. Listen, I'm sure you'd recognize her. About five foot seven, slim build, emerald green eyes."

"That sounds like Miss Bright. Stunningly green eyes. I noticed them when she—"

"That's great. What room?"

"Checked out an hour ago."

"Any forwarding address?"

"No, I'm afraid not."

"Can I get a look at her room?"

"Well I…"

I showed the clerk my identification and a five-dollar bill. "It's really important."

He turned and retrieved a key and handed it to me. "Third floor to your left."

I carefully searched room 312 for anything left behind. When I inspected the bathroom, I hit the jackpot. In the wastebasket was a bright red woman's wig. I was set up. I headed down to the lobby and questioned the doorman.

"Yeah, I remember her. Those green eyes, I'll never forget. I asked if she wanted a cab and I whistled one up."

"Did she say where she was going?"

"I couldn't hear. I closed the door before she said anything."

"Which cab company?"

"Veterans. He's usually here several times during the day."

I went back into the hotel and called Doc. Twenty-minutes later Doc met me in the lobby of the hotel. I explained the situation and Doc agreed to see what he could find out about Mr. Gandel. I waited another 15 minutes when the doorman waved me over.

"Al's the cabby you want to talk to," he said. Parked four vehicles from the entrance was a red and white Veterans cab.

"You Al?" I asked as I poked my head into the cab.

"Yeah. What can I do for you mister?"

I held out a fiver. "Do you remember a fair coupl'a hours ago? Woman about five-foot seven—"

"With green eyes. Who could forget?"

"Where did you take her?"

"Hotel Boheme," he said taking the bill from my fingers and giving me a wave.

—

The desk clerk at the hotel told me that a Miss Bright had checked in, but wasn't in her room. I called my service from the booth in the lobby. Doc had left a message to call him at his lab.

"Dental Lab," Doc droned into the receiver.

"It's Wolf, I got your message."

"Jimmy my boy. I've made some inquiries for you. Gandel seems to be a straight shooter. All on the up and up from what I could discern. He owns several radio shops. Sales and repair services all around the Bay Area. End of the week, he goes around and collects the weeks tally, or someone from one of the shops delivers the cash to his office. He balances the books and deposits the cash and checks in the night deposit. Seems he got robbed last night. Over twenty-thousand bucks."

"Not the kind of guy that would run a badger game?"

"No. Upstanding member of the community. Church goer. Real family man. Probably boring as hell to be around."

"Thanks Doc."

"Anytime Jimmy."

I went out to my car to think things over. I drummed my fingers on the wheel for a moment when I noticed Sully in the back seat.

"I don't know this dame from the man in the moon, I swear. What the hell's she got against me?"

Arrested her husband, or boyfriend?

"Adams, Bright. The names aren't ringin' any bells."

You think she's working alone?

"My gut tells me no."

Stick with your gut. It's usually right.

"Just like the old days on stake-out." I said, but Sully must have had plans because he disappeared. Half-dozen cups of coffee, two donuts and a salami sandwich later, the late afternoon mist turned to rain. One of those warm summer rains that occasionally invades the Bay Area. The ragtop on the old Ford leaked and water dripped on my right shoulder, left knee and left ankle. No matter what position I assumed, drops were establishing themselves somewhere on my body. My thoughts focused on Sully.

My mom always believed in Angels. My Pop fished out by the Farallon Islands one night in November. It started to storm with rain and winds. Two years old at the time, I developed an awful cough. By midnight, my fever had spiked to 102 degrees. The phone lines went down and mom decided to wrap me up in a blanket and slicker to take me to San Francisco General. No one in the neighborhood had a car so she took to the street. Walked nearly six blocks before a taxi driver pulled up and opened the car door. Mom told the driver she didn't have any money but the driver, Raphael was his name, put us into the cab and drove to the hospital. Twenty-four hours later, my fever broke and I was going to be fine. The following day my mother called the taxi company to thank their driver Raphael and pay him for the ride. The taxi company said they didn't have a driver by that name. With all her calls to cab companies that day, no one claimed to have a driver named Raphael. Mom was convinced that the Angel Raphael the patron of physicians and travelers saved me.

Two more hours had passed and I needed to stretch my legs. I got out of the car, crossed the street, and positioned myself under an overhang of the building next to the hotel. I lit a cigarette and fixed the collar of my raincoat tighter around my neck. Close to fifteen minutes later a tan 1941 Plymouth Coupe stopped at the entrance of the Hotel Boheme. As soon as the passenger exited the vehicle, I recognized her as the woman who came to my office. She darted into the hotel and I started to move toward the entrance, but the driver of the coupe appeared to be waiting for Miss Bright to return. I crossed the street and got back into my car. The rain on the windows obscured my view. The driver, a man with no recognizable facial features, sat behind the wheel, motor running. I started my engine and waited.

Miss Bright came out of the hotel ten minutes later, bag in hand and got into the waiting car. Rain came down a little harder and my left shoe stared filling up with water. The coupe pulled away from the curb and headed north. I swung my heap around and followed at a safe distance. They turned east on Union and then left on Grant. Continuing on Grant, they made a right turn onto Edith Street. To call Edith a street is an exaggeration. It's no more than a narrow alley with no outlet. The car crept along the alley then turned left at the dead-end. I eased my machine forward and through the wet shimmering glass of the passenger side window, I could see the man walk to the rear of the vehicle, then disappear from view when he turned to the left.

Parking two doors down on Grant, I removed my .38 from under the dash. Slipping my piece into my raincoat pocket, I walked the length of Edith Street. The apartments butted up against each other on both sides of the alley. When I reached the end, to the left, set back about twenty feet, stood a small bungalow. The tan coupe, parked next to a flight of stairs. The living quarters were on the second floor above a garage. I climbed the stairs mindful of any excessive noise, but the sound of the drizzling rain masked any creaking sounds my steps prompted from the old wood as I approached the entrance.

I outsmarted the lock on the door and entered quietly. As I closed the door behind me I could hear voices coming from somewhere inside the house. My left foot squished as I took careful steps into the small vestibule of the house. The vestibule led into the living room of the flat. An old worn couch occupied an area in front of the fireplace. The walls were void of any decoration. The room had a sad look, almost depressed in a way. Voices were emanating from the right where I could see an archway that led into the kitchen. I took a step toward the kitchen and my wet left shoe gave an excellent impression of the creaking door on the *Inner Sanctum* program. I bent down, slipped off my shoes and crept closer to the kitchen.

"It's twenty-five thousand dollars Connie. You don't want any of it?"

"I just want to get out of here. I'm scared Earl."

As I got closer to the kitchen, I could see Connie standing next to a small table.

"There's nothing to be sacred of. It was perfect!" the male voice said with punctuated emphasis.

"I should have never come up here," Connie said.

The gun felt cold in my hand as I caressed the .38 in my pocket. I inched closer.

"I'm gonna' use some of this money for a lawyer for Vic. One of those high-priced shysters," Earl said.

"Vic doesn't need a lawyer. He's only got eight months left."

"Shouldn't got any! Four goddamn years in Chino. That stupid public defender made him cop a plea, for chrissake."

"There's no talkin' to you. I'm leaving. I booked a flight for L.A. at eight."

"Whadaya' wanna' leave for? Stay for the fun. I bet that mook Wolf is sweatin' bullets right now. Set his ass up, but good!"

"Not so fast there Ace," I said as I stepped into the kitchen, my gun at my hip.

"Jesus!" cried Connie.

"What the...Wolf!" Earl exclaimed as he stood over the two-burner stove holding a coffee cup in his hand. He had a puzzled look like a dog that didn't understand his master's command.

"Yeah. Put the cup down and grab air, I don't want anything to happen to you before I find out just what the hell is going on here." Earl set the cup down and raised his hands above his head. The pot of coffee under the flame started to make bubbling noises. "You're up to your earrings in this too sister. No one in this town can forget those green eyes. You left a trail a mile wide."

Connie dropped into the chair next to the table. "I had a bad feeling about this."

Earl stood about five-ten, with curly light brown hair. He looked about 30, thin and wiry, dark brown eyes deeply set into his face; dark circles accented both of them. It appeared that he hadn't slept in days.

"Who the hell are ya pal?"

He just stood there, looking at me, fists clenching and then stretching in a rhythmic fashion. Several moments past before Connie broke the silence.

"Earl Dexter," Connie said solemnly. "Vic Dexter's brother."

"Who's Vic Dexter?"

"He doesn't remember!" Earl said throwing his hands out to the sides and turning to Connie. "The sonofabitch doesn't remember. Victor Dexter, you bastard. You shot him three years ago."

"I shot him?"

"The hold-up at Stone's Market on Ocean," Earl said.

"Your brother musta' been the one drivin' the getaway car."

"He didn't know what those mugs were up to. He had no idea they fingered the place for a heist."

"He tried to run me down!"

"He panicked! He was just a kid. He piled the car up around a pole. Smashed his head through the windshield. He's scarred for life, because of you."

"So you thought you would set me up on a bum-rap to get even. Smarten up kid. You'd better end this right now before someone else gets hurt or worse."

"Listen to him Earl."

"You still have all the money, right?"

"Yeah."

"How did you know that Gandel was carrying all that cash?"

"I worked at one of his stores for a few months. Everyone knew that he would take all the receipts back to the office to count it up and then drop the cash bag in the night deposit at the Hibernia branch."

"What you're lookin' at right now is an assault charge and grand theft. If you return the money, you may be able to get Gandel to vouch for you. As for myself, I figure the two-hundred Connie here fronted me, will be compensation enough for the lump on my head."

Earl thought for a moment and leaned back against the refrigerator. He rubbed his hands over his face and took a deep breath.

"Don't make this any worse than it already is pal. You have a shot at only gettin' probation. That goes for you too," I said to Connie. "Don't be stupid."

"What do you want us to do?" she asked.

"Call the police right now. When they get here, you give them the whole story. I know a lawyer that could help. He's not one of those high-priced shysters, but he's good. If you want, I'll call him right now."

"Do what he says Earl. Please! I don't want to be in jail when Vic gets out. Call the police!"

Earl nodded. "I was just so angry. I... I didn't know what I was doing. You know when you get blinded by anger and you do dumb things? Vic's the younger, smarter brother. Goin' to make somethin' of himself but was hangin' with the wrong crowd."

"He's young. He's got plenty of time to turn things around," I said as I holstered my gun. I called the best mouthpiece I knew, Sid Bergson and explained the situation. He told me to give him ten minutes then call the police.

—

I'd never seen Lieutenant March look so upset. He thought he had me. I'm sure he had already written up a report to get me indicted for grand theft. As Earl told the story, March became more frustrated every time Sid interrupted the questioning, advising Earl not to say anything else about certain aspects of the case. After a half-hour of this, March finally gave up and had the duo brought downtown for booking. March only had one question for me. Why didn't I want to press charges? I told him that I was feeling somewhat benevolent that evening. Emerald eyes and I exchanged glances and gave me a knowing smile.

—

When I got outside the drizzling had stopped and the air had that clean aroma that follows a rain. I got into my car and headed for home.

Benevolent, huh, Sully said from the back seat. *I didn't know you knew the meaning of the word.*

"There's a lot of things you don't know about me. I think I even surprised March. He had no idea that two-hundred dollars' worth of benevolence rested comfortably in my office drawer."

Sully let out a guffaw of derision. Death tends to harden a man.

Pearl of Great Price
Phil Giunta

THE FIRST OF THE two dead men was sprawled just inside the door, the front of his white shirt matted in crimson from the bullet hole in the middle of his chest. Across the room, the other guy sat slumped against the couch, head tilted back and cocked to one side. A stream of dried blood ran down the upholstery. On the floor beside each body lay identical semi-automatic pistols.

As he entered the rental house on New Castle Street, Detective Kurt Vandermoor snapped on a pair of Nitrile gloves before joining Sergeant Eliana Velez in the middle of the living room. "And who do we have here?"

Velez held up two driver's licenses and nodded toward each body in turn. "Seth Manning, thirty-seven, and Dino Quintana, thirty-four. Both from Long Island. Found their wallets on the dining room table along with several interesting photos."

Kurt crouched down beside the younger victim for a closer look at his head wound. "Anyone hear the shots?"

"No. Most of these rental houses are empty this early in the year."

"Then who called it in?"

"A woman named Yasmine Kadara came into the station early this morning claiming she was supposed to meet these two here yesterday, but when they didn't answer the door—or her subsequent calls and texts—she became concerned and asked us to check on them."

Kurt stood. "From the looks of things, they've been dead for at least that long, but I'll leave that to the medical examiner."

"On his way from Georgetown. Should be here in about twenty minutes." Velez shook her head. "We haven't had a murder in

Rehoboth for over a decade. Now we get two in one day."

"At least they're both in the same house. Makes things convenient. Where's Ms. Kadara now?"

"Staying at the Beach View for the week."

"I'd like to have a conversation with her when we're done here." Kurt held out his hands. "This scene is too perfect."

"Meaning?"

"Meaning that either these two really shot each other, or someone went through the trouble to make us think they did."

"If that's the case, it might have been someone they knew," Velez suggested. "There's no sign of forced entry anywhere in the house and no indication of a struggle."

"Well, if we don't find a second set of prints on those Glocks, we'll figure out who they're registered to and go from there." Kurt sauntered into the dining room and sifted through several photographs strewn across the table. Some were pictures of a small, sleek yacht called *Charisma Nova*, while others were closeups of a gold crucifix bejeweled with rubies at the ends of the arms and feet and a pink pearl above the head of Christ. Kurt turned over one of the photos. The words 'Pearl of Great Price' were scrawled on the back.

As he reached for one of the dead men's wallets, his phone buzzed. He snatched it out of his belt holster and peered at the screen. It was Police Chief Thomas Miles. Kurt put the call on speaker. "Good morning, Chief."

"You might not think it's so good after this conversation. There's been another murder."

"Where?"

"Coast Guard was checking on a yacht about six miles off Whiskey Beach. They found a body aboard, shot three times, and we think the suspect might have gone ashore on a raft."

"Anyone find the raft?"

"Not yet," Miles replied. "When you're done there, come back to the station. I'll brief you in my office. There's more to this than just a murder. It's high profile. The yacht belonged to Max Trevani from Montauk."

"Name's familiar."

"He's the treasure hunter from *Oceans of Gold* on Nat Geo."

Kurt snapped his fingers. "That's right! My ex-wife watched that show all the time."

"We just notified Mr. Trevani's family. They're on their way. At some point, I'll need to speak to the press, but I intend to hold them off as long as possible until we have a lead."

Kurt picked up one of the photos from the dining room table. "What about the *Charisma Nova*?"

"DNREC will tow it in—wait, how did you know the name of the yacht? I didn't mention it."

"Just a hunch, Chief, but I might have found our first lead."

———

"Coast Guard boarded the boat at 4:40 a.m. and found Trevani on the floor of his cabin. They recovered a watertight lockbox containing relics bound for the Shipwreck Museum in Fenwick." Chief Miles pushed a photograph across his desk. "According to the cargo manifest, this item is missing—a solid gold crucifix studded with gems. Look familiar? That picture was in the lockbox."

"Same one from the house," Kurt confirmed.

"I have a call into Denny Clifford to see if he can shed more light on it. He owns the Shipwreck Museum."

"So, either our two dead guys were aboard with Trevani or there's a third person involved. They waited until the yacht reached our waters, killed him overnight, and took off on the raft with the crucifix. They probably ditched the raft somewhere around Gordons Pond. They could be anywhere now."

"I want you to take lead on this case," Miles said. "State Police and Lewes PD. requested our help to search that area. Velez is already out there with Gemell, Lonakis, and a few others."

Both men glanced up at a knock on the open door. A uniformed officer leaned in. "Sorry to interrupt, Chief. Denny Clifford's here."

"Perfect timing. Send him in."

The officer stepped aside and waved forward a middle-aged man with short cropped platinum hair, wrinkled polo shirt, and faded jeans. The chief stood and extended a hand. "Denny, thanks for coming in on short notice." He gestured toward Kurt. "This is Detective Kurt Vandermoor. He joined us at the end of last year."

The two men shook hands before Denny settled into the seat beside Kurt. "Any leads on Max's killer?"

"We're working on it," Miles assured him.

"How well did you know Mister Trevani?" Kurt asked.

"We were like brothers. Max and I went on shipwreck dives together all over the world for almost thirty years before I opened the museum. In fact, he was coming here to donate one of his recent finds, a gold crucifix recovered from a wreck in the Alboran Sea."

"That's why I called you," Miles said. "Coast Guard found a lockbox half filled with small relics, but the crucifix was nowhere to be found aboard the yacht."

"So, it was stolen?"

"Seems likely." Kurt nodded. "What can you tell us about it?"

"Other than the fact that it was named for one of Christ's most famous parables, it's worth nearly twenty million dollars." Denny picked up the photo from the chief's desk. "This crucifix dates back to August of 1415 when King John of Portugal and his sons Edward and Henry led an armada to conquer the city of Ceuta along the Strait of Gibraltar. The siege was swift with almost no casualties.

"History attributes that to the fact that Ceuta's defense was caught off-guard, but there were many who credited three gold crucifixes gifted to the king and his sons by a Portuguese craftsman. As they embarked on the raid, King John carried the largest crucifix aboard his ship while his two sons each carried a smaller one aboard theirs. King John's was the only one adorned with jewels.

"Over time, all three crucifixes were lost at sea. The two smaller ones were recovered in the Indian Ocean in the 1980s, but of course, they're only worth about three million each."

"Only." Kurt said. "I'm in the wrong line of business."

"I've had those two on display in the museum for years, but this summer, Max and I planned to exhibit all three crucifixes at once. It would be the first time they were together in over six hundred years."

"If we find it, we'll let you know," Miles said. "But keep in mind that it's evidence in a murder investigation. You'll need to postpone your exhibit."

"I take it this thing was insured?" Kurt asked.

"Absolutely." Denny nodded. "And I suspect you'll hear from an insurance investigator before the day is over."

———

An hour later, Kurt trudged across the cool sand toward a relic of a more recent era. The Delaware coast was home to a series of concrete fire control towers constructed during World War II to prevent enemy ships from invading Delaware Bay.

The majority of them had weathered time and tide to remain standing seven decades since. Two in particular, Towers Five and Six, had been built 300 yards apart like twin sentinels along Whiskey Beach between the sea and Gordons Pond Wildlife Area.

As Kurt approached Tower Five, Velez met him halfway. "We can call off the search. Bunch of kids managed to dig their way under the door and into the tower. They found this." Velez gestured toward a partially deflated raft lying in a crumpled heap on the sand. "We got here just as they were dragging it out."

"So, the scene's been contaminated."

"Unfortunately." She handed Kurt a pair of Nitrile gloves. After slipping them on, he crouched down and unfurled the raft until his fingers found a series of long gashes that just happened to slice through the name *Charisma Nova*.

Kurt glanced up at Velez. "Did these kids happen to find any—"

She thrust two plastic and aluminum oars toward him.

"How about a solid gold crucifix encrusted with precious gems?"

Velez shook her head.

"Didn't think so." Kurt nodded toward the tower where several other officers were milling about. "Let's take a look around. How did these kids get inside the tower? I thought the entrances were sealed."

"They are, but years of high tides deteriorated the bottom of the sheet metal, creating a gap."

"So I see." They stopped in the shadow of Tower Five where a trench in the sand vanished beneath the rusty, corroded door. It was nearly large enough to allow an average adult to crawl inside. Kurt pointed at Tower Six to the north. "What about that one? Same thing?"

"Yep. Kids get in there, drink, smoke weed, graffiti the walls."

"Now you got me curious." He leaned forward to peer beneath the door. "Think I can fit under there?"

Velez held out one of the oars. "You'll need to dig a deeper trench."

Kurt ignored the laughter from the officers gathered around them. "I'll bet you a drink I can squeeze under there."

"You're on."

He lowered himself to the sand and slipped his legs under the door. With a final glance at Velez, he wiggled his upper body through the shallow gap. A moment later, Kurt stood inside the tower. "You owe me a drink, Velez."

"See anything interesting?"

"Just a few cigarette butts, some trash, innocuous graffiti." High above, sunlight from a series of narrow rectangular windows, spaced evenly apart, illuminated three levels of circular wooden platforms— floors that hadn't endured the weight of a human being in generations.

Surrounding him, more such windows, barely wider than his arm, had been sealed with brick and cement, with one exception. The top half of the window to his immediate right was unobstructed, permitting a modicum of sunlight.

"Velez, slide one of those oars under the door."

Kurt grabbed the contoured blade as soon as it appeared. "Got it."

After a moment, Velez stood at the window.

"You're blocking my light, Sergeant."

She stepped to one side. "What are you looking for?"

"Buried treasure."

"You can't be serious. Whoever took that crucifix is in the wind."

"Call it a hunch." Kurt poked the oar's shaft into the sand a few times before striking something solid directly beneath the partially sealed window. Flipping the oar over, he dug frantically with the blade before reaching into the hole.

A moment later, he thrust an empty beer bottle through the opening in the window. "So much for that. Hey, Velez. Recycle this, will ya?"

———

Kurt stood outside the tower, brushing sand from his clothes with one hand while pressing his phone to his ear with the other. "The raft confirms that someone else was definitely aboard Trevani's yacht. I asked Velez to contact Montauk Beach Marina. Maybe someone there knows who accompanied Trevani yesterday or, if we're lucky, they have security footage."

"Good. Keep me posted," the chief said. "One last thing. Denny was right, you're about to get a visit from an insurance investigator. Her name's Brenda Lambert. She showed up at the station a few minutes ago, so I sent her your way."

Kurt turned in the direction of the parking lot to find a petite woman scurrying onto the beach clutching a black portfolio in one hand and a pair of suede pumps in the other. "She about five four, strawberry blonde, wearing a pale green blouse and jeans?"

"That's the one. Be careful. She's a barracuda."

"No worries, Chief. I may be new to Rehoboth, but this ain't my first time swimmin' with sharks. I'll be in touch." Kurt lowered his phone and stepped forward to greet the woman. "Good afternoon, ma'am."

"Please don't call me that, it makes me feel old. Chief Miles said I would find Detective Vandermoor here."

"And here I be."

She tucked her shoes under her arm and extended a hand, followed by her business card. "Brenda Lambert, investigator for Coastline Insurance."

Kurt glanced at the card before slipping it into his shirt pocket. "Yes, I was warned you were coming. What can I do for you, Ms. Lambert?"

"My company sent me out here when we were informed of Mr. Trevani's death and the subsequent theft of a highly valued artifact from his yacht." Brenda produced a photograph from her portfolio. "It's called the—"

"Pearl of Great Price," Kurt finished. "Worth about twenty million dollars. You know, that's the third photo of this thing I've seen today. Maybe third time's the charm and we'll actually find it."

"Got any leads?"

Kurt swept his hands over the raft. "We have this. It's from the *Charisma Nova.*"

"You found it in the tower?"

"Yes, ma'am."

"So, the murderer took the crucifix, fled the yacht on this raft, and came here."

"Looks that way."

"What's your next step?"

"Find out who it was."

Brenda's shoulders slumped. "Okay, I get it. You don't want to deal with me, but we need to work together to find—"

"Look, lady, there's more to this than some expensive insurance claim. This is a murder investigation."

"First of all, sir, please stop cutting me off when I'm talking. Secondly, I appreciate the sensitive nature of this case, but Mr. Trevani's decision to transport a multi-million-dollar artifact on his private yacht without any security beyond a couple of Glocks was reckless to say the least. If he had made the proper arrangements, there wouldn't have been any murders."

Kurt folded his arms. "You're going to be a pain in my ass until we find this thing, aren't you?"

"Just doing my job."

"Then let me do mine."

"Fine. So let me ask again, Detective. What's next?"

"I need to question a woman named Yasmine Kadara at the Beach View Hotel."

"Was she on the yacht with Max?"

"I don't know. That's why I'm going to question her."

———

As Kurt reached the top of the stairs at the Beach View, all irritation toward his unwelcome sidekick faded at the sight of two toned and bronzed gams topped by a perfectly round pair of Daisy Dukes.

The young woman stood barefoot on the concrete promenade hunched over the railing that overlooked the empty pool below. She took a long drag from a cigarette and flicked the ashes into a paper cup. Her slim face was partially concealed by a leonine mane of disheveled chestnut hair that cascaded over her shoulders and back as she drew herself to her full and considerable height.

After wiping her eyes with a finger, the woman turned away from the railing, revealing a yellow tank top that left even less to the imagination than her shorts. Kurt nearly dropped his ID as he pulled it from his pocket.

Beside him, Brenda cleared her throat, which served the dual purpose of snapping Kurt back to the task at hand and gaining Ms. Kadara's attention. She looked from one to the other with swollen gray eyes and dropped her spent cigarette into the cup.

"Yasmine Kadara?" Kurt held up his badge as he introduced himself and Brenda.

"You're here about Seth and Dino. I already heard the news from their families." Her voice was soft and husky, whether naturally or from crying Kurt couldn't determine. "My phone's been on fire all morning with calls and texts from people asking me what I know about their deaths."

Kurt gestured toward her room. "May we go inside?"

"Sure." Yasmine entered first and dropped onto the couch by the window while Kurt and Brenda took seats at the table just inside the door.

Yasmine rubbed her eyes and sniffed. "Sorry. I know I look like shit right now. How can I help you, Detective?"

Brenda handed her a box of tissues from the table. "So, I understand you're from Smyrna. Did you drive down?"

Yasmine shook her head as she accepted the box. "Took the bus. Two of them, actually."

Brenda glanced at Kurt. "Your turn."

He shot her a sidelong glance. Although he had briefed Brenda on the way to the hotel, Kurt made it clear that he would be the one to ask the questions. "How did you know Seth and Dino?"

"We grew up together. I'm originally from Long Island. My family moved to Delaware when I was fifteen. I fell out of touch with the guys for a while until I found them on Facebook. A few months ago, Seth mentioned that he and Dino were coming to Rehoboth this week on business. Seth's uncle owns the house they were staying in. They invited me to join them."

"What kind of business?" Kurt asked.

"They were working with a local museum on a new exhibit."

Brenda leaned forward. "Did they mention the name Max Trevani?"

"Sure. They worked for him. Seth said that Max was bringing a new artifact down to the museum and that I might get the chance to meet him."

"You've never met Mr. Trevani?"

"That's correct."

Brenda held up a photo of the crucifix. "Do you recognize this?"

Yasmine shook her head. "No. It's beautiful, though. Is that the artifact?"

Brenda opened her mouth to respond until Kurt nudged her foot with his. "Would you mind if I looked around? You have the right to refuse, of course, in which case I would probably return with a warrant."

Yasmine's eyes widened and she sat ramrod straight. "Am I in trouble? I didn't do anything. Like I told Officer Velez, I didn't even enter the house. It was locked."

Kurt held up a hand. "You're not under suspicion right now but allowing a brief search would help ensure that you stay that way."

Yasmine shrugged. "I have nothing to hide."

"Thank you." Kurt donned a pair of Nitrile gloves and moved from chest of drawers to closet to bathroom before peering under the bed. Yasmine stood by the window as he searched beneath and behind the couch.

Finally, he pulled off the gloves and shoved them back into his pocket. "All good. Thank you for your time, Ms. Kadara. How long will you be in town? Just in case we have more questions."

"I'm here for the week. Will you please keep me informed if you find out anything about Seth and Dino?"

"Oh, I'm sure we'll speak again."

———

"You didn't think she'd be dumb enough to keep the crucifix in her room?" Brenda asked as they walked across the parking lot of the Beach View.

Kurt shook his head.

"So now what?"

"Wait here. I'll be right back."

He made his way into the lobby and presented his badge to the middle-aged woman at the reservation counter. "I have a question about one of your guests—Yasmine Kadara in room two-twelve. Can you tell me if she registered a car?"

The woman flipped through a small stack of paperwork and pulled out a sheet. She shook her head. "No, actually she didn't."

"Were you here when she checked in?"

"No. She came in late, after we closed. We left the room key and paperwork in the mailbox for her."

"I see. Thanks for your time."

Outside, Kurt found Brenda sitting on a bench scrolling through email on her phone. She looked up as he approached. "What did you find out?"

"At least one part of Ms. Kadara's story was true. She didn't drive here. I noticed bus schedules in her room, but anyone can get those."

"You think she lied? That she came here with Max on his yacht?"

"Not sure yet. Can't think on an empty stomach." Kurt glanced at his watch before nodding toward Gus and Gus Hamburgers across Wilmington Avenue. "How about lunch? My treat."

———

"This is all too surreal. Ancient artifacts, three men killed, that raft inside the tower." Brenda paused as the waitress brought their drinks. Even after the girl was out of earshot, she lowered her voice. "Even the name of the thing—Pearl of Great Price. It's like something out of an old movie. The only thing missing is buried treasure."

Kurt swallowed a sip of iced tea. "It's a unique case, but I believe we're close."

"Close to finding the crucifix? Who has it?"

He held up a hand. "I don't have enough evidence yet and I don't want to risk accusing the wrong person." Kurt pulled his buzzing phone from his belt holster. "Excuse me. I need to take this." He pressed the phone to his ear as he slid out of the booth and hurried toward the boardwalk. "Velez, what do you got for me? "First, the Glocks that killed Manning and Quintana were registered to Max Trevani. Secondly, the manager of the Montauk Beach Marina confirmed that Trevani did bring a guest aboard his yacht for the trip to Fenwick. They didn't recognize her—just figured she was one of Trevani's trollops of the week—but they got one decent close-up on their security cameras."

"Can you send it to my phone?"

"On its way."

A moment later, Kurt stared at the picture. "Damn, that's disappointing."

"She sure fills that bikini nicely, though. Do you have enough for an arrest?"

"Not yet. You got any plans tonight?"

"You want that drink I owe you?"

"Later. I need your help to chase down a hunch."

"What else do I live for?"

"Thanks, Velez." The waitress had delivered their sandwiches by the time Kurt ended the call and rejoined Brenda in the booth.

"New development?" she asked.

"With another case. I hate to eat and run, but I need to get back to the station as soon we're finished. How about if we regroup tomorrow morning?"

"Sure. Just tell me one thing. Do you really suspect that woman?" Brenda waved in the general direction of the Beach View.

Kurt slumped back against the cherry red vinyl seat and wiped his mouth with a napkin. "I'd say the woman is high on my list."

—

Silhouetted by the lights from the Rehoboth boardwalk in the distance, Tower Six stood tall beneath a crescent moon. Kurt stared at it through the windshield of the unmarked SUV. "My first beach stakeout. This is wild."

In the driver's seat, Velez drummed her fingers on the steering wheel. "You sure about this hunch?"

"She'll be here, trust me." Kurt glanced at the dashboard clock. It was 10:31 p.m.. "High tide's in about twenty-two minutes."

"And you think she knows that?" Velez had barely finished speaking when a flashlight appeared several yards ahead, approaching Tower Six.

"Apparently." Kurt snatched up the radio. "Lonny, suspect just arrived. As soon as I give the signal, move in quietly."

"Roger that."

"The light just dropped to the sand and disappeared," Velez said. "I think she crawled inside."

"Give her a few seconds." Kurt counted to ten then raised his radio. "Okay, Lonny. We're on."

Kurt and Velez exited the vehicle and gently closed their doors. Beside them, Officer Lonakis did the same while his partner remained behind the wheel. The trio marched across the sand toward Tower Six. White light was visible for a moment beneath the jagged bottom of the corroded door. As Kurt and the others drew near, the light shifted, and a pair of dark shoes emerged followed by black jeans.

Kurt nodded to Velez and Lonakis. Each officer gripped an ankle and dragged the squirming body out of the tower. The woman screamed and thrashed until Velez shined a flashlight in her face.

Kurt leaned forward and snatched the crucifix from Brenda Lambert's clutches. "Let me help you with that. It's a bit heavy. I know because I dug it up myself four hours ago."

"Son of a—" She shielded her eyes from the light. "I thought Ms. Kadara was your suspect."

"I specifically said the woman was high on my list. I just didn't say which woman. Truth is, you gave yourself away. When we first met, you immediately assumed that I'd found the raft inside Tower Five, even though it was sitting out on the beach when you arrived. Then you said that Trevani's murder wouldn't have happened had he taken better precautions beyond carrying a couple of Glocks. How did you know what kind of guns he carried on his private yacht unless you were on board?

"You were familiar with these towers, so you waited until the yacht reached Whiskey Beach before gunning down Trevani. Then you fled with the guns," Kurt hefted the crucifix, "and this. After slashing the raft and shoving it into Tower Five, you knew you couldn't traipse through town carrying a massive gold crucifix, so you came up here and buried it inside Tower Six. You then met with Manning and Quintana at the house on New Castle. They knew you, so they let you in. You promptly murdered them, repositioned the bodies, and planted the Glocks to make it appear that they'd shot each other."

"That's a good story, but you can't prove I killed anyone."

"I admit, it was all just a hunch at first, but then we got this." Kurt crouched down and held out his phone. "This picture was taken by security cameras at Montauk Beach Marina yesterday as you joined Max Trevani aboard his yacht to come here. You planned to steal the artifact by romancing your way into Trevani's life. Wasn't too hard given that he never met a bikini he didn't like."

"I want to call my lawyer."

"I bet you do. You're under arrest on three counts of murder, theft, conspiracy, and insurance fraud. Officer Lonakis will escort you to his vehicle and inform you of your rights."

The patrol officer stepped forward with a pair of handcuffs.

"Take her to the station. Velez and I will be along soon." Kurt leaned against the tower as Brenda was led away. "I have to admit, Sergeant, if the marina's security footage turned up nothing, we might have ended up staking out Ms. Kadara tonight."

"Did you have a hunch about her, too?"

Kurt grinned. "Honestly, no, but she was my only other suspect."

"And quite the hottie," Velez added.

"Really? I didn't notice."

"Liar."

As they trudged back to their vehicle, Kurt held the crucifix out before him, illuminated by Velez's flashlight. "Got any plans tomorrow night, Velez? I could use that drink you owe me from our little bet this morning."

"I'll buy you two drinks if you let me carry that to the car. I'll never see that much gold again in my life."

Kurt handed her the relic. "You can hold it all the way back to the station and do the honor of checking it into evidence."

"Lord, have mercy." She cradled the crucifix in her left arm and blessed herself. "It's beautiful. Just a shame three men had to lose their lives over it."

"Gives a whole different meaning to Pearl of Great Price."

Profit and Loss
Dianna Sinovic

THE LATEST SHIPMENT was waiting to be unloaded from the trailer: 300 pounds of raw coffee beans from Central America that Elijah would later feed into the roasters batch by batch. But he knew he had to be careful. Paul, his boss and the one who owned Wake Up, Lil' Suzy, didn't know about Elijah's plan for the fifty additional pounds of a very special bean. Still, he had Paul's trust, something he had patiently tended over the last year.

Maneuvering the mechanized hand truck to the trailer, Elijah moved the bags a few at a time to the storage area at the back of the building. In that garage-like space, the hulking roasters took up the center of the floor, flanked by bag after burlap bag of raw beans on one side and on the other, shelves filled with half- and full-pound packages bearing the Lil' Suzy blazing sun. The odor of coffee so strongly permeated the air that the staff joked about the dangers of inhaled caffeine.

The staff would show up later, when Lil' Suzy opened at seven for the going-to-work crowd. The sun was just edging above the Chicago cityscape as Elijah removed the last of the bags from the trailer.

On his latest trip to Ecuador, he'd met a new grower. Vallejo had greeted him cautiously in the market square of the small town Elijah always stayed at while buying. He turned out to have a sizable patch of coffee trees. The sample of roasted beans he handed over to Elijah that afternoon smelled of the future—Elijah's future as a premier coffee buyer. He and his driver followed the old man the nine kilometers to his ranch. The cup that the old man had placed before him on the rough-hewn table outside his casa entwined with bougainvillea

147

steamed with a fragrance that made Elijah's heart race. When he sipped from the chipped white cup, tasting the bitter but not too bitter brew, he made the deal on the spot.

Now he parked the hand truck and unzipped his jacket. The late winter day's warmth was trying to poke its fingers into the building. The high ceiling of the warehouse section made it difficult to keep the area comfortable in the cold months even with a half-dozen ceiling fans whirring and three roasters running.

Elijah was still alone, more than an hour before Caroline and Josh and Brittany, his girlfriend, showed up to start the brewing and prep for the clientele. Paul never arrived before mid-morning.

He slipped a plastic covering over his curly brown hair, donned a pair of vinyl gloves, and opened the fifty-pound bag marked with a winged lizard. Lagarto volando, the old man had said, grinning widely, his eyes disappearing under dark brows. Elijah had felt disgusted at the crude joke Vallejo seemed to be implying about lizards. Dipping his gloved hands into the beans, he let them pour through his fingers. A pale green, they were not much to look at, but they held so much potential.

Carrying a bucket of the new beans to one of the roasters, Elijah dumped them in and switched on the unit. On the electronic display, he chose "dark roast." It's what Vallejo had advised. Tostado oscuro, he'd said with a quick dip of his head. And even with Elijah's limited Spanish, he understood.

Back in the cavernous room, on a still-quiet downtown street, Elijah waited down the minutes until the first batch was done. He started the two other roasters with beans from Colombia and Costa Rica. He measured out portions of beans from several other bags for Lil' Suzy's Ooh La Blend.

When the timer beeped to let him know the initial batch had finished, he quickly emptied the roasting bin so the beans could cool. He scooped up enough beans for a pot, ground them, and carefully cleaned the coffeemaker they kept in the warehouse section for taste testing—and late-afternoon pick-me-ups.

The rumble of the roasters hid any other sounds, so he didn't notice Paul until his boss was pouring himself a cup of the Ecuadorean coffee.

"What's this?" Paul said, passing the cup beneath his nose to sniff and then taking a sip. "Good god, this is good. These are the new beans, right?"

Elijah blanched. "Yes," he said, and poured himself a cup, using his standard mug emblazoned with Lord of the Beans. "You're here early." Too early.

Paul smiled. "You talked up this shipment so much I wanted to be one of the first to try it." He took another drink from his cup. "You're quite the pitchman, Elijah. Maybe we should consider moving you over to Sales." His tone was genuine, not joking.

"And give up buying?" Elijah's shoulders sagged slightly. His future depended on making the next trip south to Vallejo's hacienda.

Paul was silent for a few moments, studying Elijah, then nodded, as if to himself. "I'll admit you also have quite a knack for bringing home some of the best beans." Another sip, another pause. "Relax, Elijah—let me just say, if you get tired of the buying work, you'll have other choices here."

"Thanks," Elijah said, relieved. "I'll stick with the buying for a while yet." He picked up the carafe and motioned at Paul. It was too late to turn back the clock on that morning, so better to play with what he had. "Refill?"

Paul accepted the additional cupful and then sauntered off toward the front office. "Great brew, Lige," he called over his shoulder.

Just wait, Elijah thought.

—

It was after making the deal with the coffee bean farmer that Elijah's life slipped sideways. He shook hands with Vallejo beneath the canopy of banana and palm leaves, a whisper of sultry breeze cooling the sweat on his face. The old man drained his cup of Arabica coffee, and following his lead, Elijah did the same. A stocky middle-aged woman took away the cups and disappeared into the house. Elijah wasn't sure if the woman was Vallejo's daughter or his housekeeper— or possibly his wife. Neither spoke to the other.

The old man said a few words in Spanish to Elijah's driver, David, and walked to a mud-caked Jeep as ancient as he was. David responded with a few words of his own and then shrugged. When he turned to Elijah, his look was concerned.

"Are we done here?" Elijah said. "I'm ready to head back."

From the Jeep, the old man shouted and waved his arm. Árboles was the one word Elijah caught in the rapid-fire speech. Trees.

"He wants you to go with him," David said. "He'll bring you back to the market square, where you met him, when he's done."

"Why?" Elijah was trying to read between the lines, but they seemed blurry. On past buying trips, he made all of his deals in town. He seldom visited the coffee farms themselves. It saved time and seemed safer.

David's gaze slid away from Elijah's. "He wants you to see a special grove of trees. 'Very special,' he said."

"I don't speak much Spanish," Elijah said. He felt both wary and eager. If the old man had a special kind of bean, and he made a deal for those before anyone else could get to him...

"You're a coffee buyer," David said, "and he wants to make a sale. You'll be fine." David got into his Nissan and soon was out of sight, down the winding road back to the town.

As Elijah walked toward the ancient Jeep, he wondered at the truth of that prediction.

But despite the old man's bent posture and densely wrinkled face, he drove competently over the dirt path that led deeper into his farm. The pot-holed track means it's a regular route, Elijah reassured himself. Just like any other proud farmer taking a visitor on a tour of his property.

A quarter of an hour passed and the old man pulled off the rutted path into a clump of wild cashew, switching off the engine. In the sudden silence, Elijah was aware of birdcall and the screams of small monkeys high above them, in the trees. Despite sitting next to Vallejo, Elijah felt very alone, far from anything familiar.

The old man grinned and slapped his thighs. *"Un secreto,"* he said in a mock whisper. *"Para ti solamente."*

Elijah understood the word secret and his ambition fired up again. "Yes," he said, nodding vigorously in case that helped the old man with his answer. *"Sí."*

The old man dug around in the rear of the Jeep and brought out a small burlap bag, empty, waiting to be filled. Placing the bag in a small knapsack, he said a few words to Elijah, who had exhausted the little Spanish he knew. With no response, the old man added gestures along with the words and started down a footpath into the thick of the forest.

"I'm coming," Elijah called, quickly falling in behind the old man.

The air was sticky with humidity, and insects buzzed into his ears and eyes. The path smelled of sweet decay and honeyed essence.

Deeper and deeper into the green realm they walked. When Elijah was about to protest at the distance, the old man held up one hand and stopped. He moved closer to the trunk of a tree and unfastened his pants.

"Here we go," Elijah muttered, as the old man peed against the tree, laughing softly to himself. Now he's going to tell me this is the secret to his coffee.

Elijah realized how thirsty he'd become, his tee-shirt soaked with sweat. His bottled water sat in the Nissan that David, his driver, had taken back to town.

"*Señor,*" he called to the old man. "How much farther?"

"Eh?," Vallejo said, his face scrunching up into puzzlement. He seemed as fresh as when they had started their walk.

Elijah grudgingly admired the old man's stamina. He mentally searched through the few phrases he knew. "*¿Cuándo?* When do we get there?"

"*Sí, sí, pronto.*" The old man waved his hand vaguely back at Elijah and set off again on the path.

Elijah had had enough; he no longer cared about the "secret" the old man wanted to show him. It was probably just a bean grove blessed by a local priest. Or maybe the beans grew in the shade of a volcano that supposedly made them more robust. The legends that circulated in the region were as rich as its fertile soil, David had told him.

But when he turned to retrace his steps back to the Jeep, the path wasn't as evident as it had seemed, following Vallejo. Spinning back around, Elijah spotted the old man already disappearing around a tree, and he sprinted to catch up to him. Getting lost in the dense growth would be his death; he would never find his way out.

Panting and so sweaty that his curly hair had turned to ringlets, Elijah fell in behind Vallejo once more.

The old man seemed to sense what had just happened and waved his arm, gesturing Elijah forward. "*Llegaremos pronto,*" he said.

"Please," Elijah muttered. "*Por favor.* I'm so tired."

When the old man finally halted, he did so abruptly. Elijah's momentum carried him into the old man's back side.

"Sorry," he said, shaking his head from the impact.

The old man turned so fast, Elijah almost missed the movement. Vallejo held him tightly by the arm, his face inches from Elijah's. His breath was of coffee and unwashed teeth, and his eyes bore into Elijah's. He spoke a few words, none of which Elijah knew, and leered. With his other hand, he grabbed Elijah's groin.

"No, no," Elijah said, pulling out of the old man's double grasp. "Get away from me."

"Está bien," Vallejo said, with a shrug. He spread his outstretched arms toward the forest and shouted a few more words. Café was among them.

"This is it?" Elijah surveyed the coffee trees in the grove, each woody evergreen pruned to a good picking height. Red cherries choked the branches; the trees were loaded with coffee fruit.

"Sí." The old man took out his small burlap bag and shook it at Elijah. He was no longer leering, but serious. He reached into the branches and plucked the red cherries interspersed with the still-green ones, filling the bag over the next few minutes. "Llena," he said, patting the bag.

Full, Elijah guessed. "Good," he said, glad to get back to the deal, then added, *"Secreto?"*

"Ah," Vallejo said. But his explanation was lost on Elijah, who kept nodding as the old man's speech flowed over and around him. Vallejo shook his head at Elijah's lack of comprehension. He secured the bag's opening and said several times, again patting the bag, "Fuerte. Fuerte."

Elijah's memory of how they made it back to the Jeep was dim. He was tired, he was thirsty, and he felt torn between a deep dislike of Vallejo and avarice when pondering the deal for these "secret" beans. Above all, he wanted a shower and then a shot or two of Jack Daniels at the hotel bar.

But Vallejo insisted, through gestures, that they first stop at his casa for another cup of coffee, this one made with beans from the special grove.

"Just one—*una taza*," Elijah said, slumping into the wooden chair on the porch.

The silent woman brought him the same chipped cup, and Vallejo stood, arms folded across his chest, to watch Elijah's reaction.

Just as Paul, his boss, would do later, in the warehouse kitchen, Elijah held the cup beneath his nose to take in the aroma. Volcanic soil, the fierce sun, the swift passage of lizard feet on the tree branches. Elijah had closed his eyes to concentrate, but opened them in surprise.

How would he know this?

The old man nodded as if affirming Elijah's question. *"Bebas, bebas,"* he said, gesturing that Elijah should drink.

The first sip led to the next and the next, and Elijah had drained the cup. "Yes," he murmured. "Totally awesome." It was as if this was the first cup of coffee he'd ever had. Every other experience fell away, was forgotten. He was glad he was sitting down.

"¿Estupendo, no?" The old man winked.

"Sí." Elijah sighed. He wanted another cup, but he wanted a shower more. "Town?" he said, pointing in that direction. "Can we go back now?"

At the hotel that evening, Elijah sat at the bar, his second whisky before him on the polished wood. He felt better than he had since he left Chicago on this buying trip. And excited. That the old man was giving him an exclusive deal would make Paul happy. And impress Brittany.

When his driver, David, showed up at the bar entrance, Elijah waved him over.

"You're alive," David said, taking the next barstool.

"You had doubts?" Elijah ordered a drink for David and, downing his whisky, another for himself.

"Not really, but I've heard tales about some of these old granjeros." David sipped his drink. "You're heading home tomorrow?"

"Two o'clock departure."

They discussed when David would pick him up for the ride to the airport. And Elijah gave an abbreviated version of the unnerving hike to the coffee grove and that first, exquisite cup beneath the banana and palm trees.

"Tell me something," he said. "The old man said a lot that I didn't understand, but he kept repeating *fuerte* about the beans from those trees. What was he talking about?"

David was quiet for a few moments in thought. "It means strong, so he probably meant the brew would be strong."

Elijah nodded. It was pretty much what he'd thought. He signaled to the bartender for his tab.

David pushed his empty glass away and stood up. "But, it also can mean powerful." He smiled. "These old guys can have pretty big egos, you know. They all think their beans are the best."

—

Elijah spent the next several weeks until the shipment arrived in Chicago carefully meting out the sample of beans Vallejo had sent home with him, smuggled within a pair of athletic socks. He could not run out. The special beans, which Elijah told Paul they should call Irresistible, were so good, he kept them at his apartment instead of sharing them at work so the team could try them. He even hid them from Brittany, who slept with him more nights than not.

"Just wait," he told them, mostly for Paul's benefit. "It was that single cup at the old guy's farm that sold me. You'll be, too."

"And he can ship us more if this takes off?" Paul asked.

"The growing season will end soon, but I've contracted for as many beans as he can send us. And then we'll have next year." Elijah now knew he would follow Vallejo into any grove anywhere if it meant he could bring home more of the beans.

Paul clapped Elijah on the shoulder. "Nice job, Lige."

Elijah winced. He hated that nickname but what could he do? Paul was his boss.

Brittany gave him a hug in front of the rest of the crew. "I found your stash," she whispered. When he flinched, she added, "Don't worry. I won't drink it all." Then she smirked. "It's better than good. You were selfish."

When he looked into her eyes, he knew that she knew.

Once the beans arrived and Paul had sampled his first cup, Irresistible became the staple brew at Lil' Suzy's. Each morning, customers lined up around the block to get their cup, or more often, their Mega Cup. The company raised its prices, but the demand didn't slack. They hired three more baristas to handle the crowds.

Paul found Elijah again one morning, as one of the roasters beeped that its cycle was complete. The boss now often arrived shortly after Elijah, helping move bags and roast beans just to brew the coffee as early as he could.

Paul stood with his cup, watching Elijah pour the beans into their cooling tray.

"What's really in this stuff, Lige?" He swirled the deep brown liquid. "It's more than coffee, isn't it?"

—

Elijah thought of the trees in the coffee grove, their roots burrowing deep into the soil to draw up nutrients that fed the berries. He wasn't a chemist, but something in that hillside must have supercharged the caffeine. He shared his suspicion with Brittany, who talked to an aunt who worked in pharmaceuticals. No details, just floating a theory.

"She thought I was joking," Brittany reported. "She said caffeine can cause dependency—it is a stimulant—but it's not capable of rewiring your brain pathways like, say, meth can."

They sat at Elijah's kitchen table, each with a cup of Irresistible in their hands. The thought of giving up that cup was enough to make Elijah lightheaded. He couldn't imagine a day without it.

It was around that time that Paul hired a bodyguard for Elijah.

"We can't let anything happen to you," Paul said, introducing him to Amos, who at six-foot-five towered over both of them. "Profits are up 450 percent. If we lose the connection with your source, we're sunk."

Source? Elijah thought, walking back to the warehouse with Amos. What are we now, a drug cartel?

The bigger question, he realized, was what happened when Vallejo, who seemed at least sixty, if not seventy or older, passed on? He couldn't see the future, but who would honor his deal? Who would keep that grove tended and producing? His hands began to shake.

—

He called Paul from O'Hare. He was flying to Ecuador to secure a long-term agreement with Vallejo and his heirs, whoever they might be. Amos would run interference.

David picked them up at the airport in Quito and drove them to the town nearest Vallejo's hacienda, delivering them to a lawyer he knew. With David's help, Elijah had made the appointment before he left Chicago.

His plan was to pick up the contract paperwork and the lawyer and go straight to the marketplace to find Vallejo. They would finalize the contract there or make the journey to the farm to sign it.

The marketplace was busy—it was Wednesday, the main market day for the area—and it took more than half an hour under a heavy overcast to make the rounds and determine that Vallejo was not present. Even Elijah understood "no," as David asked vendor after vendor.

"Nobody's seen him today," David said.

Amos, equally unversed in the language, stayed by the Nissan with the lawyer and watched the crowd.

"Let's go to the farm," Elijah said when he and David rejoined the others. "You remember the way?"

"Of course," David said.

The road was muddy from recent rain, with more rain likely, and when they pulled into Vallejo's yard, they splashed through puddles that spattered the windshield. David and the lawyer conferred in Spanish for a few minutes, as Elijah peered through the streaked window at the house. No one had appeared at the door or come out onto the porch.

I'm waiting for the man, Elijah thought, reluctant to admit it to himself, just like any other addict. "Is he here?"

"*Sí, sí,*" the lawyer said, and David translated. "They're being cautious. If you get out, he'll surely recognize you. Go on up to the door."

The dense clouds released a light drizzle, but the day, even in March, was warm. Elijah walked carefully around the pools of water in the yard and stepped up onto the porch. Before he could knock, the door opened and the old man stood there. He nodded, acknowledging Elijah, then winked.

"*El lagarto volando. Te gusta mucho, ¿no?*"

"Yes." Elijah nodded. "*Sí,* yes." Whatever the old man had said, he agreed. His thermos, left behind on the car seat, was down to the last few swallows of the coffee.

Vallejo spoke over his shoulder, into the house, and stepped out onto the porch. David approached, trailed by the lawyer and Amos, both of whom skirted the puddles in the yard. David spoke quickly, with introductions, and the lawyer took over the presentation. Vallejo watched them all carefully, his dark eyes moving from person to person.

The door opened, and the same stocky woman who had served Elijah last time carried out a tray of cups. Vallejo pulled chairs from across the porch, wiped them off with a bit of sleeve, and placed them around the wooden table. Everyone sat, including Vallejo. He passed out the cups, singling out the chipped one for Elijah.

"Solamente para ti," Vallejo said, positioning the cup before him. *"Los otros beben café regular."* He gestured at the rest of the table's occupants.

"Gracias," Elijah said. He greedily sipped the bitter, dark liquid, and satisfied it was the real thing, sat back. "Now, about the agreement."

The lawyer took over, and he and the old man conversed back and forth. The lawyer became more animated as the minutes slipped by, and Vallejo more firm. David gazed at Elijah with alarm from across the table.

"What is it?" Elijah said. "He won't accept the proposal?"

David shook his head slightly. "He'll accept it, but it's the terms...."

Elijah's stomach clenched. He could walk away—it wasn't too late. But staring down at the dregs left in the chipped cup, he knew he would accept them, he had to accept them.

"And they are?" He looked at David, then at Vallejo.

"Vivas aquí," Vallejo said, tapping the table with his forefinger. *"Puedes beber el café especial todos los días."*

"You'll live here, on the hacienda," David translated for the lawyer, "and in return, *Señor* Vallejo gives Lil' Suzy exclusive purchase of the beans from the lizard grove." The lawyer shifted a few papers around in his folder.

David added, "It's not an agreement the lawyer would usually support, but the farmer won't budge."

"Why these terms?" Elijah said. "For how long?" What about his job? What would he tell Brittany?

"He..." David paused. "He's...taken a liking to you."

The reality of what was about to happen finally cut through to Elijah. He pushed away the cup and stood, poised to run. Where he didn't know. That could come later, once he was safe from the old man.

Amos rose to his feet as well.

"I wouldn't step off the porch if I were you." Amos' intimidating height was enhanced by the handgun he produced from a hidden holster.

"What the fuck, Amos?" Elijah stared at him. "Are you crazy?"

"Paul is one hundred percent behind the agreement, anything to keep the supply rolling in." His smile was not kind. "It's just business, kid. You know, profits."

"Paul wouldn't do this," Elijah said, his voice rising. Yet he knew the truth: Paul would indeed. He himself had just moments before sat staring into the chipped cup, ready to sell his soul.

"It's not forever," Amos said, motioning for David and the lawyer to head back to the car. "And you're so lucky. It's a tropical paradise." He stepped down into the wet grass, the fine drizzle dampening his hair. "Don't worry about Brittany." He laughed as he reholstered his gun. "Paul will take good care of her."

Amos got into the passenger seat and shut the door. The Nissan splashed back through the puddles, back to town, but Elijah was not in it.

Angel Delorme and the Craigflower Bus

Mitchell Toews

"SUP, MONKEY WOMAN?"

"Nuthin," she said with a start. Then her eyes narrowed to focus on me and she slid back on the bench. "Ahh, Nazi, didn't reconnoiter you right aways. How's it goin', bro?"

"All good, top of the heap."

"Not in jail…"

"Nope, not in jail. Not working, neither. Not flying to Sweden to accept an award…"

"Ha-ha. Same not here. Thanks for meetin' me, eh?"

She slid over sideways on the bus bench to make room for me. At least we were dry under the shelter's Plexi roof. "I know you and me ain't worked together before, but I have an idea I wanted you to hear."

"Sure thing. Criminal enterprise?"

A little startled, she grinned uncertainly and said, "Yeah, I guess. Crook on crook action, you could call it."

"Fair enough."

I had seen her around plenty at a lot of my usual haunts. She was the borderline type—some days she had a job, some nights she slept under the bridge. She had some issues, no doubt about that. Monkey Woman… Damned if I can remember how she got that handle. Lately I wonder if the booze and whatnot has done more to my memory than I like to admit.

I got my name because I speak German. After a few street fights I was "that Nazi." Some people say I fight dirty. Maybe. I figured if I had a hard reputation, I wouldn't get into as many scrapes.

Monkey Woman had a lean narrow frame, topped by long, flowing hair. The bags under her eyes hung loosely, the skin shop worn. She was pale, blue-eyed, hollow-cheeked and might have been beautiful once. She still was in a hard to pin down way. Drooping eyelids gave her the look of someone who had seen too much, too early. A little too dirty, unkempt and looking more like a stringy puppet than a monkey, her back was hunched and she wore three layers of hoodie-jacket-track suit. She was the kind of girl that could never warm-up during Victoria's maritime winter.

Sleety rain drummed on the clear plastic above us. My bench mate stared unblinking across the street. Exiting dump trucks at a gravel pit were lined up next to a scale shack to weigh their loads. Diesel exhaust rose black in the grey air as the drivers stopped on the platform and waited for the attendant to hand them a load ticket. Monkey watched intently, not saying a word to me.

"Jeez, don't talk so much—you're makin' my ears hoarse," I said. I was starting to think the whole thing was a waste of time. She was not known for her intellect; not a thought leader among the Bay Street Bridge crowd.

"I'm watchin' what I need to watch… THERE!" she said, almost a shout.

She was zeroed in on a heavyset man with a Canucks hat, the attendant in the booth. The fellow's arm hung out of the shack's window and as we watched, he reached up and took something from the driver before the truck drove off the scale.

"And there ya go," Monkey nodded. "That's the hustle. Right there."

I was unimpressed. It seemed routine. Still, I was here, so I may as well see things through, doubts or not. There was talk of some decent money. A bus pulled up as I mused. The door wheezed open and the driver glared down at us.

"Hey! TODAY!" he yelled. A thin blonde, the guy looked like he could have been Monkey Woman's twin brother, but in an even lighter shade of nasty. Skinny as a wet rope. "Ya gonna board the bus or not?"

"Nah, we're waitin' for a better offer," Monkey answered, looking away.

"Pathetic," the driver said, hissing the brakes and roaring off toward the bridge. Monkey stood up abruptly, strolled out onto the street behind the departing bus and held up a crooked middle finger. An oncoming car slithered to a stop on the wet street scant inches from her backside. The driver laid on the horn as Monkey sauntered back to the bench, smirking.

"Jesus H... Suicide much?" I said, palms up in a WTF gesture. The skin on my neck and back prickled. This lady is a bit unhinged. "So, anyway... What's going on? It's my day off." I added the last bit for comic relief. She sat down and leaned back, sizing me up. Then she pinned her lips back to give me the most awful felt-tipped grin. Like each tooth was wearing a green parka, the kind we used to call "army jackets" years ago in Winnipeg. I imagined not too many young fellas—or young ladies, for that matter—fell for that smile. Surely, those teeth had enjoyed better days, hygiene-wise, I thought.

For some reason, as she grinned at me, I imagined her as she might have looked in a sunny past—twenty years ago on Fair Day, sporting a clean softball uniform and braces on those same teeth. Not that I knew her as a kid—but you had to wonder how she got from childhood to this rotten present life. The rotten life we shared. I knew how I got here, but what was her story?

"Anyway, you... you up for a little cash? Say $150 for a minute's work? See, I been thinkin' I need a pards for this job I'm figuring out. Need a guy... big guy. Guy that can handle himself... You got a rep."

"That's me. What's your proposition? It's obviously got somethin' to do with that gravel operation across the road." The money was good enough to keep me here for a few minutes at least. I forgot about the rain and the cold for a minute.

"Yeah, so I been sitting here a few days watchin' this here scale shack guy. I know him from where I used to work, a service station in Vic West."

I noticed the blackheads peppered on her face. There's a nose in there somewhere, I thought. Suddenly self-conscious, I rubbed my own acne-scarred chin and neck and concentrated on Monkey's explanation.

"So?"

"The guy in the shack—his name is Hiebert. They call 'em 'Dilbert' cuz he's good with computers. Got a knack. Funny thing is he used to be a boxer and whatnot. Tough bugger."

"Yeah, he looks kinda rugged."

"He is. Anyway, he's running a shake-down on the truck drivers."

She paused and spat. "You watch… some of the drivers hand him a twenty. Twenty bucks, like we seen a minute ago. There's no charge for the scale, so…" she paused, twisting her hawkish face into a wry look.

I shrugged, shook my head. No surprise that some petty larceny is underway, I thought. vagrants like us—Dilbert included—sometimes crossed the line. I had seen it as a lawyer, in my old life. I saw plenty of it these days.

"So, he's giving them a scale ticket for a little bit more than what they really had, weight-wise. Owner-operators get paid per load—per pound, eh? Dilbert jacks their printed weigh-in ticket by a few percent so they make some extra dough when they deliver, but it don't cost 'em the full amount. They only get charged for the real weight and they grease him with a twenty to be in on the scam. Then, to even things out, he's skimming enough off'a the load tickets of the guys who don't know no different or don't care. See, he extorts—" she said the word as if it was rancid in her mouth, "the private owner-operators… he gets cash from them, and at the same time, he rips off the guys who drive company trucks, but they don't even know it."

I sighed, trying to hide it. A typical hustle, although a fairly clever one and one requiring computer chops. I feared, though, that it would be subject to a fast-eroding orbit—destined to spiral and burn.

"It's no skin off a company truck driver's ass if his load ticket is light a few pounds… he gets the same pay regardless." She paused. "You look confused, dude."

I crossed and uncrossed my legs, thinking I'd like a beer. "Math is hard," I said. "Just give me the bottom line."

"Look, Nazi, all you got to know, see, is that Dilbert robs from Peter to pay Paul. Like the Bible, man—like the Bible."

"Okay," I said. If the scam was actually run the way she described it, I might be in. I hadn't eaten in two days. I was sleeping on the lunchroom couch in a brewery where my buddy was night watchman. His shift was midnight to six and I got headaches from the stench of the yeast. I tapped Monkey with the back of my hand. "How come Dilbert don't get caught? He must need to balance the books at the end of each day, right?"

"That's true, college-boy. That's the dope part. Like I said, I know him from before. The guy is a for-reals computer whiz! You'd never guess that off'a how he looks—am I right? But he's sharp and the scam is sweet... fuckin' *Ocean's Eleven* sweet, or whatever. Plus, he did something like this at that last place where we both worked. He cooked the books so he could swipe some car batteries and sell them for cash. He can rig the computer to automatically keep track of all the over and under weights. It's programmed to keep it even, adding or subtracting as needed—"

"So, he's always dead on. Robbing Peter..."

"To pay Paul. Yep." Monkey took a big breath. Then she added, "But Dilbert did get caught—he just don't know it yet! Caught by me, a fuckin' street rat with nothing more than grade ten."

"Look at you," I said. "You're something! But how did you latch onto all this intel?" I could have also asked why she didn't turn Dilbert in over the missing batteries. Or did she? Or was she partnered in on that scam? There were red flags all over this gig.

She glared at me and sniffed. "Okay, truth be told, I was hookin' up with one of the truck drivers who's in on this deal here and he bragged about it to me. He was piss drunk—he don't remember a thing. I thought it was bull, but, knowing about Dilbert's last scam, with the car batteries, I came out here to check and sure enough."

I picked my teeth for a minute with the edge of a matchbook. "Funny that driver or one of the others doesn't try to get over on Dilbert? Extort him,"—her word. "They could, right?"

"Well, don't forget, Dilbert's an ex-boxer. Most guys ain't eager to get on his bad side."

I nodded, thinking how that was probably true and also calculating that it gave me even more bargaining leverage with Monkey. My old lawyer skills were rousing from a long hibernation.

"How much is Dilbert pulling?"

"I only been countin' the three days, eh, but he done about, $240, $180, and $320. Close as I can tell."

I gave a low whistle. My stomach made a noise too, twisting in my gut. "Cash, eh?" Not perfect, but darn near. "Now that's math I can follow. How you gonna take him down?"

"I ain't. I'm gonna make him an offer. Either he cuts me in for fifty dollars a day or I rat him out. And I been secretly filming, wit' my phone, eh? I got the goods, dude. I reckon I need the video 'cuz he won't spook easy."

"So, whattaya need me for? Film editor?" I said, knowing better but wanting to hear it in plain English. At the same time I figured for sure this racket would crash. I wanted in on a one-time basis, only, cash up front.

"You know, Nazi, I heard you could be a smart-ass, eh? Ex-lawyer and all that. But like I said, you're a big body. I ain't. You back me when I lay it on Dilbert and make sure I don't end up in there."

She wagged her head at the Upper Harbour. Monkey didn't weigh much but she still wouldn't float worth shit.

"So, my end is one-fifty?"

"Yippers. A one-time thing. If Dilbert gives me any hassle, you straighten him out. You can handle him, eh?"

"Well, ya, he's what, like, fifty? I'm a little bigger and a lot younger. But the ex-boxer thing is kinda, uhh, disconcerting…"

"Here," Monkey said and slid a set of brass knuckles across the bus bench toward me. "In case he needs re-concerting…"

———

I sat there considering my options: Case or two of beer. Some weed. Maybe see a movie or buy a warm jacket down at Value Village. One-fifty ain't that much, but with any luck, Dilbert will roll over easy at first and get rid of Monkey later on. That's the smart play for him.

But maybe I should just walk away? This was the kind of small-time crap that put losers like Monkey in jail. I'd seen it a hundred times from the other side of the table. Pleading for petty crooks who didn't mind some winter jail time and were most concerned about which lock-up they went to. They wanted to be with their friends. I'd seen it all until my own destructive appetites turned me into one of them. But that's another story and I needed cash.

I was about to stick out my hand to shake on it, "Feff on it," as I recalled from law school when it came to me out of nowhere. THAT'S where Monkey Woman got her frickin' name! I remembered, slapping my thigh. I must have forgotten it because it was so damn dismal and disgusting. Monkey Woman was Delorme! Angel Delorme. She had been down at the Vancouver Zoo, over by the chimpanzee enclosure and one of the chimps chucked a wad of feces at her. Feisty one that she is, Delorme picked it up and threw it right back. The chimps started screaming and an all-out war erupted. Havoc! Some kid recorded it on his phone and sent the video to the local TV news, who aired it about fifty times. "Excrement battle at the City Zoo… film at 10. See the

Monkey Woman in action!"

"Monkey Woman" it was, after that. I held out my hand to her, "Okay, Angel, you got yourself a deal."

She whipped her head around, giving me a pop-eyed stare. I guess I remembered her name right. We shook on the plan and she took a minute to compose herself.

"You know, I like it that you called me by my real name. I hate the nickname I got hung with."

Besides, it should be Chimpanzee Woman, I thought. "I get it," I said, reminded of my own ugly street name and my great uncles who had experiences with real Nazis, but would never have called them that to their face.

"Say, one last thing..." I asked her. "Why take the risk? You're legitimately scared of Dilbert, you could get cheated, or beat up, or arrested, or who knows what? Why not just get a fuckin' job?"

She looked puzzled. "Jobs don't like me and I don't like them. This is—... this is what I do. I'm hungry, I want store-bought smokes, I want some weed, I want to sit in a bar and drink my face off and eat a plate of chicken wings. I want to tip the bartender and feel like I'm part of all this..." She straightened her back and waved an arm at Victoria.

I straightened my back too, smiled and said, "Fair enough. Let's do it, man. Rock and roll!"

Standing up, I could smell the cat piss reek of dried sweat exhale from the open collar of my shirt. Maybe I could get a hotel room? I pondered, letting my horizons expand. I pushed aside the thoughts about the old me, and what that guy would have done, and how the hell did I wind up in a sorry scam like this, anyway?

"Say, Angel. Hey darlin', think maybe I could get two hun?" I felt sorry for her and all, but if I was going to be in this shit-show I had to look out for myself.

She stared at me, pausing. "I don't know, man... we shook!"

"Whatever! It's just fifty more and besides, Dilbert's footin' the bill—am I right?"

She rocked back and forth for a few seconds. Rain beaded on the shoulders of her jacket. "What's your name, Nazi? Your real name?"

This shut me up. In truth, I didn't mind the anonymity of "Nazi," plus it gave me street cred. But then I thought of how the hot water in the hotel shower would feel. A burger from White Spot.

"Penner. Gottlieb Penner."

"Two-hundred it is, Mr. Penner. I'm putting you on retainer, am I right?" she said, grinning back at me. She looked almost pretty just then, and I wanted to remember her this way, not with chimp shit all over her hands. She began to cross the street toward Dilbert. "Keep an eye on me, will ya? Eh, Gottlieb... you got my back?"

I watched her go. She hiked her shoulders and tried to look big, tough. But she was thin as a stick bug. She turned back to throw me a wink and I thought, we are a go!

So was the Craigflower bus, returning on its loop. It was barreling down Bay Street coming down off the bridge with a load of passengers. I could see people falling forward as the bus first screeched then slid almost silently on the slippery street. The full bus nosed down—a charging bull coming right for Angel—and I closed my eyes, not wanting to see her frail form tumble through the air like a marionette, strings cut.

With traffic slowing and stopping out on the street, I could almost taste the burnt rubber and the stench from the brake pads, a caustic reek that burned my nostrils. I feared the worst—thought she was a goner. Angel getting hit by a bus sure as hell was not part of this scheme. In that wretched moment, I thought of her, a cast-off, made famous only for being exploited and ridiculed in the most crude and cruel way by the local news and a troop of chimpanzees. I resisted this caricature and instead envisioned her as she once might have been— an innocent little kid, full of wonder, riding her bike to a softball game and not knowing the adult life that awaited her. Not guessing what she would become, not in a million years. I clenched my hands in my pockets and opened my eyes.

The skinny blonde bus driver sat motionless, gripping the large steering wheel. His arms were locked, braced stiffly forward, his face frozen in shock and confusion. I could hear passengers yelling from where I stood.

But there sat Angel Delorme, dazed but alive on the far sidewalk where she had landed after diving out of the way. I'll be damned. Agile as a monkey. Then she confirmed her condition with a slurring shout at the driver, "Are ya blind?" At the same time, Dilbert—wearing a puzzled look—strode quickly toward her.

Still glaring at the driver, Delorme let loose with an unintelligible string of profanities, then gathered up the shattered remnants of her cell phone and with a bloody hand, tossed the pieces at the Craigflower bus like so much chimp shit.

Guess that two-hun is toast. The plan had unraveled even before it began. Pivoting on one foot, I pointed myself downtown and started to leave the scene. Best get outta here.

I glanced over, side-eyed, to see Dilbert barking at Angel; recognizing her it appeared. A thick boxer's finger pointed across the street toward the bus shelter, his other hand gripping Angel's jacket in a bunched fist. Then, turning my head, I saw her eyes follow me, watching me go. She quieted and seemed smaller than ever—like a scared little girl—sitting and hugging her knees on the wet sidewalk, her face smeared with grit, and curious bystanders gathering around. At the same time I saw her there, pitiful, I remembered myself—a boy waiting in an idling car outside the beer parlor while Dad went in for "just one, I promise!"

I slowed my exit. Then, without a second thought, held up my hand in a stiff-armed salute to halt the traffic on Bay Street and began to cross.

Seeing me coming, my arm raised, Angel cracked a grin both dingy and radiant. "That's my Gottlieb," she said and then resumed cursing in a loud voice, the words spilling out of that awful mouth of hers like wasps from a well-shook nest.

"Hey!" I yelled, breaking into a slow trot and feeling the weight of the brass in my pocket. "Leave her alone! She's with me."

Tracker of Lost Souls
Robert Pope

I HAVE A HARD TIME sitting down when I'm in my office. For that reason, I knocked down the walls in the so-called suite and put equipment at the back, including a rhythm bag and the heavy-duty bag the size of a man's body for close-in practice. The stationary bike, treadmill, but who likes all that going nowhere? I have a shower in the bathroom and a bar to hang clothes while I exercise.

The desk and such sit up front without a partition between workspace and work-out space, so I can see if anyone comes to the door. I've got that rippled glass in the door window and can see if anyone's there, and the doorbell sounds like the gong that starts and ends the rounds in a boxing match. So, I was running the bag when I heard the gong and saw the shape of the woman in the red dress with very dark hair. I couldn't see her features for the rippled glass.

I hung the terry robe around my shoulders and went to the door unlacing my gloves. When I got it open, she looked like she'd been waiting for hours and might be ready for more if she had to. She had long dark hair, an unusual tawny complexion, and features dominated by a formidable, straight nose and absolutely no expression. Her eyes located me, but she didn't say a word. She wasn't in a hurry to come in. Good-looking woman, maybe even a better one a decade earlier. I put her at thirty-eight, three years older than me, and turned out to be right on the money.

I told her to come in and have a seat while I changed clothes. She looked down at my open robe, without the slightest sense of hurry. I am a bit of a spectacle, black hair on chest and belly, not to mention several old bullet hole scars, but I am not in the least shy. I keep myself in good shape, a good thing for business, the way I think of it. If they don't like what they see, they can take their business elsewhere. I figured if she got this far, her need had been great enough it would take as much to get her to back away.

She followed me without complaint and sat in the chair I indicated, to the side of my desk, nice leather chair, to make her comfortable for a stay for as long as she needed. "Be back," I told her. I set a bottle of water from my little fridge on the table at her side. She held her large, rectangular black purse on her lap. She had nice lines, and for what it's worth, I admired her quiet demeanor, which spoke of determination, stoicism, or complete loss of motivation, I couldn't decide which.

I went back to rinse in the shower, then toweled off quickly and pulled on a white shirt, tie, dark brown suit, and square-toe brogans. I brushed my hair to one side, still wet, and noticed droplets sparkling in the hair on the back of my hands as I sat behind my desk. I took the time I needed to arrange myself, turn on my laptop, and set the voice recorder to pick up everything she said. She watched with the utmost patience the whole time, as if she expected nothing less than what she got. I took my time looking back at her with the same frankness with which she appraised me.

Several minutes passed in this manner before she spoke slowly, deliberately in a voice I would call husky without any connotation of harshness. "Mr. Lycan," she said. "Amaryllis Hemming. I am here because of your track record for finding lost souls." Those pale eyes lingered on mine another moment before she looked around to take in her surroundings. "I heard of your Spartan existence, but this is quite nice. Practical, but not without its charm, considering your profession. I am not disappointed yet."

I did not take the bait at the suggestion she might be disappointed later. "I hope," she said, "that I have not made a terrible mistake." A shudder ran through her, and she closed her eyes. When she opened them, she stared at the painting on the wall behind me for a moment before she furrowed her brow. I swiveled my chair slightly to glance at it.

"Gift from a satisfied client. Copy of a painting by one Howard Pyle, for a magazine illustration in the early 1900s. A bit frightening, but I'm fond of it." When I turned back, I saw she couldn't take her eyes off it. "Has a rather long title: A Wolf Had Not Been Seen in Salem for Thirty Years. She said it made her think of me when she saw it."

"I don't understand," she said.

"Why don't you tell me what brought you here, Mrs. Hemming."

"Yes, of course. I've been distracted. I haven't been sleeping since they disappeared. I can barely eat anything. I know I must, but I'm not interested. I can't read, can't do much that I have to do. I find myself daydreaming with none of the pleasant associations of the word. I can barely stand to say their names, though I hear their voices and see their faces in my mind all the time."

This sounded like a guessing game. To play along, I said, "Is it your husband, Mrs. Hemming?"

She covered her mouth and shook her head. "My husband died a year and a half ago. He flew his own plane. It went down on a trip to Honolulu. He was an architect." She broke down again, but no tears once more. She held her head in her hands, giving in to distress. My friend Rolf, who is a psychologist, repeated a quote one night over scotch that meant something to him, "There's a kind of woe that's madness." Because of my own profession, the quote often comes to mind.

"Now," she finally continued, "my younger sister Hyacinth has gone missing. I told the police. They do their jobs, but that's what it is to them. They can't do what you can, by virtue of..."

"My not being a civil servant?"

She glanced at the painting above me again. Her eyes remained on it a moment and fell to mine once more. Those pale green eyes were so deep I thought they might swallow me. Whatever she had heard about me, I knew she came because she hoped it was true.

I stood slowly, not to spook her, and went around to the fridge. I keep a fifth of Russian vodka in the freezer compartment. I poured a couple of short glasses and handed hers off on the way back to my desk. She took a sip, though I'm not sure she knew she was doing it at the time.

Amaryllis went on in a laconic voice that nevertheless persisted even when I thought it would drop off and fail altogether. I'm going to shorten it here somewhat, cut to the chase. There was much about her sister Hyacinth, who had come to live with her the past three years, at the age of thirty-two, after a painful breakup with a fellow who seemed to want to drain her of every drop of energy she possessed. Born with the name Fritz Finster, he had changed the surname to Fenster, an alteration that took it from the German for dark to the word for window.

Hyacinth had an artistic disposition and the lack of practical sense that comes with it. But she had something that many with the artistic disposition do not, talent and a work ethic—though she called it obsession. She left for UCLA at eighteen, studied art four years, and left with a reputation for creating something new, challenging, and a bit threatening. The collector Fenster bought several of her paintings before she graduated, boosting her reputation among her fellow students and professors. Within the next couple of years, he amassed a total of twenty-two which he included in a show he produced in his gallery, The Window, which, as I have already suggested, might have been called The Dark had he not changed that one letter in his surname.

His power had quite a reach; the show got excellent reviews, some from friends of Fenster's or, more likely, acquaintances who feared or owed him. Not that she did not deserve high praise, but many have talent. Success begets success. Her backlog of completed paintings dwindled at about the pace of her new production—spurred on by her popularity. It's not difficult to understand how a young painter might be attracted to the man she considered responsible for her fame. Fenster took full advantage of this position to draw her into his web.

When he finally talked her into moving in with him at twenty-six, he claimed to be forty-two. In photos from this time, her hair is clipped close, her pale green eyes enormous, her nose small and slightly tipped, her mouth wide, lush. An odd combination, but striking, nonetheless. Though smaller than her sister, very nearly petite, she gave the appearance of vitality and physical strength, quite different from the woman who came home to live with Amaryllis and Eason at the ripe old age of thirty-two. That was two years before my meeting with Amaryllis.

Then, her sister told me, she was a bundle of nerves and tears, for it seemed that he had broken her not just in one or two pieces, but shattered her like a mirror, which, from my perspective, meant he was in for seven years of bad luck—if I had anything to say about it. She had stopped painting altogether. To get away from Fenster, she fled while he was preparing the gallery for a showing of another of his prospective victims. She took nothing more than a change of clothes and three of her favorite paintings—the ones she could not part with. These she hung in the house of Amaryllis in Santa Barbara. When Fritz

Fenster showed up at their door demanding to see his wife, Eason sent him packing with the threat of arrest. A few weeks later, his plane went down, and the paranoia Fenster created made them wonder about this coincidence.

In her escape, Hyacinth had enlisted the help of a friend from her days at UCLA who had seen her condition and whispered in her ear when she kissed her in greeting, "You look awful. Let me help, no matter what is happening." When he came home to see she had left, he called her cell phone and told her, "I created you, and I can destroy you!" She told him she didn't care anymore. Of course, he would not destroy her; he had too much invested. If she was not in his possession, her paintings were. He had the right, as her agent and her husband to hold them until she returned. In short, he told her she would never own them again.

"We will see about that," I told Amaryllis, and I meant it. I had not yet met the man in the flesh, but I suspected him for what he was, but that much I withheld from Amaryllis at our first meeting. I reminded her that since Hyacinth and Fritz were still married, she did in fact own her paintings, even the ones he purchased from years before, as communal property. Should he meet with an untimely end, they would all become her property once again, free and clear, as well as his precious gallery, The Window.

Her story touched a nerve in me. I knew more than I said, for not only was I familiar with her sister's work, but I had also purchased a painting of hers I could not do without once I had seen it. Amaryllis had engaged me for my honest pay; she had also engaged my mind and emotions and senses. I had done the barest research on Hyacinth at the time of my purchase and learned only the most basic details of her biography, none of the present truth. Her sister Amaryllis might have walked into my office unknown to me, but she brought with her a known commodity. The story she told so outraged me I could barely control myself.

I did, of course. That has been my discipline, my art if you will, for these many years. Self-control has been required of me, and I have lived up to the ideal I set for myself when I began my practice, to use unnatural powers only when there was no other recourse—or, I must admit, if I especially wanted to. In fact, my natural powers normally sufficed. This, of course, Amaryllis had heard of, the canny and uncanny elements of my person, and it was why she showed up at my door, half-afraid to speak yet feeling she had no recourse in her desperation.

When we left the office, I turned off the lights and locked the door. I had sworn to Amaryllis that I would satisfy her cause as if it were my own—if she provided an expense account. She would remunerate me as she saw fit at the end of our contract, which she signed in my office for the payment on the spot of one American dollar. Once at her home, I dismissed the guard she had hired and took his place myself, vowing not to leave her unprotected. When I left in the pursuit of my duty to her, my associate Conri would take my place, a creature in whom, I assured her, I had absolute confidence.

That evening, I searched the house, handling and inspecting every effect of the missing Hyacinth until I knew her intimately. In the attic studio, I found several abortive paintings, one splashed with red paint by none other than Hyacinth herself in a fit of despair at her inability to create something worthy of her name. If I had doubts where she had gone, they were removed by what I saw and felt, and, yes, smelled in the very air of that desolate house. The very next day I ensconced Conri—who is an intimidating seven feet tall and silent as a monk—in the house and made my way, in my black Ferrari 488 Spider, to Los Angeles, to scope out the art gallery known as The Window.

I found The Window on a street in Los Angeles which shall remain unnamed to protect the present owner of the renamed gallery. True to its name, a rather large window covered the entire front of the store, tinted so passers-by could not see inside. Odd, but fitting, a window too dark to see through. On this window, as if it commented on itself, in huge black lettering, the window proclaimed itself The Window; beneath this, three smaller lines, one beneath the other, read, Gallery of the Arts, and Proprietor Fritz Fenster.

On the door, which also featured a tinted window, a professionally made sign reflected the style of the lettering on the window proper, announcing the name of the newest ingenue Fenster had taken up, today's date, and the name of a show for the work of the young female artist who, presumably, would take Hyacinth's place. I had left Amaryllis' house precipitously because I saw online the show was planned for this very day, which meant, as I took it, Hyacinth might soon become expendable.

I tried the door, locked, and though I pressed my face to the glass, I could not see inside. I knocked on the glass, to gauge the thickness or stoutness of the glass and whether it might have been bulletproofed. I should think a glass front building would be an invitation to an intruder armed with a brick and a need for ready cash. A more sophisticated violator of the inner sanctum of the arts would know the gallery housed any number of extremely valuable paintings, made valuable through the machinations of Fritz Fenster.

I hardly expected the door to open, confronted suddenly by the proprietor himself. He must have seen my surprise, as a smile crept up the side of his face in such an odd way I had to study it a moment before concluding it must have been intended to convey a welcome of sorts. I had worn my most dapper and snug silver-gray suit and vest and carried a cane I like to think of as a walking stick. As I held it more like a baton than a cane, the silver wolf head grip became a focal point for Herr Fenster's powers of observation.

"Interesting stick, that."

"Yes," I said. "Something of an heirloom. I carry it out of habit. Respect for a tradition."

"A tradition, interesting phrasing."

"Thank you."

"I did not mean it as a compliment."

"I did not take it as such."

"May I inquire after your name and business. And, if I may be so bold, why you rapped on my door?"

"Ah, yes. The nature of the glass used in your storefront interested me. I understand your gallery specializes in the art of young women."

"It is a passion of mine to empower female artists."

"How interesting. They are females? Are they not women as well?"

"Of a certainty."

Fenster satisfied my expectations. He looked like an old movie star of the black and white era, dressed already for his showing in a stagey tuxedo with tails, a shirt with frills at the breast and cuffs, and what seemed to me thick foundation makeup of the type worn by stage actors, perhaps doubling as sunblock. I noticed further he had the red dot in the corner of each eye closest to the nose, again, in the manner of the stage actor. Broader in the shoulders than I expected, he had a triangular build down to a narrow waist. And, of course, he wore an exaggeratedly large pair of sunglasses, the glass giving off a reflection both dark and red at the same time.

"Interesting glasses you have," I mentioned.

"Prescription, I'm afraid. Made special for me. You can't buy them anywhere if that's what interests you."

"Not at all. I am more interested in the young woman whose show you have sponsored this evening. I am something of a collector myself, housed now in Santa Barbara, and I have come down to admire her work and perhaps purchase a painting or two if they tickle my fancy."

"Tickle your fancy indeed. But may I say, I find it unusual that a man of your girth would be interested in paintings."

"My girth, what does my girth have to do with my taste in art?"

"Your shoulders and biceps strain that suit to bursting. You look more like a professional wrestler than an art dealer. And that beard, cut so close along your jaw, seems designed to prevent an opponent from gripping it to pull your head up down or sideways. You look like a stand-in for the hulk. Do you have credentials I might peruse?"

"All the credentials I generally require is a stuffed bank book, which I possess. Now, will you show me these damned pictures, or must I come back in a couple of hours to mingle with the riffraff?"

"Sir, you will find no riffraff here tonight or any other night, and, furthermore, you will not be welcome should you show up for this or any other show. I turn you away, reject your plea for entry, and hasten you on your way."

"Unlike yourself, Herr Fin-ster," I said, filling the first syllable of that name with my disgust, "I do not require permission to enter your establishment, and should I decide to show up for your grand opening, I will make my presence felt in as potent a manner as you could wish in your darkest dream."

"I take exception to your blatant threat, and now absent myself, as duty calls from within. Sir, you may go to the devil and begone."

With this, he attempted to shut the door in my face. Extending my arm, I stopped it mid-slam and stared into his red-black sunglasses. "May I inquire if this is not the very space that once promoted the work of Hyacinth Hemming? And, if so, may I further inquire what you have done with her work that you are so ready to move on to your next puppet?"

"You insolent fellow," he spat. "How dare you insinuate whatever it is you insinuate. I will thank you to release this door, my door, the door to my gallery, and I will thank you not to curse the name of my wife with any foul utterance."

"Very well," I told him, "I will release your door, but understand that I know your game. I know what you are up to. I see through your plans for this ingenue. You have met your match in me. I will find you in my own time, and we shall see what we shall see. Until then, Guten abend, mein herr."

"Your German is execrable, you yourself a foul beast."

"Truer words have yet to be spoken, but I doubt they will be spoken by you, who lives in darkness."

I released the door in such swift manner he fell forward shutting it. I heard him slam the bolt to keep me out, but soon enough it would be open to the world. Meanwhile, I will have invaded his lair. I had studied blueprints for the building and knew where I would find his bedroom, in the bowels or basement of the very building in which he hid from the light.

To tell the truth, I had not expected to see him before surprising him in his lair. That trick of knocking on the glass had done it, but I did confirm what I knew, that Fenster or Finster or Fritz, whatever he called himself, had sealed the front of his building in glass, yes, but impenetrable glass. What he did not know I knew, from the way in which he altered the building, sealing the rear to ingress or egress, was that every beast must have a secret exit or entrance beyond the knowledge of the common viewer.

Earlier I had wandered behind this gallery, crawled on top of the building which faced the street on the other side of the block, and seen, from that roof, the manhole cover which could have no natural connection to sewer lines, and, thus, must be the private entrance I sought. I had only to wait until evening, festivities under way, to make my move, when Fritz became preoccupied with his newest star. I passed an hour in a dinner of rare steak to fortify myself against the night's occupation. And to pass the time, I attended an afternoon performance of short plays by Samuel Beckett abbreviated and performed by students from a nearby repertory college. I confess that I enjoyed it enormously, particularly for all the curious flaws cleverly inserted by an inept director. I got the signatures of the director on my program, and all the actors, with the intention of sending them notes on just where they had gone astray.

But when I stepped into the darkening evening, strutting a bit with my walking stick, my hour had come. I made my way back to The Window—still musing over the irony of a window through which one cannot see—climbed once more to the roof of the building from which I had earlier observed the hidden entrance, stripped off my elegant attire, folded it and packed it into a protective sack hidden in my inside jacket pocket. Determined now to transform myself in midair, I leaped from the roof to the courtyard at the rear of the gallery, which had not yet opened to the guests of Herr Fritz.

To be sure, the courtyard had been set about with perhaps twenty bottles of champagne sunk in tubs of ice, with glasses stacked decoratively on two nearby tables. Soon, several young art students posing as servers in white or black campaign jackets would appear to pour glasses and circulate them among the guests until it would require an act of magic to keep them on their own legs—the guests, I mean, and particularly those who brought the requisite passport, the checks and credit cards for which Monsieur Fritz would offer worthless canvasses he hoped to convince them were potentially priceless artifacts.

Inserting my nails into the holes in the manhole cover, I lifted it easily from its fixed position, dropped inside, pulled it back in position, and descended into the darkness of the den, where I hoped to find both the Finster lair and his wife, the languishing kidnap victim Hyacinth Hemming. I did not need a light any longer, as my eyes now glowed sufficiently to light my way, though my increased size posed difficulties in squeezing through the narrow passages not intended for the man-wolf.

I would have to be careful if I came upon Hyacinth, as in whatever state or condition I might find her, I did not doubt the sight of me, without preparation, might have a deleterious effect on her health. I knew two things by this time, as I wound down deeper into the cavern beneath The Window, and I knew them by scent. I had smelled the effects—by which I mean clothing and such necessities—of the captive Hyacinth, and I already had a snootful of Fritz himself earlier when I rapped on his door by accident. By scent I knew them to be here, that Fritz himself had frequented these dire lodgings.

By scent, I found her, chained to the wall of a sleeping chamber, drooping unconscious or semi-unconscious. Her hair, grown longer, much longer than before, hung over her face in twisted coils. Her head hung on her neck. Her body drooped from her hands fixed in their moorings on the wall. I suspected this was to be her last night on earth if this showing of his latest acquisition proved amenable to the success for which he intended her. Hyacinth had become a liability; she hated him. His habitation required wealth, and he had come to know all that the world of art might provide for him.

As I approached the hanging woman, I heard a whimper, perhaps in a fever dream in which she attempted to flee from the monster who thus imprisoned her. I easily sprung the chains from their fastenings; she fell into my arms. My hope was that she would not see me thus transformed and wake screaming, but she remained bound in silence. I lay her upon his bed, provided with dark purple and black spreads, coverlets of silk and velvet. The poor child herself wore the flimsiest of vestments yet looked like a fading angel, her eyes sunk in darkness, mouth open and gasping for air as I arranged her on the bed for what I thought must be greater comfort.

How long it would be before he returned to his prisoner, now locked in a dark silence from which he planned never to release her. Once he knew his ingenue struck the proper chord with his guests, what awaited her I could only guess. The lightness of her body as I carried her, the paleness of her skin, confirmed that he had fed on her already. I found the slashes on her arms and breast from which he drained only enough to sustain him. I knew he would not want her lingering as one like himself, but she would do for extended consumption.

I paced as I awaited his return to his lair, tended to the fair girl on the bed, gave her water to drink, slowly, carefully. Even in an unconscious state her mouth would open, her lips and tongue reach out for relief. I heard a celebration from above, the voices of congratulations, the increasingly drunken guests, as my ears had a wider range in this form. I still feared that if she woke, the sight of me would frighten her to death. I could do nothing to prevent that if I hoped to surprise him in his den. When at last I heard him descending toward us, I fixed my own arms to the chains, loosely, to free them easily, and hung there as he had hung sweet Hyacinth. As he came into his lair, alerted to my feral presence, he might have supposed his wife had died and fouled the air. I glanced up enough as I hung from the wall to see that he now saw me there, not knowing who or what I was, and just then, I gripped him by the throat and lifted him off his feet.

Oh, he tried to wriggle free with considerable strength, but I clutched him tight and hard, sank my teeth below, in his belly and his side, and when he screamed and tore away, I set on him again. His fangs flashed in the dark, and from the corner of my eye, I saw the girl sit up, witnessing the terrible battle. Nothing could be done to prevent her panic as I leaped at him, driving him against the wall and onto the floor, plunging teeth and nails into his neck. I felt sorry for dear Hyacinth, the sound of our deadly battle must have terrified her. I snarled and growled as I ripped at him; he screamed as he attempted to sink his fangs in me.

When at last I had his throat severed, I tore the hideous head from his body, threw it against the wall and pounced on it again. Only when I knew he could not strike back, I hung him where he had hung his wife, and chained him there, headless, for his attendant to find him when he came down to clean the mess of the monster's destruction of his wife.

With this accomplished, I turned to her, and rather than fearful and trembling or fainted dead away, I watched her rising from bed, now coming to me, grabbing my fur to cling to me in such a manner I thought my heart would break. I would have preferred at that moment to show myself in human form to ease her fears, but what she said shocked me as much as I had feared the sight of me would terrify her.

"I saw you just now. You ripped the head off the monster. Make me as strong as you. Give me the gift that you possess, that I might never be as weak as I am now."

She leaned her head to one side, as if I might sink my teeth into the tender flesh, as the vampire might have done. I felt such urgency and pity. "We must leave now. Others may come, we must be gone when they arrive. Hold to my back, and I will take you home. Cling to me tightly, the passageways are narrow."

She did as I asked, but once on my back she never ceased imploring me to make her like myself. I could neither deny nor provide the boon that she requested. Emerging from the opening in the courtyard, I leaped onto the building behind, onto the roof, with Hyacinth still clinging to my back. As I allowed myself the painful transition to my human form she stood back and watched, and I wondered if at last she feared.

I wiped the blood from face and hands as well as I could, dressed, and entered the building through a roof door, holding the walking stick ahead now for protection. Together, we descended stairs onto the street, and ran the streets until we found the parking deck where I had left the car. Once inside, and on the road, headed back to the house where she was born, she made me promise I would make her as myself, so she would never have to fear again. As we sped along the highway, gazing at the shining ocean below us on the left, I made a solemn promise if she made the same request in one week hence, I would grant her fondest wish. In the interim, it would be Amaryllis who nursed her back to health, and, at last, to talk some sense into her human sister.

It wasn't one week hence, but months, that Hyacinth stood at my office door. I saw her through the rippled glass. I knew she came to claim a promise I had made. Her sister now had given in, to let her do as her heart would. The hidden basement is sealed off; no one knows where he has gone. But life is short, and art survives. New life now thrives within the convoluted streets where lust and greed and hunger had once ruled; Hyacinth sits upon a throne I cleansed for her. She tells me don't go, Harry, stay with me. I tell her, Sweetie, don't tempt me, I've got an agency to run.

Dig Two Graves
Andrew R. Mikos

"I WAS ONLY fucking around with the kid. You gotta remember, this was my third tour. There wasn't anything I hadn't seen happen in that jungle. I'd watched my brothers shot to pieces and blown to bits. And here's this kid, couldn't have been 25 years old. And he's a lieutenant, that was the worst part. This kid fucking outranks me and here he is shitting himself." Charles continued, "This kid was fresh out of OTS. Real green, ya know?"

"OTS?" she stubbornly asked.

"Officer training school. That's where they cram six days of material into twelve weeks to teach them the difference between bars and oak clusters, I guess. He was an electrician or something back in the world, so they put him in the Engineer Corps. See this was supposed to be a humanitarian mission. Hearts and minds bullshit. We were gonna turn someone's power back on, or their water, I don't fucking know. Basically, our job was to protect these noodle-armed guys so they could fix shit in this shitty town in shitty South Vietnam. We were supposedly in 'safe' territory. What a joke. Anyone who spent any time in that jungle knows there's no such thing as safe territory."

The soft lights of Dr. Leslie Graham's office were designed to mollify her patients, but this never had the desired effect on Charles Dotson. Some sessions, Charles wouldn't even sit down, what the hell were some stupid scarves thrown over a lampshade going to accomplish? No, he was the opposite. He needed to be coaxed. Leslie had been planning this for years, and she had been seeing Charles every week for the better part of four months. This was the first time she had gotten him talking about the day of the incident. He seemed so close now. She had to push him. "So why did this.. lieutenant, you said?

Why did this lieutenant make you mad?"

"I don't know that he made me mad, it just... seemed so stupid, you know? Here we are marching from our base to some little piss-ant village... for what? To fix their fucking lights? Fuck do these people need lights for?" Charles began to knead the flesh of his palms with the tips of his fingers, a technique Leslie had taught him. She was close. She pressed on.

Perhaps imprudent, but Leslie proclaimed, "And you blamed this young lieutenant, so you tried to scare him."

Charles scoffed at her phrasing before taking a contemplative pause to lie back on the couch. "He was already scared. I could tell just by how close he was keeping to me. He knew I didn't get the stripes on my sleeve being a fucking pussy. I got them in the shit. He wanted my protection. If he'd asked me what I wanted to do, we'd be about facing right back to the damn base, but orders are orders, and lieutenants don't ask sergeants what they think we should be doing. They tell them what to do."

Leslie watched the back of his head and bit her tongue. She waited to see if he would continue, not wanting to break his train of thought. She focused on the sliver of light from the crack in the curtains and the dancing motes of dust within. The pigeons outside her office window flapped in and out of the light as they tended to their daily business.

Just as she inhaled, he broke the tortured silence, "I don't know why I thought it would be funny. We'd done it before to other guys, rite of passage, ya know?"

"What was it?" Leslie pressed.

"Well me and the boys knew the kid was scared. Must have been his first time in the field ever, so I decide to try to, I don't know, freak him out a bit, a prank, ya know? We had this... charm... that had been with the company for a while."

"What kind of charm?" She asked, both eager and frightened to hear his answer.

"It was a nose," Charles stated somewhat matter-of-factually.

"A... nose?"

"Yeah. Well, it started as a nose. And then a couple more noses got added, so it was like... a clump of noses. Shit had pins, glue, whatever holding it together. Thing was fucking gross, but someone always carried it. No one ever got hit who was carrying those fucking noses. Not once."

Leslie tried not to think about what it takes to normalize grown men carrying around a clump of noses, or whose noses we were talking about here. She didn't care. All she could think about was young lieutenant David Baldwin. He was so striking at his graduation. She waited for Charles to continue.

"Well I had 'em with me, so I pull the noses out and pass it over to the lieutenant. I said something like 'try this, sir.' and I think he thought I was passing him chaw or jerky or something cause he doesn't even look down at it, but starts peeling one of the noses off it and shoves the fucking thing right in his cheek. Well he must've thought it tasted funny or something cause he finally looks down at what I handed him and sees what it is. I mean, it took him a second for his brain to figure out what his eyes were fucking looking at, ya know, but he just let's out this little noise, like a dog's squeak toy or something and he drops them. The other nose plops out of his mouth onto the ground and he's about to puke, but instead of just puking, he tries to run off into the brush, like he was embarrassed or something. And that's when it happened."

"When.. what.. happened?" All these years searching for it and Leslie could reach out and touch the truth now.

"Well as he runs into the bush, he steps on a landmine. Couldn't tell you if it was one of ours or one of theirs, but it doesn't really make a difference once you step on it. That was the end of the lieutenant. Probably could've added his nose to the rest if we wanted. He shouldn't have dropped them. If he'd carried them into the brush, I'm convinced that mine would have been a dud. Or maybe he wouldn't have stepped on it at all."

"You think the lieutenant just had bad luck?" Leslie asked, almost mockingly. She felt a sudden surge of splenetic spite for sergeant Charles Dotson. Before she could form her next thought, he continued.

"I don't know the guy. That was the first time I'd met him. We just got our orders that morning and we were probably only five clicks out from base when this all went down, so it's not like I got to know him. He seemed weak to me." Charles pushed his guilt further down.

"You think he was weak? Because he saw something horrific and reacted like a normal human person would?" Leslie gritted her teeth but the words still found a way past them.

"We've all seen horrific shit. That's the point. You can't forget your training and run off into the woods like a goddamn toddler." Charles said with a cold terminality.

"You were trained in how to handle being handed severed human body parts?"

"Kind of. All of the training is designed to numb us. I never did OTS, but I gotta imagine some of it focuses on being a good officer, and a good officer doesn't run into the brush to puke, no matter what he's seen—"

"Or bitten into?" She interjected.

Charles shrugged his shoulders but didn't say a word. If he had experienced any guilt in divulging the details of that day, he had already dispensed with them. Unburdening himself of this anecdote seemed to have no effect upon him, but it engulfed her. She stared at the back of his head as she felt her rage wash over her like the curling crests of the Pacific as they crashed onto the rocks at Big Sur. She thought back to the summers when her family would go there. She would run down to the waves as soon as their parents' Buick came to a halt, but David always liked to spend some time looking through his binoculars first. He would start by looking around for the sharks that were never there, but eventually he would always end up with his eyes in the sky searching for condors. One time he had actually spotted one and they all marveled at the majesty of this prehistoric descendant of time. By the time David had made his way down to the water, their father would be helping Leslie build another sandcastle and their mother would be sunning herself like a bird, her arms stretched to the edges of her limits.

And then she thought again of David when he had told the family he was joining the Army. He didn't want to wait to be drafted and get stuck in some infantry unit. He intended to make the most of it. If the Army was going to use him to fight a war in Vietnam, then he was determined to use the Army to get what he wanted as well. He had already been working with Gus Erickson for a year on account of his friendly relationship with his daughter, so David already knew just about everything he could about being an electrician. When he got a 99 on his ASVAB, the highest score possible on the Army's entrance exam, they assigned him to the Army Corps of Engineers and he was off to basic training and officer training school.

And then of course, it was off to Vietnam. But it was going to be different for David. Those first few letters home filled them with hope as he talked about helping the local people rebuild their infrastructure. He talked about how freedom could really take root here if the people didn't have to rely on the government for things like electricity and running water. He was going to rebuild this place for the better.

But instead of receiving more letters from David, they received a telegram and a folded American flag.

She rubbed the barrel of the .38 special in her desk drawer as her mind came back from her nostalgic sojourn. All her efforts culminated here, Sergeant Charles Dotson, before her eyes. Leslie had researched tediously the men involved in that operation that day, and she encountered difficulties at every turn, but she finally found someone in Dotson's unit who was willing to discuss her brother's death. Of course, she didn't tell him she was his brother. She wanted their unabridged accounts of what happened. Her parents hid from the truth, but she would not. She intended to find out exactly what had happened to David, and after over a year of disappearing leads and abruptly-ended phone calls, he fell right into her lap. One of the men she had been treating attended the same Alcoholics Anonymous meetings as Charles Dotson, and she guessed he was the one to convince him that she was a safe person with whom to talk. She wondered what that man would think when he heard that Sergeant Dotson met his untimely end in the very office of the woman to whom he had referred him. She lifted the revolver and placed it in her lap, feeling its gravity upon her.

"Anyways," Charles broke the now-awkward silence hanging in the room like a wisp of smoke, "That was too bad about the lieutenant. I hope his family got a big check out of it."

She sat suspended in stupefying silence. 'A big check?' Is this how this animal rationalizes away his role in her brother's death? By creating a magical 'check' that wafts in and disperses the cloud of endless grief and remorse? She could feel the heaviness of the gun in her lap. She began to gently run her fingers down the silver barrel until she rested her hand upon the trigger. She thought about the simplicity of her solution. All she needed to do was lift the gun and ever-so-slightly squeeze and it would be over. David's death would be avenged. Her life would be over too, but she hadn't cared about that in a long time. Her obsession with her brother's death drove her friends away first, followed soon after by her husband. The endless stream of doctors that examined her called it by different names: depression, bipolarism, paranoid schizophrenia; they never called it what it really was. Now she carried her vengeance around her neck like an albatross, refusing to part with it for fear of even worse consequences.

She pictured David's face on the beach, the ocean spray glistening on his skin. She raised the gun and pointed it at the back of the sergeant's head. As she closed her eyes, she could hear the birds fluttering outside her office window and she thought of the condor her brother had found and shared with her all those years ago.

Rock Bottom
Quintin Peterson

AS THE UNMARKED police vehicle sped away from the bloody crime scene into the night, AC/DC's "Highway to Hell" blaring from its factory-installed radio perpetually tuned to Classic Rock 105.9, the hurtling black Crown Vic equipped with the Police Interceptor Package and permeated with the acrid aromas of blood and sweat turned off Chesapeake Street, SE onto Southern Avenue on two wheels and burned rubber when the other two tires finally returned to the asphalt. His dirty blonde hair matted to his feverish head by cold perspiration, the right sides of his gray polyester sport coat, button-down powder blue shirt, body armor, underwear and blue jeans wet, warm and sticky and stained a deep burgundy, the undercover narcotics officer flew like a bat out of hell. His mouth and throat filled with the metal-like taste of his own blood, his mind on the satchel stuffed with cash and Crack rocks resting on the front passenger seat, Detective Moe Bundy made his getaway.

One hand gripping the steering wheel and the other pressed hard against the oozing bullet wound in the right side of his neck, his bloodshot eyes stinging from the saline-rich sweat flowing from his furrowed forehead and constantly blinking, swiftly closing to slits and then opening wide, Moe fought not only to maintain control of the careening getaway car, but also to simply remain conscious. Blood-drenched and woozy, he struggled to focus. Like a trucker who had been on the road for far too long or a drunk driver, he fought second by second to keep his eyes open and to keep his vehicle on the roadway. Regardless, he was dying for just one hit of one of those big, fat Crack rocks beckoning to him from the satchel on the seat next to him; ached for it deep in the pit of his belly.

He had polished off a pint of Smirnoff's Vodka and hit his last rock in his unmarked police cruiser just moments before he walked into the four-unit apartment building on Condon

Terrace, SE, up the stairs and into apartment 202, and opened fire on "The Devil" and his crew, and his high had worn off long ago, five minutes or longer. An eternity. And the numbness brought on by shock coupled with the charge of the Crack cocaine seemed to be wearing off. Along with the throbbing in his neck he felt with each heartbeat just like with a toothache or a hammer- struck thumb, twinges of pain now seemed to be encroaching. But now definitely wasn't the time to take a hit and take away the pain. Damn it! He had to keep his head, plot his next move, he had to concentrate! Severely handicapped by massive blood loss, he made a Herculean effort moment to moment to focus. His eyes watering, constantly blinking, and swiftly closing to slits and then opening wide, he struggled to decide, *Right or left onto Wheeler Road? Right.* At the last second, he slammed on the brakes and yanked the steering wheel hard over, tires screeching as he whipped right onto Wheeler Road, out of the District of Columbia into Southern Maryland. He stood on the accelerator pedal, still fleeing when no one was chasing him, leaving a trail of smoke and burned rubber as he fishtailed up the road, bobbing and weaving through traffic. He had to put distance between him and the bloodbath he'd left behind on Condon Terrace, but more importantly, he needed immediate medical attention, though he had no idea where to get it off the books. His squeeze Sizzle would know. All he had to do was get to her.

The job his squeeze Sizzle laid out for him was supposed to have been a cakewalk, but the robbery of drug dealer Marcus "The Devil" Delaney had gone horribly awry. Typical. This fiasco was another fine mess his self-serving side piece had gotten him into; yet another precarious predicament. But, as always, he chalked it up to bad luck, not bad planning.

—

Moe Bundy had been kickin' it with Sizzle for about a year, ever since he'd made her acquaintance at the Ragin' Cajun Supper Club up on Mount Olivet Road, an eternally dark and smoky Ptomaine

Domain specializing in so-so pseudo Cajun cuisine and outstanding authentic pole dancing.

The night he met her, Moe was sitting at a table in the back of the club when he raised his bottle of Budweiser to his lips, but stopped in mid-drink when he caught sight of the luscious and leggy scantily glad beauty strutting out onto center stage on three-inch stiletto pumps.

Curvaceous and caramel colored; she stood five feet, six inches tall, and weighed about 120 pounds. Her hair was long, lush and dark, her breasts ample and firm, her stomach flat, and her legs shapely and strong. He couldn't put his finger on her race. Brazilian? Pacific Islander? East Asian? Middle Eastern? (Much later in their affiliation, she had told him that her father was a Seminole Indian and her mother was Sri Lankan. Once he researched Sri Lanka on the Internet to learn where the hell it was, her extraordinary beauty made sense to him then.)

The young honey's age was questionable. Her fake ID said she was twenty-one, and she looked it, but that's how old one legally has to be to strip. But the truth was she could have been anywhere between fifteen and twenty-two. Moe didn't let that bother him though: he wanted her. And what Moe wants, Moe gets. He had no qualms about being a bad man and cheating on his wife to get what he wanted, which was pretty bad in the scheme of things, so he didn't let the possibility that Sizzle was underage hold him back. It didn't really matter; bad is bad…and he'd already done worse things. And if being bad was all it took to get next to the fresh and tender stripper, he didn't want to be good.

"Gentlemen," said a baritone announcer with a mic inside of a booth, "Please put your hands together and give a warm welcome to our newest dancer, the red hot and smokin', Sizzle! Yes! If she was a car, she'd be a showroom fresh little red Corvette!"

Holding but not drinking from his bottle of beer, Moe left his Marlboro smoldering in the ashtray, mesmerized as Sizzle, nimble and lithe, alternately had sex with the pole center stage, then moved closer to the oglers hanging close to the periphery of the stage, her garter filling with lengthwise folded one dollar bills, gyrating and then posing her way all the way through the pulsating rhythms of "Nasty Girl," a song written by Prince for his protégé girl group Vanity 6.

True to form, Sizzle didn't reveal to Moe that her real name was Rachel Young until about six months into their relationship, which began the night they'd met. Their first, and many subsequent dates, cost him $200 and the price of a dime bag of weed, a bottle of Moët champagne and a room at a cheap motel on New York Avenue, NE. But in a month or so when their relationship blossomed, he rented her an apartment on the 4100 block of Georgia Avenue, NW, across the street from the *Foxy Playground* where she also danced whenever she needed some more quick and easy cash. After that he no longer had to put cash on the barrelhead…at least not every time he stopped by. It came out cheaper for him in the short run…but not in the long run when he started dabbling in Cocaine with her and graduated to Crack Cocaine a month later.

Moe had thought snorting Cocaine and having marathon sex with Sizzle was the pinnacle, but powder paled by comparison to Crack. Inhaling the pungent smoke of the far more potent rocks of Crack Cocaine provided an immediate, euphoric rush. He'd let Sizzle hit the glass pipe first. When she gave him the nod, he'd hit the pipe and then she'd mount him as he lay on his back holding deep in his lungs the intoxicating vapor for as long as he could, exhaling the cool smoke slowly as she rode him like a Preakness jockey. And on and on long into the night, stopping briefly now and again as needed to reload Crack rocks into their ubiquitous singed glass pipe and inhaling the acrid vapors to refresh their insatiable lust. It was heaven. The Crack all by itself was almost better than sex, but Sizzle had skills like no other woman he'd ever encountered, especially his timid spouse Martha, whom he had grown up with in Crofton, Maryland and had been his Arundel High School sweetheart. Sizzle was magnificent. The one- two punch of Sizzle and Crack had Moe twisted.

Moe swerved to avoid a white Chevy Tahoe that seemed to come out of nowhere and stood on the horn. He swore under his breath. Classic Rock 105.9 broadcasting the Eagle's "Life in the Fast Lane" as his eyes watered, constantly blinked, and swiftly closed to slits and then opened wide, Moe Bundy sped away up Wheeler Road.

Even when Moe eventually became strapped for cash to pay the mortgage on his home in the suburbs, the rent for his lust nest on Georgia Avenue, the utility bills at both places, his car notes, food, formula and diapers for baby Moe, and his pudgy, white bread wife's

Pilates classes, he always found a way to cover it all plus the price of heaven…until the overtime money he was making dried up. Without it, he was close to hitting rock bottom and being on skid row.

Regardless, he kept on a good face at work and at home, for the most part, and continued to make solid drug busts and excuse his long absences from home by claiming to his wife that he was working overtime to fight the good fight in the War on Drugs. He was a frontline soldier and all hands were needed on deck. And it worked. Even when he hit a rough patch and his police powers were revoked and he was placed on non-contact status and was actually working day work at the Property Division, his wife Martha had been none the wiser.

Moe's suspension came as the result of a stupid move he'd made after bingeing on Crack and working for three days straight. His mind muddled, he had left behind his notebook at a Crack house where he'd served arrest and search warrants. When he realized his mistake an hour later, he returned but could not find his notebook. Later that night, streetwalker Zenaida Austin, his confidential informant for the raid on the Crack house, was found horribly murdered in a cheap motel on New York Avenue and his notebook was left at the gory crime scene. Distraught and remorseful, Moe had confessed to Detective Dave Crawford that he had inadvertently left his notebook at the Crack house, but it wasn't he who had ratted him out. On the contrary, Superintendent of Detectives Ray McCann was advised by Commander of Homicide Branch Jed Cullinane that Moe's notebook was found at the motel room murder scene, and McCann had then advised Moe's boss, Lt. "Blackjack Zack" Braxton. Blackjack Zack in turn revoked Moe's police powers and placed him on limited duty, non-contact status while the Internal Affairs Division investigated the matter. As Blackjack Zack so eloquently put it, "Whether you blundered and accidentally left your notebook at the Crack house, left the notebook there intentionally to surreptitiously pass on the identity of your CI for the raid to a third party, or chopped Zenaida Austin to pieces personally, it is evident that you are responsible for that young woman's death. An Internal Affairs investigation of the matter is warranted to determine if your act was one of criminal intent or merely gross negligence. And if, God forbid, the press gets wind of this and this mess gets out, the fact that we investigated this matter will not only help the department defend itself if the victim's survivors file a lawsuit against the department, but against an allegation that the department doesn't protect witnesses and informants. Hell, it's hard enough to get people to come forward for fear of their lives." However, Moe had weathered the storm. IAD detectives determined that he had been exhausted from working overtime fighting the War on Drugs in the weeks prior to the unfortunate incident and had merely made a mistake when he left his notebook at the Crack house. He was reinstated to full duty status, with only a reprimand placed in his personnel file, which would be removed after one year, provided he kept his nose clean during that time period.

The beauty of being placed on limited duty though was his non-contact assignment at the Property Division: he stole dozens of seized handguns slated for destruction and sold or traded them on the street for Crack. The downside was that months after he worked there, ballistics in nonfatal shootings and murders all over the city were being traced back to guns that had supposedly been melted down at a smelting plant in Baltimore, Maryland and turned into manhole covers. IAD was all over it, looking at everyone who worked there prior to the scheduled destruction date of the firearms in question, and the Chief of Police had ordered new security measures be implemented, including the installation of additional video cameras throughout the Property Division.

Yeah, it was a real hustle coming up with all his other expenses and the price of heaven. But that was cool. All that really mattered to him was a handful of Crack rocks and Sizzle and a few hours to enjoy them in. He was flying high and never feared hitting rock bottom.

His cash flow problems generated by his and Sizzle's drug addiction dictated a series of desperate acts to make ends meet that were inevitable, if the good times were to continue to roll.

Although he had thought up a few moves on his own, Sizzle had been the mastermind of most of their moves, including the debacle on Condon Terrace. It was she who suggested that he short the cash and product he seized during drug busts, pocket the difference, and place into evidence less than half of what was actually confiscated. So far, not one of the defendants had complained and even if one did, it would be the word of a scum sucking drug dealer against the word of a decorated and celebrated narcotics officer. In fact, he had the best arrest record in the Narcotics and Special Investigations Division.

The thought of his sterling reputation among his peers in law enforcement caused Moe to involuntarily stick out his chest with pride for an instant, but he was immediately jolted back to the stark reality of his present dire situation, bleeding profusely from the neck and fleeing from a multiple-murder scene in an unmarked police car.

Classic Rock 105.9 broadcasting ZZ Top's *Me So Stupid* as his bloodshot eyes watered, constantly blinked, and swiftly closed to slits and then opened wide, he whipped the rumbling Crown Vic left off of Wheeler Road onto St. Barnabas Road and then decided it was best that he slow his roll so he wouldn't draw attention to himself. He eased up off the gas and cruised slightly above the posted speed limit. No worries. At this speed, he should rendezvous with Sizzle on the parking lot of the Arbor View Apartment complex on Brinkley Road in Temple Hills, Maryland in about ten minutes or so, traffic permitting. She'd know what to do…

—

Sizzle had known what to do when drug runner Blinky Felder bragged to her about his standing in notorious drug dealer Marcus "The Devil" Delaney's organization and blabbed the man's entire operation. "The Devil" had a hell of a set up.

Delaney had a fleet of candy trucks operating all over DC, but they dispensed more than just goodies for the kids, the drivers also sold Crack. He also had a fleet of "pizza delivery" vehicles operating all over the city, complete with fake roof signs declaring, "Mama Mia's Pizza." The "pizza deliverymen" carried empty insulated pizza cases to customers' homes and delivered significant orders of Crack cocaine.

In different neighborhoods all over town, he had apartments where he transacted business personally, picking up cash and dropping off product. Sizzle learned the time and the place for tonight's business on Condon Terrace, as well as how many people would likely be there. Yeah, that dummy told Sizzle everything and then Sizzle told Moe. Moron.

Yeah, Sizzle had given him the lowdown on The Devil's operation and his rep didn't scare Moe one bit.

Marcus Delaney had gotten his well-deserved street name the instant he torched Francisco "Big Boy" Longus a couple of years back. Everybody knew the story, but Delaney had gotten away with the gruesome murder because witnesses were too terrified to finger him.

Big Boy had been ducking Delaney for some time because Delaney had discovered that Big Boy had been peddling Crack on Delaney's turf. Big Boy was as nervous as a hooker in church. No, scared shitless was more accurate. He kept moving around, never spending more than a few hours at any one place. If he kept moving, he was sure, Delaney wouldn't find him. He also changed cars frequently. The night Big Boy got burned; he was going to borrow his boy Pee Wee's car, a rusted, blue 1970 Chevy Nova.

After looking the area over carefully for a while, Big Boy exited Pee Wee's place located in the Barry Farm public housing project and walked briskly to the Nova, key in hand. He unlocked the door, but before he could climb into the car and squeeze behind the steering wheel, someone behind him yelled, "Hey, muthafucka!"

Big Boy spun around and stood face to face with Marcus Delaney, who held a…mayonnaise jar…filled with liquid. A burning rag, which was soaked with the liquid, hung from a hole cut into the lid of the jar. Big Boy's eyes widened in terror when he realized that Delaney was holding a big ass Molotov Cocktail.

Delaney whispered, "Just so you know, your boy Pee Wee dimed you out for an eight ball of crack. Welcome to hell!"

With all of his might, Delaney hurled the incendiary device at Big Boy's forehead, making sure that the glass would shatter and cover the fat boy's nappy head and bovine shoulders.

The Mega Molotov Cocktail was Delaney's Special Blend of gasoline, soap chips, and Joy dishwashing liquid. It was perfection. Delaney swore by it. "Accept no substitutes," he always said.

The fat boy instantly burst into flames. Big Boy, a huge fireball lighting the night, wailed like a banshee as he ran blindly, bouncing off of parked cars and utility poles, and falling and getting up and running and falling and getting up and running until he disappeared out of sight around a corner and all that remained were his diminishing screams.

All the while, Delaney laughed raucously.

Those who observed the horror exclaimed:

"Daaamn!"

"Oh, shit!"

"He set that mu-fu on fire!"

"He's the Devil!"

Delaney didn't give a damn who witnessed it because he knew not one of them would have the nerve to tell Five-O what they had seen. Whether Big Boy Longus lived or died, it didn't matter to Delaney; he had made his meaning plain: DON'T CROSS MARCUS DELANEY!

Moe was annoyed by a slow-moving silver colored Lincoln Continental in front of him and stood on the horn. He took advantage of the Crown Vic P71's 4.6 L Modular V8 and whipped around the luxury car, passed it on the left, and then abruptly whipped back into the right lane in front of the Lincoln, cutting it off and forcing its operator to brake to avoid a collision.

The sights and sounds of the swaying Lincoln's screeching brakes and smoking tires behind him, Classic Rock 105.9 still broadcasting ZZ Top's "Me So Stupid" as his bloodshot eyes watered, constantly blinked, and swiftly closed to slits and then opened wide, Moe Bundy sped away down St. Barnabas Road.

———

Yeah, that stupid-ass Blinky's info had been dead on and Moe had fearlessly gone up against The Devil and his minions. The only trouble Moe encountered couldn't have been foreseen; it had just been bad luck. Moe had made a big mistake when he believed that all five of the men he'd shot were dead. One wasn't. While Moe frantically removed rubber-banded stacks of filthy and wrinkled one, five, ten, twenty, fifty, and one hundred dollar bills from one gym bag and stuffed them into another gym bag containing a large quantity of packaged Crack, The Devil shot him in the neck while he wasn't looking. Moe instantly drew his service handgun and shot the dirty bastard in the forehead. He then quickly moved to him and kicked the shiny gat from Delaney's dead hand.

Funny thing was Moe thought he recognized The Devil's gun. Could it be? Yes. That nickel-plated Colt .45 semiautomatic handgun with the cracked ornate Ivory grip was unmistakable; it was one of the guns he had stolen from the Property Division and sold on the street for Crack a few months back. Son of a bitch. Imagine that. Sizzle would get a kick out of that one! Moe had laughed aloud right there in the room full of bloody corpses.

Like he always said, "Never underestimate the power of bad luck."

———

Classic Rock 105.9 broadcasting Jimi Hendrix's "Purple Haze" as his bloodshot eyes watered, constantly blinked, and swiftly closed to slits and then opened wide, Moe whipped the growling Crown Vic off of St. Barnabas Road right onto Hagan Road, bobbing and weaving through the traffic. It wouldn't be long now; he'd be reunited with Sizzle soon and everything would be alright.

His squeeze Sizzle would get him medical attention, he'd clean up the police cruiser, and they could play with their money naked on the king size bed in the lust nest and smoke crack and screw to their hearts' content and then he could take Moe Junior and the missus on a trip to Disney World next week, like he'd promised...

———

Jimi still belting and strumming *Purple Haze*, his bloodshot eyes watering, constantly blinking, and swiftly closing to slits and then opening wide, his neck throbbing beneath his hand, Detective Moe Bundy, blood-drenched, woozy, and cold like in the dead of winter even though it was summertime, turned off Hagan Road right onto Temple Hill Road. He travelled a short distance and then turned right onto Fisher Road, and navigated the winding road a while and then made a left onto Brinkley Road. Finally, he turned left into the Arbor View Apartments complex. He drove to the back of the parking lot to a poorly lit area, pulled next to a dumpster, and put the cruiser in park. His left hand fell from the steering wheel to his wet lap. Shivering, Moe rested his head against the headrest, closed his bloodshot eyes, and sighed. He'd made it. Pale as Nosferatu, his teeth clicking like castanets, his eyes watering, constantly blinking, and swiftly closing to slits and then opening wide, Moe spotted Sizzle dressed in a black mini skirt and red tube top walking toward the police cruiser and he smiled a weak smile, teeth stained with thick, frothy blood. Everything would be alright now.

As soon as Sizzle reached the police cruiser, she snatched opened the driver's door and eyeballed him unsympathetically.

Eyes half-closed and wandering, Moe gurgled, "Siz-zle, hel-help…"

As though she were far away, Moe heard her say, "Put away your gun, Blinky. The Devil and his boys saved us the trouble. Grab the bag off the front seat and let's get out of here!"

His squeeze Sizzle slammed the door in his face and Blinky Felder, armed with a semiautomatic handgun and wearing a Redskins jersey and half-wearing baggy stonewashed jeans hanging far beneath his ass, quickly opened the passenger door and grabbed the satchel from the shotgun seat. Moe tried to go for his service handgun in the holster on his left hip, but his arm would not move. Blinky smirked at him and slammed the door.

His bloodshot eyes watering and constantly blinking, his vision blurred by stinging teardrops, Moe watched helplessly as his precious squeeze, her luscious ass filling out her miniskirt nicely, her stilettos clicking on the pavement like cat claws; and Blinky, holding up his sagging jeans with one hand and carrying in the other the bag containing all of Moe's hopes and dreams, ran away together back the way the girl of his nightmares had come. He moaned.

Moe felt like he was falling, falling…

—

Classic Rock 105.9 broadcasting Three Dog Night's "Mama Told Me (Not to Come)" as Detective Moe Bundy, blood-drenched and woozy and unable to move, his vision blurred by stinging tears, watched Sizzle and Blinky run off into the night and disappear around the corner of one of the apartment complex's many buildings. The narcotics officer's cold white hand stained with streaks of burgundy finally fell from the bullet wound in the right side of his neck. His bloodshot eyes watered and constantly blinked, closed to slits, opened wide, and then closed.

The Bullet Train
R. David Fulcher

THE LONG FLIGHT from New York to Frankfurt had left me tired and feeling disheveled. As a private investigator, I instinctively felt for the reassuring bulge of my snub-nosed .38 revolver under my left shoulder, only to remind myself I had left my piece back in the Big Apple before embarking on my vacation.

I hadn't gotten a break in over five years, not since Delores had convinced me to take her to the Bahamas. I should've known she would split right after the trip. This time was different—just me, myself, and I. If I wanted to drink beer at a biergarten all day I could, or rent a car and speed down the Autobahn, I could do that as well. It was almost too good to be true.

I was glad to finally board The Bullet Train when I found the right platform, and gladder still to find an abandoned cabin. The Germans didn't call it The Bullet Train of course—they called it an IC or Inter-City Express. It was called that because it didn't stop at any of the smaller stations between the starting point and the destination. I called it The Bullet Train because I'd been impressed by photos of high-speed Japanese trains many years ago, and the term just stuck with me.

This particular train was travelling between Frankfurt and Darmstadt. I wanted to start my vacation in Germany in Darmstadt as it was picturesque, and small by big city standards, and believe me I've had enough of big cities.

I had just lowered my hat over my eyes and propped up my feet when I heard the cabin door slide open.

Just my luck, I thought, until I opened my eyes.

In front of me was a knockout redhead. She was easily over six feet tall, with a figure that was somehow curvy and trim at the same time. She had full pouty lips, a slightly upturned nose, and eyes that seemed to change between different hues of green when the light caught them.

"Do you mind if I share the cabin with you?" she asked. She didn't sound German, but she also didn't sound American. The only word that came to mind was that she sounded cultured.

"Of course not. I'm Nick Jansky. Pleasure to meet you," I said, sitting up and extending a hand. I felt a spark when she lightly clasped my hand in return.

"The pleasure is all mine," she replied, taking the opposite seat. I didn't escape my attention that she hadn't offered her name in reply. I didn't overthink it, however. In my line of work I had learned that people may prefer to remain anonymous for any number of reasons. In her case, I was pretty sure a man was involved.

"Are you from Frankfurt?" I asked as the train got rolling.

"I'm a bit from all over, I guess you could say," she said, laughing slightly at her own joke.

She was taking her anonymity seriously. Despite her allure, it had been a long flight, and I wasn't in the mood for games.

"Well, enjoy the trip, Miss," I said, lowering my hat back down over my eyes. She seemed disappointed that I was no longer playing along.

The gentle vibrations of the tracks helped to quickly lull me into sleep, and I wasn't sure how long I had been out before I felt a slight tap on my knee.

"Nick?" she asked.

I sat up, still groggy and unsure of my surroundings. The urban feel of Frankfurt had given way to rolling hills and quaint towns.

"Yes?" I replied, lifting my hat.

She seemed anxious and vulnerable now, no longer exuding the confident demeanor she previously exhibited, and she was squeezing her handbag for apparent comfort.

"I haven't been entirely honest with you," she began.

"Well, how bad could it be? We've only just met!" I exclaimed.

This made her show a forced smile, and she clasped my hands. Again, I felt the spark, a shiver that coursed through my being when she touched me.

"You're kind. I didn't expect that," she said, looking out the window at the landscape rolling past. Again the sunlight caught her eyes and they seemed to shift like currents in the ocean.

"What do you mean you didn't expect that?" I inquired.

"Okay, here's the honest truth. I saw you on the platform and followed you to this car. You seemed like a man who...well, who could handle himself."

"Are you in some kind of trouble?" I asked, looking directly into her shape-shifting eyes.

"Yes. There is a man following me. I think he's from the government. I think he wants to kill me," she blurted out.

"Listen lady, I'm new to Germany, but I'm pretty sure even here the government doesn't track down and assassinate everyday citizens for no reason. Tell me what you did to deserve this kind of heat," I said, squeezing her hands firmly.

"I'm telling you, I don't know! Maybe they don't like my lifestyle, my looks, who knows!"

"I'm sorry, but this makes no sense. There must be a reason," I countered. "Are you mentally stable?"

A great sadness seemed to come over her upon hearing this, and she lowered her eyes. "I'm not crazy, Nick," she said, still gazing down at the floor. "This is real."

"Okay, okay—I'm sorry. This is all just a bit much for me, that's all. I just came here for a vacation," I replied.

Suddenly she sat straight up and cocked her head to the side, like a dog tracking a scent.

"He's close Nick! I know it. Here—you might need this," she said, opening her handbag and passing me a compact Walther PPK pistol.

My eyes grew wide. "How did you...?"

"There's no time for questions. We need to surprise him before he surprises us. Take it please, and wait outside for him—please!" she cried out desperately.

I took the gun and left the cabin, not sure what else to do next. I clicked off the safety just in case we were in real danger. For the moment, the passageway was empty.

I remembered that at the opposite end of the passenger car was a bathroom.

I made my way to the back of the car. After tapping twice softly on the door I determined it was unoccupied. I quietly entered and then cracked the door open a few inches so that I could peer down the hallway. Just as I was about to give up this foolish goose chase, a man entered our car at the opposite end.

He was heavyset and wore a dark suit that seemed too small for him. His wide nose reminded me distinctly of a pig.

There was a pin on his lapel that may have been the insignia of a secret agency such as the Stasi or KGB, but he was too far away to be sure. He smoothly withdrew a pistol with a silencer from a shoulder holster under his jacket, confirming that he was armed and dangerous. As he made his way down the hall, I could discern more details.

The pistol was a semi-automatic Soviet Makarov. Its .380 caliber ammunition delivered a solid punch, especially when dispensed in bunches. This was a standard issue military sidearm of the Eastern Bloc countries, confirming my suspicions that he was possibly KGB.

The lapel pin was more puzzling. On the pin was the insignia of the planet Saturn circled by its rings. Perhaps it was some exotic offshoot of the Russian Mafia. I wasn't hanging around to find out.

The man stopped directly in front of my passenger compartment, the same compartment I had left mere moments before and that remained occupied by a desperate, beautiful woman.

He extended a hand to open the door.

If I was going to act, it was now or never. Unsure of what else to do, I reached into my suit coat and withdrew a coin. I flung it smartly at the window of the passenger car and once again closed the bathroom door, leaving it open only enough for me to watch his actions.

The coin made a satisfying *clink!* when it hit the window. It then rolled off down the corridor.

The man withdrew his hand from the door handle as if stung, his senses now alert and wary.

He advanced down the hallway in my direction, pistol at the ready. His movements were more graceful and silent than should have been possible for such a large man.

He was directly in front of the bathroom. It was now or never.

I sprang into action, thrusting open the door with all my strength. I wedged his forearm between the door and the wall and his pistol clattered to the floor.

Having been in more than a few scraps myself, I had several moves of my own. I grabbed his free wrist and spun him around, violently wrenching his arm up at the same time.

He grunted in pain and bent over to try and free his arm. I took this opportunity to knee him in the face again and again.

Soon he collapsed to the floor unconscious. I leaned against the wall to catch my breath. To me the confrontation had sounded like World War III, but, beneath the clatter of the train tracks, only the passengers in the immediate vicinity would have realized anything was amiss.

"Darmstadt zehn minuten," the conductor crackled over the loudspeaker. We were nearing our destination.

I wrestled the stranger's body into the bathroom and with all my strength hefted him onto a sitting position on the toilet seat. I tied his hands together behind his back with his own belt. These measures were meant to temporarily restrain him until the proper authorities at Darmstadt could attend to him.

I retrieved the Makarov pistol and tucked it into the small of my back. Ironically, I now had two guns—the Walther PPK from my mysterious lady friend and the goon's Makarov.

I quickly made my way back to my cabin. The woman was where I had left her, serenely gazing out of the window at the rolling landscape.

I found her calmness annoying after having committed so much violence.

"I got him," I said.

She turned from the window and drew me in with those shifting eyes. She clasped my left hand and kissed it, so deeply I felt my face grow flush.

"Thank you," she said sincerely. "May I have my protection back now, please?" she asked.

I handed over the Walther pistol with my free hand.

Shyly, I tried to withdraw my hand. But I could not. She held it in a vice-like grip.

But it was not merely her hand clasping mine. Her long red hair had also become alive, entwining itself so tightly around my arm that the veins stood out.

Her face stretched into a demonic grin.

"Now you will feed me!" she rasped, her voice sounding cruel and ancient. Her red hair began to twist together and grow thick bands like dreadlocks, but at the end of each dreadlock was an evil mouth ringed with curved fangs. The mouths hissed and clicked at me, trying to tear off a chunk of flesh.

With my free right hand, I grabbed the silenced Makarov as she drew me ever closer. Not wanting to shatter that once beautiful face, I fired a slug into her heart.

Her face at once became frozen in shock, and the dreadlocks ceased their frantic thrashing. She slumped back into the seat, and her face slowly returned to that of a beautiful woman.

"And I thought you were such a nice man," she gasped, as the splashes of color in her eyes slowly turned black. The train shuddered to a stop and her body slumped completely across the seat and slid to the cold floor.

"Darmstadt Station," the conductor announced over the loud-speaker.

I quickly left the compartment, tightly closing the door behind me. I raced to the exit and for a moment after disembarking I stood quietly and enjoyed the cool air of the open train platform.

Suddenly, I felt an uncomfortable twitching in my shirt pocket. I quickly fished in the pocket and cried out in pain as I withdrew one of the red dreadlocks, its greedy mouth firmly attached to my index finger.

I shook my hand violently until it loosened its grip and dropped to the ground. Once it hit the platform, I ground it under my heel casually as if putting out a cigarette.

I then followed the signs into town, leaving The Bullet Train and its dead behind me.

AUTHOR BIOS

Da bunch'a mugs what wrote this book

ALBERTO AMBARD

Alberto Ambard is a Venezuelan author who has published several short stories and two novels: *High Treason*, and *Dogma, Aren Door And A Birthday*. Currently, he lives in Oregon, where he is working on a new novel. More at albertoambard.com

WILLIAM F. CRANDELL

William F. Crandell is the author of The Jack Griffin Detective Series, published by Hawkshaw Press. The Griffin series is an action-packed, hard-boiled bullet train of adventure and intrigue set in the backdrop of Washington, DC, and featuring an array of fictionalized real-life historical characters. Book 1 in the series, *Let's Say Jack Kennedy Killed the Girl*, published December 2021. Book 2, *If Only Truman Were Dead*, arrives summer 2023.

Crandell served in the Vietnam War and returned home from the war with a taste for adventure, a skeptic's eye, and a hundred thousand stories. After completing a doctorate in history at Ohio State University, he was awarded a Maryland State Arts Council Individual Artist Award in 2004 for the aforementioned novel, *Let's Say Jack Kennedy Killed the Girl*. Crandell was awarded the PRIZM's Mark Twain Award for Humor/Social Commentary 2012. His short story, "The Last Lootenant Wins His Fuckin' Medal," was awarded first place by the National Federation of Press Women in 2020. More at ohthefoxwentout.com

JAMES DONZELLA

James A. Donzella lives in Northern California. He is an active member of the UCLA Wordcommandos Creative Writing Workshop for Military Veterans. He's had short stories published in *Every Day Fiction, The War Horse, Military Experience, Line of Advance* and placed second in the College of the Redwoods, Seven Gill Shark Review Creative Writing Competition. The 2023 edition of the *Cone Flower Cafe'* magazine features his short story, "Friend of Ours." He has completed his first collection of short stories as well as his first novel in the James Wolf P.I. for Hire Mystery Series, adapted from his short story "The Lady With Emerald Green Eyes." He's worked as a screenwriter, ad copywriter, and actor. More at jamesdonzella.com

BENJAMIN FINE

Benjamin Fine is a Professor of Mathematics and a graduate of the Fairfield University MFA program. He has published fifteen books and over twenty short stories and has won numerous awards.

R. DAVID FULCHER

R. David Fulcher is an author of horror, science fiction, fantasy, and poetry. Major literary influences include H.P. Lovecraft, Dean Koontz, Edgar Allen Poe, Fritz Lieber, and Stephen King. Fulcher's collection of short stories, *The Pumpkin King and Other Tales of Terror* releases from Gravelight Press in fall 2023. More at rdavidfulcher.com

PHIL GIUNTA

Phil Giunta's novels include the paranormal mysteries *Testing the Prisoner, By Your Side,* and *Like Mother, Like Daughters*. His short stories appear in such anthologies as *Love on the Edge, Beach Pulp, Space Opera Digest 2022, A Plague of Shadows*, the *Middle of Eternity* series, and more. He is a Pushcart Prize-nominated author and member of the Horror Writers Association, the National Federation of Press Women, and the Greater Lehigh Valley Writers Group.

Giunta is currently working on his fourth paranormal mystery novel while plotting his triumphant escape from the pressures of corporate America where he has been imprisoned for thirty years. More at philgiunta.com

SCOTT ARCHER JONES

Scott Archer Jones is currently trapped inside his sixth and seventh novels. He lives in northern New Mexico, after stints in the Netherlands, Scotland, and Norway, plus less exotic locations. He has completed four novels: *Jupiter and Gilgamesh, A Novel of Texas and Sumeria, The Big Wheel, And Throw Away The Skins,* and *A Rising Tide of People Swept Away,* through Southern Yellow Pine Publishing and Fomite Press. More at scottarcherjones.com

DENA LINN

Dena Linn, ex-urban, thriver, commune child, never one of "those girls." Her dark fiction, "Frost," is published in *The Chamber Magazine.* Other stories are appearing in *Down in the Dirt Magazine, Ariel Chart International Literary Journal,* and her First Place winner, "The Problem Is," appears in *Prompted,* by Reedsy. She is a short story judge for Reedsy. Dena has published six short stories in anthologies produced by Transcendent Authors. More at linnfiction.com

SUZANNE MATTABONI

Suzanne Mattaboni's work has appeared in *The Huffington Post, Seventeen, Newsday, Guideposts, Chicken Soup for the Soul, Mysterious Ways, Dark Dossier,* the '80s-themed *Pizza Parties and Poltergeists* horror anthology, 2023's *Scars* anthology, and the *Little Demon Digest* anthology. Her debut novel *Once In a Lifetime* was published in March 2022 by TouchPoint Press. More at suzannemattaboni.com

ANDREW R. MIKOS

Andrew R. Mikos is a writer and an attorney from Florida. He lives in Michigan along with his son and daughter.

QUINTIN PETERSON

Quintin Peterson is a retired Washington, DC, police officer who served the public for three decades. He is also a critically acclaimed crime fiction writer who has authored four DC-based crime novels and has contributed to several magazines and ten anthologies, including *DC Noir,* edited by George Pelecanos.

ROBERT POPE

Robert Pope has published a novel, *Jack's Universe*, three collections of stories, most recently *Not a Jot or a Tittle* (2022), and a book of flash fiction, *Disappearing Things* (2023). His stories appear in journals, including *Kenyon Review, Alaska Quarterly Review, Fiction International*, and anthologies, including *Pushcart Prize* and *Dark Lane Anthology*. His work can also be found at fictivedream.com

DIANNA SINOVIC

Dianna Sinovic's short stories have been published in anthologies by the Bethlehem Writers Group and Sunbury Press. The most recent story, "Lab Test," appears in *That Darkened Doorstep* anthology, which was released in October 2022. She's also a certified book coach and editor. More at dianna-sinovic.com

MITCHELL TOEWS

Mitchell Toews has published stories in over one hundred journals and anthologies. He is a three-time Pushcart Prize nominee and a finalist in numerous major literary contests and prizes in Canada and the US. Toews debut collection of short stories, *Pinching Zwieback* (At Bay Press) launches October 24, 2023. More at mitchellaneous.com

ALBERT TUCHER

Albert Tucher is the creator of prostitute Diana Andrews, who has appeared in more than 100 stories in venues including *The Best American Mystery Stories 2010*. Diana's first longer case, the novella *The Same Mistake Twice*, was published in 2013. Albert Tucher is a retired librarian. More at alberttucher.com

SUSAN WALSH

Susan Walsh is finally living her best life at the beach. She has published several op-ed and essay type pieces. Her first published fiction appeared in 2022. She is hoping for more fiction success ahead.

www.ingramcontent.com/pod-product-compliance
Lightning Source LLC
Chambersburg PA
CBHW022015170626
46808CB00001B/422